CLAWS

The Baron Blasko Mysteries
Book 3

A. E. Howe

Books in the Baron Blasko Mysteries Series:

FANGS (Book 1)

KNIVES (Book 2)

CLAWS (Book 3)

TENTACLES (Book 4)

SCALES (Book 5 - Coming 2021)

Copyright © 2019 A. E Howe

ISBN: 0-9997968-7-9
ISBN-13: 978-0-9997968-7-0

PROLOGUE

Seth Taylor's eyes stared unblinking at the bright February sky. The first vulture landed on him an hour after sunrise and more soon followed. It was the sight of the birds circling that alerted Ol' Man Murphy that there was something dead near the creek which formed the border between his property and Elroy Taylor's land.

Vultures weren't an unusual sight out in the country, signaling a transition in the circle of life for many animals. Being in his late seventies, Murphy decided to wait until his grandson came home before going out to check on whatever had died. He owned a number of cattle and diligently kept track of their births and deaths. *Take care of the small things and the big things will take care of themselves* was a phrase that his family had grown tired of hearing him spout. Though they were a bit more respectful now when the country was wallowing in the pit of a great financial meltdown and they still had a roof over their heads and food in their stomachs.

Seth Taylor was beyond caring about the vultures or if he was found. Many of his insides were on the outside, and when Murphy later recounted the moment when he and Todd found Seth, he'd say that as soon as he saw how far the foot was from the head, he knew something horrible had happened to the boy.

When Murphy saw the body, he jumped down from the wagon and pulled his shotgun from its leather scabbard on the side of the buckboard. He told Todd to take the wagon back and get the sheriff, which would mean pushing the horses at a trot all the way down to the Campbell place, which was four miles closer to town and had the nearest phone. Murphy cautioned the boy not to talk to anyone but the sheriff. Seth's father was a bit of a hothead and didn't care much for the Murphys. The old man didn't know how Elroy Taylor would react when he learned that his son's dismembered body had been found on Murphy land.

CHAPTER ONE

That night, Baron Dragomir Blasko sat in his wingback chair, holding a small bag. He listened to the clink of the coins inside as he shifted it from one hand to the next. He glanced up at a small brown bat hanging from the rafters of his basement apartment.

"Vasile, we are going to reach a crisis point soon. Fifty gold coins will not last very long." The bat seemed unconcerned with the baron's financial situation. "At least you can hunt your own food."

Blasko had spent the early part of the evening with Josephine upstairs, but she had planned a night out with friends, so he'd come down to his Victorian-inspired parlor to read before going out for his usual late-night walk.

"Prowling. That's what she calls it when I go out. She refuses to trust me, even after all we've been through. Bah! I'm not going to beg her to trust me, and I'm certainly not going to rely on her for money," he said to the bat, who had pulled both wings over its head. Now that it was winter, the creature wasn't very interested in foraging outside.

Before Blasko could grumble more about his current situation, there was a knock at the door that led to the back yard of the house. Vasile let out a small squeak of surprise and fluttered to a dark corner of the room.

"I doubt that it's Poe's raven knocking at my chamber door, my leathery little friend," Blasko said as he rose from his chair. When he opened the door, he was surprised to see Deputy Robert Tucker standing in the small alcove.

The deputy's expression was grim as he nodded and removed his hat. "Evening, Baron."

"Tucker, come in out of the cold," Blasko said, moving out of the way to give the large man room. As he led the way into his parlor, Blasko discreetly closed the door to his bedchamber. The deputy knew the baron was unusual, but he wasn't aware that he slept in a coffin. Blasko didn't think he needed to burden him with that knowledge tonight.

"Have a seat," Blasko said, waving the deputy to the other chair in front of the fire and sitting down himself. Bobby looked uncertain for a moment, but finally sat. Blasko noticed that the deputy's uniform was dirty and his shoes looked like he'd been hiking cross-country.

"I need to talk to you about… a boy who was killed last night," Bobby said slowly.

"Killed. Do you mean murdered?" Blasko asked, repressing the excitement he felt. Solving crimes was becoming a consuming passion for him. *What else do I have to do in this country?* he'd asked Josephine.

"Sheriff Logan says he was killed by a wild animal. A bear or a wolf. But I don't know…" Bobby shifted in the chair as though doubting the sheriff caused him actual physical discomfort. "Neither suggestion makes any sense. First of all, the black bears we got around here aren't big enough to tear someone apart like that. As for a wolf? There hasn't been one around here for as long as I've been alive."

"Go back to the boy. How old was he? Where was he found?" Blasko asked.

"His name's Seth Taylor. He was seventeen. A neighbor found him this morning down by a creek that runs along his property. I've seen a man who was attacked by a pack of wild hogs. This was worse," Bobby said with a shake of his head.

"Why does the sheriff believe that it was a wolf or a bear?"

"'Cause he hasn't seen the things I've seen," Bobby said, and Blasko realized what he was implying.

"You think this has something to do with the summoning we broke up in November?"

"What I know is that nothing around here could have done that to the Taylor boy. I wondered if something might have... I don't know... got out of that pit before it closed up." It was obvious that the strange and terrifying events three months earlier had left a shadow hanging over Bobby Tucker.

"I doubt that's the case," Blasko said, then stood up. "But why don't we go take a look at the spot where the attack took place? Perhaps I will see some evidence of who or what killed the boy." Blasko's condition enhanced his senses and he was sure he'd be able to identify the killer, by smell if nothing else.

"It's funny. You know I'm not a person to shrink from danger, but thinking about going back out there at night... I'm telling you, something tore Seth up." Bobby shuddered and put his hat back on as they walked out of the basement.

"If it is something... dark, then we can deal with it," Blasko said, though he was confident the killer was a man. He had seen men do unspeakable things to other men. He'd had to subdue human monsters many times during his years as the *voivode* of his district in Romania.

As Blasko and the deputy talked, Josephine Nicolson was driving through Sumter to pick up the Bryant sisters, Eileen and Eva. The whole night had been Alice Robertson's idea. She was the wife of the manager of Josephine's bank. Even though her father had passed away almost a year earlier, Josephine found it hard not to think of the bank as belonging to her family, though in reality it was overseen by a board of directors. However, Josephine did own a majority of the stock.

Alice had come into the bank the previous afternoon while Josephine had been in to meet with the manager. Always effusive, Alice was beside herself when she started talking about the medium who had held a séance at a neighbor's house.

"You simply won't believe what he can do. He literally conjured up my dead aunt!" she told Josephine while they stood in the lobby, waiting for her husband to come back from lunch.

"How did he do that?" Josephine asked, trying not to sound too cynical.

"Channeled her voice. It was uncanny. Took me back to my childhood. That woman has been dead for twenty years!" Alice said, going up and down on her toes. Josephine had always assumed she'd gotten into this habit because the petite woman was less than five feet tall.

"That does sound impressive," Josephine said, looking at the door and hoping Daniel Robertson would arrive soon.

"Oh! We should all go to one! I can arrange it. That would be wonderful. I bet Eileen and Eva would like to go. The poor girls never get out," Alice said, looking across the lobby.

The "poor girls" were actually two middle-aged, unmarried sisters who worked as tellers at the bank. Their parents had been friends of Josephine's father, but they'd been orphaned in their teens following a train accident. Andre Nicolson had taken them under his wing and had given them both jobs at the bank. At the start of the Depression, there had been a strong push by board members to have the Bryants replaced by men with families to support. But the fuss had been over pretty quickly once Josephine's father gave a passionate speech in their defense at a board meeting. He had argued that both of them were polite and precise in their work, two qualities necessary at the teller windows. The point he'd used to end the debate was that the middle of a financial crisis was not the time to be making personnel changes.

"The experience of talking to the dead is... so... bizarre," Alice continued. "Please say yes."

"I'm not..." Josephine hesitated.

"Oh! Your father. Of course. No, I'll just tell François that it would be too painful for you. Everyone will understand that. But you have to come. He is just the must amazing man you will ever meet. And he's got a quality about him... Well, I'll say no more!"

"All right, I'll come," Josephine said abruptly. She just wanted Alice to stop talking. The woman was as sweet as she was verbose, but there were limits to how much chatter Josephine could take. After meeting Alice years ago, she understood why Daniel Robertson would work for hours in the bank without saying a word.

Both women turned as the door opened behind them. Daniel walked into the lobby and looked a bit surprised to find both of them waiting for him.

"Miss Josephine," he said with a nod before hanging his hat on a rack by the door. Then he turned to his wife. "Alice, what are you doing here?"

"Why, I came to see you. What else?" she said as the two women followed him into his office. "Though, honestly, I was hoping to get a bit of cash. I want to pay off Mr. Decker down at the five-and-dime. We've been running a tab for months and I just heard that his daughter is engaged. The poor man is going to need every penny he can get. That girl is bound to want the sun and the moon for her wedding."

"Very thoughtful," Daniel said, and gave her a light kiss on her forehead. He was slightly above average height and had to bend down to do it. Then he took out his wallet and gave her a twenty-dollar bill.

"Don't you think Eva and Eileen should go with us tomorrow night?" Alice asked him.

"What? Where?" he said, having not been privy to the

earlier conversation.

"To a séance with François, of course. Josephine is going to come."

Daniel looked at Josephine, who smiled and gave a slight shrug of her shoulders.

"If they want to, of course," Daniel said, looking down at the papers on his desk. Josephine could tell that his mind was already drifting away from the conversation. "You should go ask them," he said to Alice in an obvious ploy to get his office back.

"I'll do that!" Alice said. She touched Josephine on the arm as she went toward the door. "I'll call you and arrange everything."

"I want to get a list of the loans that are in default," Josephine said once Alice had left.

"You can't keep bailing people out," Daniel told her.

"I don't bail many people out. What I do is try to keep people from being humiliated. If I can help them find a new home or help them move someplace else where they have family, it makes me feel better. I don't think the bank needs to push anyone off a cliff."

"You're as kind as Alice. Just not as talkative," Daniel said with a rare smile.

CHAPTER TWO

Sure enough, the Bryant sisters were excited at the prospect of a night out. Josephine picked them up in front of the small bungalow they shared.

"I've never been to a séance," Eva said, pushing her sister across the back seat as she got into Josephine's car. "I admire you so much for driving your own car. I keep telling Eileen that we need to learn to drive."

"Why would we do that?" Eileen, the dour one of the pair, asked. "What would we do with a car?"

"We could go places and we wouldn't have to rely on others to drive us." Eva leaned over the front seat. "Thank you so much, Miss Josephine. We never go out."

"Now that's not true. We got out to dinner every Saturday," Eileen said.

"Yes, that's true, we do. We go to the same old place. Winnie's Diner. Someday I'd just like to get in a car and drive away... maybe to Montgomery. Wouldn't that be something?" Eva said with a world of wonder in her voice.

"Pick a day this summer and I'll be glad to drive us all over to Montgomery for a shopping trip," Josephine offered.

"Oh my, that would be a dream. Did you hear that, Eileen?"

"What do you want from Montgomery?" Eileen asked. She sounded genuinely puzzled, trying to imagine why anyone would go to the big city of Montgomery to shop.

"Because the trip would be something different. That's all. My gosh, can't a person want to do something they haven't done a million times before?"

"That's what we're doing tonight," Eileen argued.

"True enough. I can't wait. Mrs. Robertson said François knew everything about her and the other people at the séance. He could talk to the dead." Her voice held the awe of a ten-year-old talking about Santa Claus.

"I doubt that. Besides, what she said was that the dead talked through him," Eileen said matter-of-factly.

"That just gives me the shivers," Eva said with an excited tremor.

The séance was being held at the home of the MacDonnells, elderly neighbors of Daniel and Alice Robertson. Josephine knew them only as acquaintances of her parents and patrons of the bank. They'd had a son, several years older than Josephine, who had been killed in the Great War.

Once Josephine parked the car, the three women made their way up the driveway to the large craftsman-style house. The broad front porch was dimly lit by a small bulb above the door and soft yellow light came through the house's windows.

"Looks like they've got the whole place lit by candlelight. Hope they don't burn the house down around our ears," Eileen said.

Josephine knocked on the door.

"Come in, come in," said Mr. MacDonnell. He was wearing an old-fashioned waistcoat with a plaid bowtie. "You ladies are in for quite the evening. We saw him last night. It's really rather amazing," he said as he took their coats and scarves.

Mr. MacDonnell led them into the parlor where a large, round oak table had been positioned in the center of the room with seven chairs around it. The burning candles added a spooky element to the atmosphere. Standing by a bookcase and talking with Alice and Mrs. MacDonnell was a short man whose black hair was a little longer than the fashion of the day. He was dressed in a conservative suit and looked for all the world like a college professor.

"There they are!" Alice said as the women approached.

Josephine took a moment to observe the man as he looked at Eva and Eileen, a slightly amused expression on his face. When his eyes met Josephine's, she felt an odd chill. He seemed to be looking past her social façade. "Like he knew more than he should have," was how she would later describe it.

"What a delight!" François LeSauvage said after Alice had made the introductions. His smile made Josephine think of a cat, reaching out with claws extended, to pull them into his world. "We are going to have a fascinating evening together."

Alice was acting as hostess. Mrs. MacDonnell seemed frail and slightly unfocused. Josephine tried to figure out her age, deciding that both she and her husband had to be well into their eighties.

As Alice started to seat everyone around the table, François gently took control. He guided each guest to a chair he chose for them. Josephine felt him touch her arm lightly and indicate the seat to his right. Once the table was arranged to his satisfaction, he sat down beside her.

"Tonight we will ask our astral guides to bring us word from our loved ones who have crossed over and gone beyond the veil." François paused and looked around the table. "The power that we use should not be squandered or misused for gain or revenge. You may ask questions, but it should be done in the spirit of *bonhomie*."

Josephine refrained from rolling her eyes, barely.

François turned to her and put his hand out, just short of touching hers. "I understand you recently lost your father. We won't reach out to him. He's been on the other side for a relatively short time. Occasionally, when you call a spirit back too soon, they can become disoriented, even angry. So no fears, Mademoiselle Josephine." He paused and looked around the table at the eager faces.

Josephine found herself being drawn in against her will, not to the ritual itself but to the theatrics. She'd read about séances. Would there be beating drums and blowing trumpets? Would she be able to see through whatever conjuring tricks he used to fool the others?

"Do you want me to blow out the candles?" Mr. MacDonnell asked.

"Yes, but bring one candlestick over to the table," François told him. "I will warn you, this is not a theatrical performance. Those of you who were with me last night know that I am not an entertainer like so many spiritualists. There will be no drums, levitating tables or rapping on the walls."

Josephine had the uncomfortable feeling that he'd read her mind.

Mr. MacDonnell snuffed out two dozen candles before he carefully carried the remaining candlestick over to the table.

"Now we begin," François said, reaching out to Josephine on his right and Alice on his left. Everyone joined hands.

François's head drooped down to his chest and his breathing became heavy. Josephine could feel him swaying rhythmically as his hand tugged back and forth on hers.

"Spirits, you know me. You trust me. I ask you to reveal yourselves to me. We have visitors tonight who wish to speak with you," he intoned.

To Josephine, he sounded like he was talking to beings he could actually see. *A good actor*, her skeptical side concluded.

He continued to call on the spirits for several minutes until a chill descended over Josephine. She glanced around the table and saw that the others looked uncomfortably cold.

"Eva! My Eileen!" came a strange female voice from

Josephine's left. Her head whipped around and what she saw almost caused her to drop François's hand. He was looking up now with a smile on his face, but for a minute she'd thought he'd changed into a woman. She quickly decided that it was just the effect of the feminine voice coming from his mouth. It was uncanny in that it didn't seem to be coming from him at all. It was more like it was coming *out* of him. It was unnerving.

"It's your mama. Don't you know me?" the voice asked. Eva and Eileen were staring at François, open-mouthed.

"Mama?" Eva asked slowly.

"Yes, I'm here. I've missed you both so much. I remember the sound of your voices around the kitchen table when we snapped peas in the summer. I'm happy on this side, but I miss those days with the two of you."

"We miss you too, Mama," Eva said, sounding just like the young girl who'd seen her mother come home in an oak box.

"Eileen, has the cat got your tongue?" the voice asked.

Eileen looked puzzled and suspicious in equal measures. "Maybe it has."

"You doubt that I'm your mother. Do you remember the spring day when you were ten and wanted to wear your church dress to school?"

"I... do," Eileen said cautiously.

"But I wouldn't let you so you cried and begged until I got it out of you that you were sweet on Ethan Tibbets."

At this, Eileen's jaw slowly went slack. She looked at her sister, who was staring at François with a mesmerized expression on her face.

"It can't really be you," Eileen said. Her voice carried more wonder than accusation.

"Yes, my dear little flower, it really is me." And with those words, Josephine watched as Eileen became a believer. Tears started to stream down both women's cheeks.

"I can't believe this. I didn't dream..." Eileen said.

"What about Father?" Eva burst out.

"Yes, your father is with me."

"Can I speak to him?" Eva asked.

"What's up, puddin' head?" A deep male voice floated from François's mouth. Josephine felt like she had been transported to some strange world that she didn't understand.

"Oh, Papa!" Eva said, wiping the tears from her cheeks. She dropped Mr. MacDonnell's hand and reached toward François.

"We must go," the man's voice said.

"No!" Eva and Eileen said together.

"We came hoping to bring you comfort. We're happy, and the only thing that will make that happiness complete is when you join us. But there is nothing more we can do now. We love you." The words seemed to fade as if down a long tunnel.

Both women were openly crying now, but Josephine thought they were tears of happiness. *Whatever that was, it has brought these two women a peace they haven't known since they were young,* Josephine thought.

"Josie?" Like before, the words came out of François's mouth, but not from him. Josephine's head snapped toward him. The voice was familiar.

"You don't remember Petey?"

"Uncle Petey?" Josephine couldn't believe she was being pulled into this, but the voice had taken her by surprise. She hadn't thought of her father's brother in years. Uncle Petey had been a gangly man who'd seemed to her like a human-size marionette. Later she'd learned that he was the black sheep of the family, accused of jilting a woman he'd promised to marry. Her father had always called him a rogue. She knew he'd died young, but couldn't recall how.

"Little Josie, I want you to know that I'm sorry for not being a better uncle and brother. I know I was a disappointment to Andre and our parents."

"He always smiled when he spoke of you," Josephine said, barely realizing that she was accepting the voice as the spirit of her uncle.

"I feel him on this side. I will see him soon. That makes me glad. Our parents are here. All together again. All the strife ends in peace."

"That's good, Uncle Petey. I'm glad," Josephine said, feeling slightly foolish. The surprise of hearing his voice was wearing off and some of her skepticism was resurfacing.

"Oh, I left something for you," the voice said. "In your father's library. I put a note in a book, a collection of Edgar Allan Poe's stories. You'll find a letter there. I must go now." The voice ended abruptly.

François's body shook in what looked like a cross between a convulsion and someone shaking off a nap.

"He needs a break," Alice said. "François, would you like something to drink?"

"A brandy would be divine," he said, opening his eyes. Everyone relaxed and Mr. MacDonnell stood up.

"I've got some excellent brandy that I saved from the revenuers," he said with a twinkle in his eye. "Orders all around?" he asked, looking at those seated at the table.

"Yes, something please," Eileen said, sounding as tired as François. Eva, on the other hand, shook her head. Her face still wore a wide grin while her eyes looked happily into the distance.

"I'll help you, and you can make me something that will warm me up. I'm chilled to the bone," Alice said. Her excitement hadn't dimmed at all. She got up and followed Mr. MacDonnell over to a large mahogany cabinet.

François looked less fatigued as he turned to Josephine. "Not what you were expecting?"

"I can't believe that I spoke to my Uncle Petey." But even as she said it, she knew she'd be going straight to the library when she got home to pull down that volume of Poe's works.

"It doesn't matter whether you believe or not."

"How do you find our relatives?" Josephine asked, half curious and half unconvinced.

"I don't find them. You all draw them here. I am just a conduit. Like a telephone."

"You're saying that they sense us?"

"Exactly. Your family is always with you. I open the gateway and they come forward with their messages."

"You ever run into angry spirits?"

"Yes," he said with a look on his face that didn't encourage further inquiry. "Again, it depends on the people around the table."

"How long have you had this… talent?"

"Since I was a small child. My mother used to have me open the gateway for people when I was only nine years old."

"Where are you from?"

"France. Many years ago."

Josephine wanted to ask him how he made a living. As far as she could tell, he didn't charge for these sessions. There hadn't even been a pitch for a tip or donation. But she couldn't quite compose the right question. Even she couldn't bring herself to just blurt: *Where do you get your money?*

"You were shocked when your uncle spoke to you," François said.

"I hadn't thought of him in a long while," she said, wondering if that was part of the trick. By conjuring up relatives who were long dead, it was less likely that the participants in the séance would remember what they had really been like and call his bluff. That sounded like a good explanation, but even so, how could François have learned that she even had an uncle, let alone any details about his life and personality? Josephine doubted there were more than half a dozen people in town who would remember Petey.

"You find it hard to believe in my power."

"I'm skeptical."

"There are many things that are beyond our understanding," François said.

Reflecting on the past year and her experiences since meeting Blasko, Josephine couldn't argue with that statement. "Skeptical doesn't mean closed-minded," she said amicably.

"Caution is seldom a fault."

Josephine saw Eileen walk toward the kitchen, looking upset. She excused herself and got up to follow her. On the way to the kitchen, she passed Eva, who was talking excitedly with Alice.

Eileen wandered through the kitchen to the back door and Josephine followed her onto a small porch. The air was cool, but mild for winter.

"Mind if I join you?" Josephine asked.

Eileen hesitated for a moment, then shook her head. "I don't mind if you join me if you don't mind if I have a cigarette," she said, flashing the unlit cigarette in her hand.

"I didn't know you smoked."

"I'm the bad sister," she said, rooting around in her black sequined purse for a lighter. With the cigarette burning, she inhaled deeply. "That sounds bitter. I'm not really. Eva is so sweet; I just look bad in comparison." There was both melancholy and affection in her words.

"You're the strong one," Josephine observed.

"I almost got married ten years ago, but I kept thinking what Eva would do without me. Silly, really. Once in a while I see beneath all her naiveté to the strong little fortress she has built. Still…" She took a few more drags on the cigarette. "Do you think he's for real?" She nodded back toward the house.

"A year ago, I would have said no. But now…" Josephine tilted her head to the side. "I don't know."

"I'm just worried that Eva will get too caught up in all of this. Hell's bells, he had me going for a while. My mother… I can't be sure which are real memories and which are ones that we've dreamed up or embellished over the years."

"By channeling people who've been dead for decades, he's making it more difficult to call him out as a fraud," Josephine agreed. "But then again, it's hard to imagine how he could have dredged up so much information about events that took place so long ago."

"The voices… They were… eerie, like echoes of our parents' voices," Eileen said, taking another deep drag on the cigarette and reducing it to a stub which she put out and dropped in a pot by the door.

"Eva is smart and clever. She'll be okay," Josephine assured her.

Eileen nodded and opened the door.

When they returned to the parlor, everyone else had finished their drinks and were taking their seats around the table for the second half of the séance. Again, François called to the spirits.

"Alice, what are you doing back here? You are such a bother," said a female voice.

"Mother! You don't mean that," Alice said, sounding even more giddy than usual.

"No, I don't, honey bee. You were a wonderful child. Even now, I can see you playing in in the front yard with your puppy. What was his name? Speedy!"

"That's right. He was the fastest dog I've ever seen. I still haven't met a dog that can run faster than him," Alice said.

They talked for a few more minutes about Alice's childhood and several of the milestones of her early life before her mother said she had a favor to ask.

"Anything, Mother," Alice replied.

"I want you to give my bible to your sister." The voice sounded very earnest.

"Which bible?" Alice asked, sounding puzzled.

"My communion bible. It's in the chest up in the attic of your house."

"Oh yes, it might be. I think my wedding dress is in that old trunk too," Alice said, sounding surprised.

"Take the bible to your sister as soon as you can."

"Why?"

"It is important, little one." Then the voice was gone. Josephine and the others watched as François's head nodded down to his chest like a curtain going down to end a show.

"Hey, Dad!" A voice suddenly boomed out of François's mouth and his eyes shot open, unfocused. The loud cry made everyone around the table jump. Several dropped the hand of the person next to them, but they quickly regained their composure and grasped hands again.

"Son?" Mr. MacDonnell said timidly. Josephine remembered that Alice had told her how disappointed the MacDonnells had been that their son hadn't made an appearance at the séance the night before.

"You got it on the first try," the voice joked. The joy in his voice was uplifting.

"I... We..." Mr. MacDonnell was clearly stunned.

"It's okay. I know I died. I'm so sorry that I left you both. I... In the last moments, I thought of you and Mom. I just couldn't hold on."

"When we got the telegram, our hearts were broken," Mr. MacDonnell said as though he and the voice were the only ones in the room.

"I did my best, just like you taught me. The sounds are what I remember most. The artillery was like all the gods of ancient Rome and Greece having the final battle of the world. Terrifying and electrifying all at once. The ground shook, the air pulsed and the noise... everything else was drowned out. Time seemed to stand still while the artillery barrage of the German trenches went on. Then, in an instant, the world went silent. No noise at all. The men in my regiment were sure that no German could have survived. But as soon as the thought was formed, the whistles sounded. All up and down the trenches, the officers blew their whistles. When no one moved, the sergeants started shouting and shoving us toward the ladders. The Germans weren't dead.

"The first man up my ladder fell back on us with a rifle bullet through his neck. Blood flew in my face and, I think as much to get away from that dying man as to obey any orders, I climbed up and out of the trench. Then I saw hell. Surely men had never faced such carnage. We moved forward as one chaotic mass. I'd say we moved toward the

German trenches, but I couldn't see anything but smoke and blood and dirt and men. Dead men, running men, falling men, struggling men, screaming men and men who were out of their minds with terror.

"I stumbled forward. One of my mates was next to me. I wrote to you about him—Albert. A second after I recognized him, he turned toward me. I thought it was odd that he had changed into a red shirt, but then I saw the pieces of flesh hanging from his chest just before he collapsed to the ground. I ran. I don't even know if I still had my rifle in my hand, but I ran away from Albert. I tripped over some barbed wire and fell to the ground. I thought, *Good. I'll lay here on the ground and wait for all of this to be over.* Then I felt something hit my helmet and fall beside me. A potato masher. That's what the guys called the wooden-handled German grenades. I tried to scuttle away, but the barbed wire snagged my clothes and then the grenade exploded. There was no pain, just the realization that I was going to die. The moment stretched out and that's when I thought of you and Mom. I thought of warm summer days and the smell of your library. All I wanted was to come back to you."

The voice had mesmerized everyone around the table. When it faded away, they were left speechless. François's head sank down to his chest again.

"Wait!" Mrs. MacDonnell yelled. She half rose out of her chair, but her husband's hand on her arm kept her from reaching out to François.

"Is that all?" Mr. MacDonnell said, his voice cracking with emotion.

"I want to talk to him," his wife said. "Please."

François opened his eyes and looked at her. Then he said, his voice weak, "Sometimes the spirits only want to have their say."

"No, no, please," she cried, looking more like a woman who'd just lost her child than one mourning the loss of a son who'd died sixteen years earlier.

"Madam, it is no use. He wished to share his last moments on this earth with you and that is what he did," François said, his voice calm and soothing. "We cannot command them. I know that hearing them speak can cause us to forget they are no longer of this world."

Mrs. MacDonnell began to weep. Her husband pulled her into his arms and hugged her tightly as tears rolled down his cheeks and fell upon his wife's shoulders.

"I regret the pain this has caused you. However, you have to remember that you've helped your son to rest easier," François said, then stood up.

Josephine could tell that Alice wanted to ask him to continue, but the sound of Mrs. MacDonnell's sobbing kept her enthusiasm in check.

"I'll get everyone another drink," Alice said, getting up from the table.

"I'll help," Eileen said and followed her. Eva looked at the MacDonnells with eyes that reflected their sadness. She reached out and patted Mr. MacDonnell's arm.

François had walked over to the window and was looking out into the dark. Josephine joined him.

"Your… gift holds great power. It must be a burden on your shoulders," she said.

"Years ago I found it more difficult. Now I forget that others who join me around the table are novices. To them, all of these experiences are new and difficult to understand." There was an edge to his voice that Josephine couldn't quite interpret.

"I don't know how I feel about the voice that spoke to me."

François turned and looked at her. "You are different. Your soul is open to new experiences, which means your potential for growth is almost unlimited. You have been incubating in this small town."

"I don't know about 'incubating,'" she said with a smile. "I like it here."

An odd look passed over his eyes. "This place may be in

the middle of the pine woods, but I think there is something special here."

His words seemed to echo a discussion she'd had with Blasko after they'd confronted that strange cult at Mrs. Rosehill's. The baron thought there might be a force drawing odd occurrences to Semmes County.

"What brought *you* here?" Josephine asked. Behind them, Mrs. MacDonnell's sobs had turned to soft whimpers.

François smiled. For a moment, Josephine didn't think he was going to answer. Finally, he said, "I have an old friend in town."

He turned around and went to the MacDonnells, kneeling down beside them and putting his hand on top of theirs. "The Great War and the flu that followed left the dead stacked high in the churchyards. Far too many died without being with their loved ones as they crossed over, and their families were left without knowing what their last moments were like. You've been allowed contact with your lost son and have given him peace by listening to him one last time. He longed to reach out to you again as he did when he was a child. Accept this small token for what it is and don't disparage it for what it cannot be."

The MacDonnells looked at him and Josephine saw them both relax. François stood up and turned to the rest of the group. "I'm sorry we had to cut the night short. I'd be happy to meet with you all again anytime."

Alice and Eva joined him at the front door, thanking him effusively. "Can I drive you back to the hotel?" Alice asked.

"No, I think a walk in the night air will do me good." He shrugged into a coat that seemed to envelop him, then disappeared into the night.

Someone turned on the electric lights and the strange mood that had settled upon the house was lifted in an instant. *Was it the light or did the mood come and go with François?* Josephine wondered.

CHAPTER THREE

Blasko and Bobby drove out to the Murphy farm in the deputy's patrol car. During the first part of the drive, neither man spoke. Despite everything they had been through together, the two men still weren't completely comfortable in each other's presence. Bobby didn't know Blasko's past or his true nature and Josephine, who had been courted by Bobby for years until she had finally broken it off, had insisted that telling him would be a bad idea. It hadn't been a hard argument for her to win. Blasko had never found that divulging his origins was a good idea.

Bobby eventually broke the ice. "Mrs. Rosehill's is open for business again."

"With the end of Prohibition, won't her business suffer?" Blasko didn't fully understand the vagaries of the American political system.

"Only the federal law changed. It's going to be a while before Alabama gives up being dry."

"And I'm sure the salacious story of the deaths at her house won't stop people from taking advantage of her hospitality," Blasko said. Human nature was human nature. Even in his superstitious homeland nestled in the Carpathian

25

Mountains, people found death and scandal more attracting than repelling.

Bobby slowed the car as they approached the farmhouse. "We better tell Ol' Man Murphy that we're going onto his property. I imagine he's pretty trigger-happy with whatever-the-hell-it-is on the prowl."

Blasko got out of the car and watched as Bobby approached the front porch. He didn't get far before Murphy stepped outside with a double-barreled shotgun cradled in his arms.

"That you, Bobby?" Murphy asked, looking around as though he expected to be jumped at any moment.

"Yes, and I brought another fellow with me. We're just going down to look at the spot where it happened."

"I don't care what the sheriff says, that weren't no bear or wolf," Murphy said defiantly.

"I'm inclined to agree with you," Bobby told him. "That's why I wanted a second opinion."

"What is he, some kind of animal expert? Someone from the government?" Murphy asked, squinting in Blasko's direction.

"He's seen a few murders. I expect we'll be done within the hour."

"You stop by here and let me know when you leave, 'cause I ain't takin' no prisoners tonight," Murphy said, his tone leaving no room for doubt.

"Don't blame you. If we aren't back in two hours, send for the cavalry," Bobby said, trying to make it sound like a joke. He waved to the old man and went to the trunk of his patrol car.

"I'm not arguing with a good idea," he said, pulling his Winchester '97 shotgun from the trunk. He turned it on its side and ejected the shells that were in the gun before reaching for a box of ammo and pulling out seven new shells. "I think I'd rather have slugs than buckshot," Bobby said, grabbing a flashlight for himself and handing a lantern to Blasko.

The baron didn't bother to tell him that he didn't really need the light. A full moon was rising and, to his eyes, the landscape was as clear as a summer's day.

As they walked through a fallow field toward the creek, Blasko discreetly sniffed the air and detected a peculiar odor, something wild. It was a smell that was familiar to him.

"You say there aren't any wolves around here?" Blasko asked, his eyes on the far tree line where the creek ran.

"Hasn't been a wolf in southern Alabama in decades. There might still be some up in the hills in the northeast part of the state, but not down here. 'Sides, red wolves don't get much bigger than a dog. There'd have to be a pack of them to do the damage I saw. And this didn't look like the work of a pack. If it had been a bunch of critters, they would have dragged the parts all over and fought for them. But there was none of that. Seth was just ripped apart and left there."

Bobby slowed as they neared the area where the body had been found. "We're getting close now. That's one of my markers." He shined his light on a stick with a piece of cloth tied to the top.

Blasko quickly picked out three other sticks marking off an area about fifteen feet square. The creek was only about thirty feet from the closest marker. Blasko could still smell the blood and offal. The sheriff, Bobby and men from Connelly's Funeral Home had tried to find all of the body, but there were too many small pieces. The birds had picked at the remains during the day and the worms had worked diligently to clean up the ground, but even these industrious efforts had failed to erase all traces of gore.

"We scoured this area looking for tracks. The ground is just too dry," Bobby said, moving his light back and forth around the area.

"This way," Blasko said and moved off toward the creek. He could smell the trail of blood left by the killer. "The creature moved parallel to the creek."

"How the hell do you know that?" Bobby asked, but still fell into step behind him.

Blasko moved with the assurance born from centuries of hunting prey. Even before he had become a creature of the night, he had been trained by his father's men and had gone on dozens of hunts.

They walked for a few hundred yards along the edge of the trees that bordered the creek before Blasko veered into them.

"The beast went down there," he said, putting his hand out to stop Bobby from going down the slope toward the water. "You wanted a print. If it left one, it would be in the mud at the edge of the creek."

"Good thinking," Bobby said. He used his light to search the bank as he carefully walked a path a yard away from the damp ground. "There!" The light illuminated a dark spot only a couple of inches from the slow-moving water. "Damn it. I should have brought some plaster," he grumbled as he carefully stepped down closer to the print.

Blasko followed him. When he saw the elongated print with deep claw marks at the end of each digit, he immediately recognized it. Not the individual, but the species.

"That print looks like a cross between a bear and a wolf. Damnedest track I've ever seen. Could be a deformed or crippled animal... You have any ideas?" Bobby asked.

"Perhaps. But I believe I'll keep my opinions to myself for the moment."

"Come on, now. If we've got some killer animal roaming around here, I need to know what it is," Bobby said, shining his light on Blasko.

"I'm not sure what it is. I just have a theory. As soon as I know for sure that I'm on the right path, I'll tell you." Of course he was lying. Blasko already knew what the creature was, but he also knew that even Bobby wouldn't believe him. Plus, Bobby would want to know how he knew, and that wasn't a conversation Blasko was ready to have.

"I hope no one else gets hurt while you're making up your mind," Bobby said. He took out his handkerchief and tied it to a tree branch so he could easily find the spot in the morning. "I'll get some plaster and make a cast of it first thing tomorrow. You got any more ideas where this animal went? You tracked it this far."

"I assume it went into the water to clean itself," Blasko said. His nose told him that the blood trail ended here.

"I've never heard tell of any animal that cleans itself off after a kill. Most creatures love the smell of blood and meat," Bobby said suspiciously.

"I agree," Blasko said.

"What are you saying?" Bobby was beginning to have a suspicion. One he didn't like.

"I'm not saying anything more. Except that, if I'm right, everyone needs to stay in at night. Or at the very least, go out in pairs and be well armed."

"Now you listen here. You can't give a warning like that and not tell me what you think this thing is," Bobby said, moving closer to Blasko. He was taller and, now that he'd stepped up from the creek bed, he was looking down at the baron.

Blasko straightened his back and met his gaze. "When I'm ready. Or I should say, when you are ready."

"What does that mean?" Bobby asked, his voice louder than before.

Blasko sighed. "It means that I don't think you would believe me if I told you my suspicions."

"Try me," Bobby shot back.

"Bah! This is getting us nowhere. I've already told you my decision." With that, Blasko wheeled around and strode off back toward the scene of the attack.

"You're worse than arguing with a woman," Bobby said to his back.

"You should thank me for finding the track for you," Blasko responded without turning around.

"I guess you got me there." Bobby looked at the sky. The wind was picking up and clouds drifted across the moon. "Front's moving in."

Before the words were out of his mouth, they heard an eerie howl in the distance.

"What the hell was that?" Bobby asked, startled.

"Exactly," Blasko said. "It's too far away for us to go after it."

"You mean that's what did this?" Bobby waved his arm at the area marked off by his stakes, his voice an octave higher.

"That is my theory."

"When you said that it washed off the blood, you made it sound like it might be human."

"I've told you all that I'm going to tell you," Blasko said and turned back toward the farmhouse.

"I drove you out here. The least you can do is answer my questions," Bobby muttered as he followed the baron.

When they got back to the house, all of the lights were on. Murphy came out from the barn, holding a lantern high in one hand and his shotgun in the other.

"Y'all hear that?" The old man's voice held a slight tremor.

"You need to stay inside tonight," Blasko told the man.

"Who in damnation are you?" Murphy asked, holding the lantern up to get a better look at Blasko.

"He's Josephine Nicolson's cousin from Europe," Bobby said.

"Whatever that was has my animals spooked," Murphy said, deciding to ignore Blasko.

"You best look after yourself and your family," Blasko warned him again.

"Now see here. I don't care whose cousin you are. Looking after my animals is part of looking after my family," Murphy said defiantly.

Blasko stepped toward the man. "I understand you found the boy's body."

"Yep, that's right."

"Do you remember what you saw?"

"How... How... could I forget that? He was all tore up,"

Murphy said softly.

"Stay inside with your family," Blasko repeated.

Murphy shifted nervously, but didn't answer.

"You got plenty of ammo for that shotgun?" Bobby asked.

"Buckshot," the old man said.

"I got some slugs in the trunk of my car." Bobby gave the man half a box of ammo and Murphy just stared at him in the lamplight, dumbfounded.

They drove back to Josephine's house in silence. When Blasko got out of the car, he turned back to Bobby. "I'd tell you anything I thought might save lives." He started to walk away, but stopped. "There *is* one thing you can do. Check if there are any strangers in town."

"Now you sound like Sheriff Logan," Bobby said under his breath.

CHAPTER FOUR

As Blasko walked up the driveway toward his basement entrance, he noticed Josephine's car parked in front of the garage. Looking up, he saw that a light was still on in her bedroom window. He changed direction and headed for the door into the main house.

He assumed she'd be in her room, but as he came in through the kitchen and entered the dining room, he heard a noise from the other side of the house. He could see light coming from the library.

"I didn't think you would be up," he said, watching her from the doorway.

Josephine jumped at the sound of his voice. "You know, it wouldn't kill you to let your feet drop a little heavier when you walk," she said, trying to cover her embarrassment at being caught unaware.

"Walking softly has served me well over the centuries," Blasko said with a slight smile. He turned his head to read the title of the book she was holding and, perhaps, half hiding. "Poe. I approve. But his stories might make it a little harder to sleep."

"Since meeting you, his stories don't scare me," she parried.

"Did you just get back from your ladies' night out?" he asked. "Can I fix you a drink?"

"I've had enough to drink tonight." She paused. "Or maybe I haven't had enough. The man conducting the séance was rather unusual."

"I told you, séances are nonsense." Blasko waved his hand dismissively.

"I would have agreed. I would have…"

Blasko was ready to launch into a discourse on the foolishness of trying to summon the dead when he noticed her pensive attitude. "This… event affected you," he said, moving closer to her.

Josephine held up the book and let it fall open to the start of "The Purloined Letter" where someone had placed a handwritten note.

"My Uncle Petey had a strange sense of humor," she said.

"What does your uncle and this letter have to do with the séance?" Blasko asked with genuine interest.

Josephine described the evening's events. As she spoke, she couldn't help but notice Blasko's expression become more distracted.

"Mediums. Bah, they are only charlatans. Don't think any more about it. Let me tell you where I've been." With that, he went on to explain his journey out to the scene of Seth Taylor's murder.

"An animal killed him?" Josephine asked.

"Not a natural animal. I've seen something similar." He started to pace back and forth and Josephine could see his green eyes take on a strange red glow. She had seldom seen him this angry since the night they'd met, when her trip to spread her grandfather's ashes had ended with an unexpected detour to Blasko's mountain fortress.

"Sit down," he told her brusquely.

"I'm fine standing." Josephine wasn't about to let him order her around.

Blasko took a deep breath. When he had more control over his emotions, he tried again. "Please, have a seat. I have some information that might be of interest to you."

Josephine detected a hint of sarcasm in his tone, but decided to go along anyway. Once she was seated, Blasko pulled a chair up close to hers.

"You have accused me of killing the peasants in your grandfather's village. My village, if we're being fair. It was on land that I controlled, and my family before me."

"You're picking at a scab," Josephine said, feeling the blood rise in her cheeks.

"Hah! You want me to be the villain in your story, but I was not the killer. An animal was stalking the village. I tried to hunt it down. It was my duty to protect those people. My honor was at stake. I spent months trying to catch the creature. One time I was sure that I had mortally wounded the monster, but when it fell into the river, swollen by the spring rains, I never found the body."

"But the killings stopped."

"They stopped in the village. I found out that they started up again a few months later, about two hundred miles away from where the wounded monster went into the river."

"Monster? What type of monster?"

"A month before the killings in the village started, a band of gypsies had made camp between the village and the town of Capataneni. Items went missing. A ring, a chicken, a couple of knives. The villagers were quick to blame the gypsies and chase them out of the valley. That's when the killings began. The first to die were the ones who had been the most aggressive in chasing the gypsies away."

"But the villagers blamed you," Josephine said, remembering the words in her grandfather's diary.

"Some did. After the first death, I spent my nights hunting the beast. Several times I was sighted near where the deaths had occurred. To many of the villagers I was just a legend, having given up most of my duties and retreated to my castle decades before. So when villagers were killed, and I was seen nearby, they came to the conclusion that I was responsible."

"Why did you let me believe it?"

"How could you really think I was guilty?" Blasko said, looking offended. Josephine wanted to point out that he was a vampire and had tried to kill her the first time they'd met, but if he didn't see the irony in his question then she could only shake her head.

"So what did attack the village? A gypsy?" She couldn't keep the doubt out of her voice.

"A werewolf!" he said with unnecessary dramatic flair.

"What? Oh, come on." Now she didn't even try to hide her skepticism. "I read a book last year called *A Werewolf in Paris*. It was... fanciful. You seriously think that's what was stalking my grandfather's village?"

"I saw it! You forget who I am," he said, then added with less pride, "What I am."

"You have a point." She paused, trying to decide if she was being pulled into some delusion of Blasko's. But thinking back over everything she'd seen and experienced during the last year, she had to conclude that a werewolf running loose in Semmes County no longer seemed improbable.

"This... thing ripped men, women and children apart. At the time, I was helpless to stop it. If the creature had appeared a hundred years earlier, I would have had a thousand men at my command. Nothing would have stopped me from destroying it. But by the time the attacks started, I was alone."

"You could have told me all of this earlier."

"You wouldn't have believed me. You had already made up your mind."

"I'll admit to being a bit hasty in my judgment. I'm hundreds of years younger, but I'll be the mature one and apologize."

"None of that matters now, but we have to catch the monster this time." Blasko looked thoughtful. "This medium you went to visit... What do you know about him?"

"Just what I've told you," she said, seeing where he was

going. "How fair would it be to cast François, the stranger in town, as the villain? Isn't that the same position you were in not long ago?" she reasoned. "Wait. When did you say the boy was killed?"

"Last night."

"Everyone said François was conducting a séance last night."

"It could have been very early in the morning."

"Maybe. But if he has an alibi, then he can be eliminated as a suspect," Josephine said firmly, trying to back Blasko down from whatever direct action he'd been planning.

"We must pursue this with great haste. If this animal is anything like the beast I knew then, there will be more killings... soon."

"If François *is* the man you're after, he's not stupid. He spent most of tonight ingratiating himself with the people at the séance. He's been performing séances in town for almost two weeks now. Whether you or I believe it's possible to talk to the dead, he's making believers out of a lot of people," Josephine said.

"Where is he staying?"

"The Magnolia Hotel."

Blasko nodded.

"Look, let me check into his alibi. Maybe Bobby will have a better idea of the boy's time of death after Dr. McGuire has looked at the body. And I can talk to the people who were at the séance last night. If his alibi holds up, then you'll have to admit he's not your man... or monster." Josephine's voice was slow and firm. She didn't want Blasko doing anything rash.

"I'm not focused solely on the medium. He just seems a likely suspect," Blasko said begrudgingly in his best Sherlock Holmes impression. "Check and double check his alibi," he added.

"A werewolf. I can't see how that's possible," Josephine said as all the implications of what Blasko was suggesting sunk in. "Though I have heard that Native Americans believe in shapeshifters. The Seminoles have a legend about an owl man. I can't remember all of the details, but it eats the hearts of its victims."

"I don't think a giant owl did this," Blasko said dismissively.

"Of course not, but some of the other tribes, particularly those out west, have legends of shamans who could shift into other creatures."

"I need you to send a telegram for me tomorrow. There is a manuscript in my castle that might be helpful." Blasko didn't add that he planned on requesting that a large sum of gold coins be included in the shipment. He tried not to dwell on the fact that he would be relying on a group of bandits to pack the gold into a crate and send it to him. They had been willing to work with him and had been loyal when he was in residence, but with him gone he wasn't sure they would continue to do what he asked.

"I'll send it first thing," she agreed. "Then I'll talk to Bobby."

"Be careful," Blasko said, taking her hands in his. He leaned forward and lightly kissed her cheek. "Don't take any risks," he whispered affectionately.

Josephine looked into his eyes and smiled. "I almost think you care about me."

"You know there is a blood bond between us."

"If you want to believe that's all there is, then go ahead. I'm hundreds of years younger than you and I know better." She reached up and stroked his cheek. For a moment he leaned into her hand before standing up abruptly.

"I'll leave the telegram in an envelope outside my door," he said and walked out of the room without another word.

Josephine shook her head. She was having a hard time understanding what she felt for Blasko. At times it seemed to cross the boundary into love, while at other times it was more like what she would feel for a very old and dear friend. And sometimes she just found him incredibly irritating. As for how he really felt about her, she had no idea.

She remembered the reason she'd come to the library in the first place and looked down at the letter, still sticking out of the collected works of Edgar Allan Poe. She hadn't read past the salutation when Blasko had shown up. She picked up the note and unfolded it.

My dear brother,

I wish I could hand you this letter in person or, better yet, speak these words to you. We both know I'm no good when it comes to dealing with the things that really matter in life.

I'll start out by saying that I'm sorry. Sorry for what I put you and the rest of our family through. I've never been the man I wanted to be. What a sad statement. I'm going to make one last effort to redeem myself. If I'm successful, then I will be providing a small legacy to you and my niece. I know that you will think I'm being ridiculous. You have been successful while all I've been to our family is a great sinkhole for money, time and effort.

I want to feel like a success just once in my life. And yes, I want to have something tangible to show that I am worthy of the affection and trust you all have repeatedly given me.

Okay, enough wallowing in self pity. If you've found this note, then it means I was never able to return to your house. I can only assume that I'm dead. If I'm dead, does that mean I have failed in my endeavor? I've planned on the possibility that I won't survive. See, your old brother isn't so stupid. I will leave another note for you at the post office on Cedar Island.

I hope you will never read this letter. Please remember that I always meant to do the right thing by my family. I just found myself wanting.

Your loving brother,
Petey

Josephine looked at the date at the top of the letter. It had been written twenty years ago. She tried to remember the details of her uncle's death. All she had were vague memories that he had drowned. Why had he placed this note in the collected works of Poe? It was all very odd. How much did this validate François?

I've stepped into one of those Gothic novels I read as a girl, Josephine thought. She turned off the lights and headed upstairs. She spent a restless night divided between periods of nightmares and dreams, and longer periods of wakefulness as she tried to understand everything that François and Blasko had told her.

CHAPTER FIVE

Blasko went down to his apartment, intending to read for a while and not dwell on his suspicions about what was lurking in the woods. But after sitting down with Ellery Queen's *The Roman Hat Mystery*, he couldn't get past the second chapter.

"I need to take a walk," he told Vasile. The bat was lapping up water from a small bowl that Blasko had placed on a high shelf.

Once outside, Blasko considered his destination. As always, the first thought that came into his head was the need for fresh blood. What Josephine provided for him was old and didn't contain the nutrition his body craved. He'd gone around and around with Josephine about his needs, but she still demanded that he not use the citizens of Semmes County as his personal blood donors. Even the bad ones. She had lifted the prohibition a few times when it had been absolutely necessary, even going so far as to let him drink from her. But the best she'd been able to offer as a long-term solution had been to find a medical supply company closer than the one she'd been using in Atlanta, so the blood was now marginally less stale.

Blasko sighed and turned toward the local boarding house. He would ignore his body's desire for the moment.

Instead he would talk to Matthew.

Matthew Hodge was a veteran of the Great War who had sunk into depression and alcoholism when he came back from overseas. Blasko had used his powers to hypnotize Matthew in an effort to cure him of his desire for drink. In exchange, Blasko had used Matthew as his eyes and ears in the community. But their relationship had been strained since November when the events Matthew had witnessed had left him in a state not much different than when he'd returned from the war.

Blasko saw the red glow of a cigarette on the porch of the boarding house. "I assumed it was you," he said once he was standing on the porch. Matthew hadn't said a word or given Blasko more than a glance.

"And I assumed you were lurking somewhere in the dark shadows," he finally said, stubbing out the cigarette and dropping it into an old coffee can beside his chair.

"Are you doing better?" Blasko asked awkwardly.

"Haven't seen you in a while."

"We talked after the... affair out at Mrs. Rosehill's."

"Yeah, great talk."

"You were still recovering."

"Yeah, crazy me needing to recover after being abducted and forced to watch... that crazy stuff." Matthew searched his pockets for another cigarette. "I wanted to help." He found a half-smoked cigarette and lit it. "But just watching... I thought the stuff I saw in the war was bad. This was the same in some ways. Feeling like I and everyone else were just pawns at fate's mercy."

"Battle strips away the veneer that allows us to feel like we are in control. Once you accept that you are never fully in control, you can go into battle with clear eyes," Blasko told him.

"I went into this last battle tied to a chair. And thanks to you, I can't get drunk."

"I've heard people claim that they drink to forget. That's a lie. When you constantly get drunk, you mire yourself down. Your life never moves on. You can't recover."

"Thanks for the pep talk. Glad you came by. Oh, wait, I bet you got something you want me to do. Right?" Matthew said with bitterness.

Blasko moved forward suddenly and grabbed Matthew by the collar, pulling him up out of the chair.

"What the..." Matthew flailed his arms, hitting at Blasko ineffectively. "Let go of me!"

Blasko released him. Matthew just managed to keep from going all the way down on his knees. Lights came on inside the house.

"Now you've done it," Matthew said.

"You are a stupid man. You have greatness in you, but you squander it."

The door flew open before Matthew could respond.

"What the hell is going on out here? It's the middle of the night!" Paul Kowalski, the manager of the boarding house, yelled. "I ought to kick you out," he said, looking at Matthew and then at Blasko. "And you. What kind of freak are you, wandering around town at all hours of the morning?" He turned back to Matthew. "I let you have a key and this is how you treat the privilege?"

"I'm sorry. He's just leaving," Matthew answered.

"*We're* leaving," Blasko corrected him.

Matthew looked at him and, for a moment, they all thought he was going to argue about it. Instead he looked at the old landlord standing in the doorway in his robe and nodded.

"Sorry. It won't happen again."

"Better not," Kowalski said. He stood there staring angrily at the men until they'd walked down the porch steps and away from the boarding house.

"What do you want?" Matthew growled.

Blasko stopped walking and turned to him. "Enough. Don't blame me for your troubles. Fate is the defining force in our lives, but you can control many things. You could have been more vigilant when you were guarding Josephine."

Matthew bowed his chest angrily. "Don't think I haven't blamed myself for letting Josephine be taken by those degenerates. I know I should have been more careful."

Blasko shook his head. "I'm not blaming you. I'm trying to get you to see that you must take control of everything you can. Fate might still send that bullet with your name on it, but at least you will know you did everything you could before it happens. The same fate that sent you to war guided events so that you would survive and we would meet."

"Great," Matthew mumbled.

"At that moment our destinies intermingled. Yes, I need you. I admit it. But look me in the eye and tell me that you didn't need me when I found you lying in the gutter."

Matthew stared back at him. "Maybe I did need a slap in the face or a helping hand. I'm not sure I needed you."

"Yet here I am," Blasko said.

Oddly, this seemed to get at the heart of the matter. Right or wrong, it was what it was.

"Fine. Just tell me what you want now," Matthew said, resigned.

"This time it is about protecting this town. Did you hear about the boy who was killed?"

Matthew looked sharply at Blasko. "I heard. The rumor is he was killed by a bear."

They resumed walking toward Sumter's town square.

"It wasn't a bear. I know this animal," Blasko said gravely.

"I should have known," Matthew said, but his anger had drained away.

"It is a man, at least partly. He has the ability to change into a monster capable of ripping a person apart." Blasko watched Matthew, wondering how much he should tell him.

"I heard that it was brutal."

"The boy was gutted and his limbs torn from his body."

Matthew suddenly stopped walking. "I saw a monster during the war. It's strange… What I saw was terrifying, but it blended in so well with all the other grotesque outrages that were taking place around me. It just seemed like one more horror of war."

Blasko stopped beside him and waited for him to continue.

"I guess I'd blocked the memory until now," Matthew said softly.

"Tell me what happened."

"It wasn't just one monster… We had jumped into a German trench. They were on the run by this time, so entering the trenches wasn't as dangerous as it sounds. We found occasional pockets of resistance, not much more. I was on a shotgun squad, so we were the first ones in the trench. My job was to jump in with my buddy and we'd stand back to back, pumping off buckshot in both directions. After we fired three rounds we'd each go our own direction, clearing any dugouts we found until we met up with some of the other squad members.

"I came around the corner in the trench and saw this… thing lifting Stacy Martin above its head. Six foot in the air and then it just pulled him apart. I was stunned and stood there for a second. When it threw Stacy down, the thing turned and looked at me. That's when I started pumping buckshot from my Winchester into it. Had absolutely no effect. The thing took a step toward me. I knew right then that I was dead when another one of the creatures jumped down on top of it. I turned back and ran in the direction I'd come. Before I got very far, a shell went off and caved in part of the trench. I was knocked out for a few minutes before my buddy found me and pulled me out."

"What did these creatures look like?"

"Both of them had muzzles like wolves and their hands—hell, paws—were oversized with three-inch-long talons for claws. I might have dreamed it. There was gas still lingering in the lower parts of the trenches and the artillery left me dazed. Fear, adrenaline. I never saw anything like that again, so I just wrote it off. I didn't go back to that part of the trench, though. When they told me later that Stacy had been killed, I just let it drop. I'd been in the Army long enough to know you didn't volunteer for trouble."

"You saw a werewolf. Actually, two werewolves," Blasko said bluntly.

"What are you talking about?" Matthew asked. He was irritated and confused, both by the return of memories he'd thought were long buried and by the absurd emergence of monsters that he didn't think existed in the first place.

"You described them," Blasko said with a shrug. "I just gave them a name."

Matthew looked like he wanted to argue, but instead he started walking again. "Before you arrived, before I saw what I saw at Mrs. Rosehill's, I would have sworn I'd imagined those two creatures in that trench. Now... I don't know."

"I don't have much experience with them. Only once back in the Carpathian Mountains did I have to deal with one. What I've read suggests that they are drawn to slaughter. Wars are natural hunting grounds for them. A place where they can let their inner nature out without fearing discovery."

"But you think one of those things is loose and hunting in Semmes County now?"

"I do."

"I shot that beast with several rounds of buckshot and it didn't even flinch."

"I need to do more research on how to combat it when it's in wolf form," Blasko said. "But I'll tell you one fact. I've never met any creature that didn't die when you cut off its head." He paused for a moment. "Which brings us to a question. Where can I buy a good sword?"

"What? Are you kidding?"

"I'd prefer a heavy sword and not a sabre."

"Just head on down to the sword store across from the courthouse."

"You're not taking this seriously."

"That you want a sword to kill a werewolf? No, I am not."

"You saw them during the war."

"And my suggestion would be a howitzer. Something with a little range."

"I think a more portable and discreet weapon is needed."

"Then I suggest a twelve gauge with slugs."

"A headshot with a shotgun slug *might* do the job," Blasko mused.

"This is crazy. I hope you're wrong about this."

"Possibly. The real reason I came to you is that there is a stranger in town that I want you to keep an eye on."

"Who is he?"

"You are not to approach him."

"I guess you don't trust me after last time," Matthew said with an edge to his voice.

"I trust you, but this man could be a werewolf. If he is, then I don't have to tell you that he is very dangerous. His name is François LeSauvage and he's presenting himself as a medium."

"A medium what?"

"A spiritualist. Someone who can talk to the dead," Blasko snapped, not sure if Matthew was kidding or not.

"That guy! I've heard people talking about him. He's made quite an impression in the last couple of weeks."

"He's staying at the Magnolia Hotel."

"I guess it's just a coincidence that we're walking in the direction of the hotel now."

"I want to look it over. Again, don't go near him. Don't let him see you. I just want you to talk to people who've talked to him. Find out what his routine is."

They had reached the square and could see the hotel on the other side of the courthouse.

"Is that him?" Matthew asked, nodding to a dark figure walking toward the hotel.

"Blast!" Blasko hissed when he saw the man stop. He looked around, hoping there was some concealment available, but there was nothing. And in that instant Blasko knew it was too late. The man had sensed them watching him. François turned slowly and looked across the courthouse grounds. He hesitated for a moment before striding purposefully in their direction.

Blasko didn't want to confront him, but they didn't have a choice. "There's nothing for it now," he muttered under his breath.

"What?" Matthew asked.

Blasko whispered, "It is a shame there *isn't* a sword shop nearby."

"Don't try to be funny."

"I don't like the look of him," Blasko said, and squared up on the figure marching toward them. François was only twenty paces away now. *Dueling distance*, Blasko thought.

"Gentlemen," François said, tipping his hat as he came closer. "You're out late. You must be the baron I've heard so much about." He stuck out his gloved hand to Blasko, who just looked at it until François pulled it back. "Manners in your country must be slightly different than where I come from." François's voice was more than a little snarky.

"France," Blasko said as though he were cursing.

"I have offended you in some way?" François asked.

"I have no wish to play games with you," Blasko said, knowing that he should be more polite but finding it impossible. Something about the man set his fangs on edge.

"Games can be an amusing way to pass the time. I would think that, at your age, you'd be looking for diversions. I know I am."

"Why are you here?" Blasko asked.

"And who is this fellow?" François turned to Matthew and stuck out his hand. "François LeSauvage."

Matthew took the hand and shook it. "Matthew Hodge. I've heard about how you can talk to the dead."

"Just one of my talents." He turned back to Blasko. "Your henchman has better manners than you do."

"Hey, what do you mean 'henchman?'" Matthew said. François gave him a withering look.

"We've gotten off on the wrong foot," François said,

changing tack so quickly that it caught Blasko by surprise. "You and I are two strangers in a strange land. We should become fast friends."

While Blasko stood there trying to decide how to reply, François turned to Matthew. "Henchman was too strong a word. I'd just heard that you… help the baron out on occasion. Pardon my clumsy use of the language." He stuck out his hand again in apparent apology. Matthew didn't know how not to take it and accepted the light shake. "There, all forgiven, I hope."

"I've never met a spiritualist who wasn't cheating villagers out of their money," Blasko stated, then added, "But who knows…" He shrugged.

"I understand. I've been chased from one town to another across whole continents. You're from the old country. Those ways can be hard to give up. But this is a new land. All I do is provide a service to people who long for their lost loved ones. You and I don't have to be friends, but I hope you'll give me the courtesy of allowing me to prove myself." François looked straight into Blasko's eyes.

Blasko stared back and tried to read the man. Nothing. Blasko gave him a nod.

"Then I'll bid you all goodnight." With that, François tipped his hat and turned on his heel.

Once Matthew decided that the man was out of earshot, he turned to Blasko, who huffed.

"He seems like a piece of work," Matthew said.

"Watch him."

"Yeah, sure. Hey, you *do* know it's winter, don't you?"

CHAPTER SIX

Sunshine streamed through the bedroom window. Josephine tried to ignore it, but eventually she started thinking about all of the chores she had planned for the day. *It's too cold to get out of bed*, she told herself before she heard the rattling of the steam radiator which promised to warm up the room. One foot over the side at a time, she managed to crawl out.

Josephine sat down to a hearty breakfast with her cook, Anna Durand, and her maid, Grace Dunn. Grace was the only other person in Semmes County who was privy to Blasko's true nature. She'd accompanied Josephine to Romania and had helped bring Blasko to the United States. Her knowledge of the situation had elevated her from Josephine's maid to a confidant. At first, Grace had been sure that the baron was Satan's first cousin, but after he had helped get her brother released from jail a few months earlier, she'd settled into a more accepting attitude, though she still wasn't sure how to reconcile her faith with his condition.

"Everyone is talkin' about that boy bein' killed," Grace said.

"Who's talking about it?" Josephine asked, curious about what rumors were going around town.

"Well, Ronnie told me they were all talkin' about it at… that place."

Ronnie was Grace's brother and he was a skilled carpenter. He was currently working on repairs at Mrs. Rosehill's, the illegal drinking and gambling establishment that had been heavily damaged by a supernatural portal back in the fall. Mrs. Rosehill took everything in her stride and had reopened the business while the renovations were taking place. While the private club didn't allow women of low repute to operate out of it, most people, Grace included, considered the place too scandalous to name.

"I'm surprised your brother would work there," Anna said. The older woman liked to gently poke fun at Grace when she had the chance.

"The way things are, he's got to take work where he can find it. Mrs. Rosehill came to him and asked him special to do the work," Grace said. From her tone, it was clear she had very mixed feelings about the situation. "With some help from above, he'll be done and out of that devil's den soon."

"What did he hear?" Josephine said, trying to get back to the attack.

"Ronnie heard that that boy was torn all to pieces. Maybe a bear or something. That's all we need. Bad enough we got murders and all goin' on; now wild animals are comin' to get us." Grace had a knack for the hyperbolic.

"I don't think you need to worry about wild animals," Josephine said, causing both Anna and Grace to look at her.

"You know something about that boy's death?" Grace asked.

"The baron went out with Bobby to look at the spot where Seth Taylor was found," Josephine said, receiving an incredulous look from Grace.

"Mr. Bobby took the baron out there?" Grace reached for another biscuit.

"He wanted the baron's opinion," Josephine told her.

Grace didn't look happy. She had always hoped that Josephine and Bobby Tucker would get back together, and that Bobby would intervene somehow to get the baron out of Josephine's house. While she had almost given up on that, finding out that Bobby was seeking out the baron's assistance wasn't good news.

"So what have *you* heard about the death?" Anna asked Josephine.

She gave them a quick accounting that left the identity of the killer open to interpretation. When she finished, both Anna and Grace were shaking their heads.

"I hear that there's a spiritualist in town," Anna said, causing both Josephine and Grace to look at her, but for different reasons. Josephine hadn't told either of them about the séance last night because she hadn't wanted to hear their opinions on the matter. She already knew that Grace would disapprove.

"Yes, I've heard about him," Josephine said cryptically.

"That's witchcraft. As bad as that witch down by the river," Grace huffed. The witch by the river was Sissy Lylou Masson, a bone doctor who, Josephine had been surprised to find out, served a large cross section of the county.

"She did sort of help to free your brother," Josephine said, trying to avoid any talk of François.

"That woman didn't do much," Grace grumbled.

"I have an aunt who is very involved in the spiritualist movement. She moved up to Tennessee with her husband and they conduct séances there. They are also very devout Christians," Anna said, giving Grace a challenging look.

Grace looked like she wanted to say something, but apparently thought better of it. Grace respected Anna both for her age and her good cooking.

Josephine got up and put her dishes in the sink before anyone could ask her what *she* thought about spiritualists. In the back of her mind she made a note to talk with Anna about her sister and her experiences when Grace wasn't around to disapprove.

An hour later, Josephine was out the door with Blasko's telegram in her hand. The weather was sunny and brisk, so she decided to walk downtown. After stopping by the Western Union office, Josephine looked up and down the main street. Instead of stopping by the bank, she headed straight for the sheriff's office. Luck was with her and she found Bobby outside next to his car, talking with a man whom Josephine didn't recognize. The man was dressed in an ill-fitting suit and was shaking his head as Bobby talked to him.

Josephine caught Bobby's eye. He nodded to her and inclined his head in an invitation for her to join them.

"Mr. Taylor, this is Josephine Nicolson," Bobby said when she approached them. She could see that the man's eyes were red and weary, half hidden in a rough complexion that spoke of many hours working in the sun.

"Miss Nicolson," the man said with a nod.

"Mr. Taylor. I heard about your son. I'm so sorry."

"He weren't killed by no animal," the man said, as much to Bobby as to Josephine.

"I'm looking into Seth's death," Bobby assured the man.

"You ain't goin' to get any help from the sheriff. He as much as told me that he wasn't lookin' no further than a bear or a cougar. That don't make no sense. I've hunted this land since I was knee-high to a mule. There aren't no animals that would do that to a man." Elroy Taylor looked ready to fight anyone who disagreed with him.

"I believe you," Bobby said.

"You better mean it. I don't want you tellin' me one thing and doin' another," Elroy said, staring Bobby square in the face. "Look hard at the Murphys. Our family has had nothin' but trouble from them since they moved in."

"When did they buy the land next to yours?"

"Ahh, that was when my grandfather was farming it. Just before the War." Both Bobby and Josephine realized that Elroy was referring to the Civil War, almost seventy years earlier.

"What have you been feuding about?"

"It's the property line. That creek has moved a couple of times. They just aren't reasonable about it."

"What specific trouble have you had?" Bobby asked, not because he really thought it had anything to do with the boy's death, but more because he was fascinated by an argument that had gone on for so long.

"They've stolen our cows, for one thing."

"I don't remember seeing any reports about that."

"Well, the last time was back in the nineties."

Bobby had to work hard not to roll his eyes. "Anything recent?"

"We pretty much stay away from each other. When I took over, I farmed that bottom land. I keep my cows on the west side away from the Murphys. It's a damn nuisance to have to haul water to them."

"Do you know why Seth was on the other side of the creek?"

"He must've been dragged over there. He's known since he could walk not to go on Murphy land."

"Can you think of anyone else who would have wanted to hurt him?"

"Tear him apart, you mean. Who could do something like that?" the man said, confused.

"Let's not worry about how he was killed right now. I'm just trying to find out who would have wanted to do that to him."

Elroy sighed heavily and shook his head. "Truth is, I want it to be them Murphys, but I just don't see it. Anyone else... I just... Seth got into some scuffles when he was in school. Don't see how that can mean much. He quit school when he was sixteen and went to work with me full-time on the farm. We work hard. Not a lot of time to be gettin' into trouble."

"Did he have a girlfriend?"

"Nothin' serious. He courted Millie Campbell for a couple of years when he was goin' to school. Never went no place, though. His momma tried hitchin' him up to some girls from church." Elroy shrugged.

After Bobby asked a few more questions, Elroy Taylor got into his old Model A pickup and started it up.

"That was his only child," Bobby said as he and Josephine watched the old man drive away.

"I can't imagine the pain he's going through."

"His wife couldn't even come into town. He told me she's laid up in bed with her sister watching over her." Bobby turned to Josephine. "I guess you heard that I talked to the baron last night."

"He seems convinced it was some kind of monster." Josephine watched Bobby's face closely, curious what his reaction would be.

"I gathered as much. Anyone who saw the body would think the same thing," he responded with a complete lack of skepticism.

"Except the sheriff."

"He's in denial. Ever since what happened out at Mrs. Rosehill's, I think he's been living more and more with his head buried in the sand."

"Connelly have the body?" Josephine asked.

"What's left of it."

"I want to take a look at it," Josephine said with more confidence than she felt.

"No you don't," Bobby said firmly.

"Blasko said the boy was torn apart."

"Which is why you don't need to see it. You don't need those images in your head."

"Were there teeth or claw marks on the... parts?" Josephine persisted, though she had to admit the thought of it was making her stomach roll over.

"Both, and they weren't like anything I've ever seen. Trouble is, I need to convince Sheriff Logan."

"We could talk with Colonel Etheridge."

"Why in the world would we want to do that?" Bobby asked, surprised by this suggestion.

"He spent ten years in Africa. He might be able to give us some information about what attacked the boy."

"Maybe," Bobby said. He actually thought it was a good idea, but he just wished he'd been the one to come up with it.

"He lives a few doors down from me," Josephine pushed.

"I know where he lives. Now that I think about it, he and the sheriff are friends."

"Etheridge will help us if I ask him to."

"I didn't know you were so close with him."

"He and my father were good friends. Went hunting together. Like Papa, he was a widower. He never had a child of his own, so maybe that's why he doted on me when I was young."

"The things I learn about you. Come on then," Bobby said, indicating his car.

Colonel Samuel Etheridge's house looked like a cottage next to most of the surrounding homes. There was a storybook quality to the design that had always reminded Josephine of an illustration from a Grimms' fairytale. The home was filled with items the colonel had collected during his lifetime of traveling the world and it had fascinated her as a child.

"Well, call out the brass band and play a tune, if it isn't little Josie!" shouted the stout, leathery man who answered the door in a voice that could be heard across the street. "Get in here, girl!" he said, giving her a big hug and bussing her cheek with his walrus mustache.

Bobby followed her inside, though he hadn't been invited or, apparently, even noticed.

"I'd ask you why you're here, but I don't give a darn. Sit. You too, sir, sit," Etheridge said, finally acknowledging Bobby.

"Do you know Bobby Tucker?" Josephine asked by way of introduction.

Etheridge peered at the deputy. The mahogany paneling and the heavy curtains over the windows made the room dark and it was hard for him to see.

"Yes, yes, works for Logan. Of course. You all were courting, the last I heard. That was before your father..." He let the last sentence trail off and sadness cast a shadow over his features.

"He's looking into the death of Seth Taylor," Josephine explained.

"Taylor, Taylor. I don't think I know any Taylors," Etheridge said, stroking his chin in thought.

"He was killed outside of town yesterday morning. Early, before the sun rose," Bobby said.

"By gosh, that's right. My coal man came by this morning and was talking about it. Some rot about a wild animal. Nothing 'round here is going to do that," Etheridge said, waving his hands dismissively. "Told him so, too."

"Would you be willing to look at the body and give us your opinion?" Josephine asked.

"Be delighted."

"You shoot all these animals?" Bobby's eyes had adjusted to the dim light and he was looking around at the animal heads on the wall of the parlor.

"Yes, I did."

"Colonel Etheridge served as attaché in several African countries during Teddy Roosevelt's administration."

"Don't think I'm one of those big game hunters who go around shooting animals to show off. Every one of these animals was too sick, too injured or too dangerous. See that lion head over there? He'd been crippled when he was young. Don't know what he did for the first ten years of his life, but when I showed up he was eating women and children. The village asked me to help them. That rhino had a broken leg. When I came upon him, he'd lost a third of his weight. I don't kill anything that doesn't need killing. Man or animal," the colonel said with a cold tone that sounded much younger than his sixty-eight years. "And I got the guns to do it." He tilted his head toward a tall gun cabinet in the corner housing half a dozen oversize hunting rifles, as well as four shotguns.

"Your professional opinion of the wounds would be helpful," Josephine said.

"Just let me get my hat and coat."

When they arrived at the funeral home, mortician Jerry Connelly ushered them in.

"Not much I can do with the boy. Never seen anything like it. Seen worse bodies, but never seen one torn up like this."

"The colonel would like to take a look at the wounds," Bobby said.

Connelly looked at both men. "The sheriff said I wasn't to let anyone see what was left of that boy. Did he send you over here?"

"Not as such," Bobby said.

"The thing is, the sheriff says it was a wolf or a bear. Maybe a cougar that killed him," Josephine jumped in.

"Yeah, he said that," Connelly said, his tone making it clear he didn't really believe it.

"So we just thought that, if he had a second opinion, maybe from someone he'd trust like the colonel... Maybe he'd look into the death a bit more," Josephine finished.

"May not be a bad idea," Connelly admitted. "Colonel, if you want to follow me."

"I'm coming too," Josephine said.

"No," all three men said in unison.

"Oh yes, I am," Josephine insisted, staring them down

"Why in the world do you want to put that image into your head?" Bobby asked her.

She looked at them, not sure she wanted to talk about Blasko in front of the colonel and Connelly. She didn't have much choice. "The baron agrees it wasn't just a bear or a wolf that attacked Seth. The baron is my... cousin from Romania. Colonel, I don't think you've met him yet. Anyway, I want to be prepared, to be able to talk with him from experience... not just what I've heard from any of you." She looked at all three of them in turn. "I want to be able to give my own opinion."

Bobby knew what she'd already been through at Mrs. Rosehill's. He figured if she could handle that, then she could certainly handle this. He gave a slight nod.

"You'll have nightmares," Connelly said with a tilt of his head. "But I'll not stop you if you're determined."

"Tough as nails and always has been," the colonel said, patting Josephine roughly on the arm.

Connelly led them into his embalming room. Inside were three white enamel tables that could be tilted to aid in draining the blood from a body and replacing it with embalming fluid. There were several boxes of Frigid-brand embalming fluid stacked up against the wall. The odor of the fluid and Bon Ami cleaning powder warred to cover any other odors in the room.

The first two tables were empty. On the third was an enamel washtub. Connelly walked over to it.

"The fact that he fits inside a washtub ought to tell you something," he said. "Mr. Taylor came by last night, but I turned him away."

Colonel Etheridge followed Connelly eagerly while Josephine and Bobby walked up to the table a little more slowly. Bobby had seen enough the day before, but he wanted to hear Etheridge's thoughts. Josephine was determined to go through with this, though she questioned her motives. Was this simply an act of bravado, or was it important to see this body to prepare herself for whatever was to come? She decided she needed to see it. If they were going to be facing anything like the last time, then she couldn't afford to be squeamish.

"I've rinsed everything off, but I haven't tried to do anything else. Mr. Taylor wants a proper burial for his son, but there isn't much I can do beyond cleaning the pieces and placing them into a coffin."

Connelly reached into the tub and took out an arm that

still had some of the shoulder attached. After he set the pale white limb on the end of the table, he took out other parts and placed them in no particular order on top of the enamel. There wasn't any blood and somehow that made the scene worse.

Josephine swallowed and looked down at her feet. She counted to ten and looked back up as Connelly stepped back from the tub. "I'll leave the larger pieces of... meat in the tub," he said.

The colonel had already moved in close to the table and was inspecting the various parts of Seth Taylor. Occasionally, he grunted and shook his head.

"This was no animal native to these parts. Very odd. A big predator. See here, where the canines bit into the flesh. I can guess at the size of the snout. Maybe ten inches. Over on this piece of thigh, there are claw marks. Not like a wolf or cat. More like a bear. A big bear..."

"Hold the train. This area around what's left of the shoulder looks like a bruise caused by someone grabbing the boy. Bears can't use their paws like that. Might have been killed by a man and then torn apart and half eaten by a bear. But not one of our black bears, no sir. It would need to be a Kodiak or grizzly." Etheridge stepped back from the table, his eyes still on all the parts.

"Those bears live thousands of miles from here," Bobby said, wondering if coming here had been such a good idea after all.

"Looking at the whole picture..." Etheridge went quiet and his brow furrowed. "I don't know... Nothing quite fits. I'd say it has to be two animals." He seemed unnerved not to have a clear answer. "But what type of animal is hard to say. One of them could be human."

"Will you talk to the sheriff? I need his say-so to start questioning suspects."

"I will," Etheridge said, still not taking his eyes off of the bits and pieces on the table. "A person had a hand in this. I'd bet my bottom dollar on it."

CHAPTER SEVEN

Once outside the funeral home, they discussed going directly to the sheriff's office.

"We can't wait," Bobby told Etheridge.

"You know he's right," Josephine added.

"Come on then. I'll tell Logan what I think," the colonel said with determination.

Once inside the sheriff's office, Josephine and Etheridge followed Bobby down to the glass door lettered in gold with the words "Sheriff Tom Logan." Miss Ruth Lindsey, his secretary, looked up from her typing.

"Ruth, we need to see the sheriff," Bobby told the young woman. She'd taken on the job after her mother had developed arthritis and couldn't continue doing the work.

"Bobby, I really don't think he's in the mood," she said nervously, looking at the others like she wanted to say more, but couldn't bring herself to in front of Josephine and the colonel.

"We need to talk to him," Bobby said again.

"Okay," Ruth said, getting up and walking over to the door. She tapped twice and went inside. They heard muffled voices before the sheriff exclaimed loud enough for them to hear, "Damn it! Why do you ask if you aren't going to give me a choice? Send them in!'"

Ruth came out looking grim and held the door for them. Josephine saw the sheriff for the first time in weeks. His eyes were puffy and circled with dark shadows, while his hair and clothes were unkempt.

"This is a crew!" Logan said, looking up from his desk. "A loyal deputy, a loyal friend and... a banker. To what do I owe the honor of this visit?" He wasn't slurring his words, but Josephine had the feeling the sheriff had already had a drink, or possibly two, this morning.

"Sheriff, I took Colonel Etheridge by the funeral home to look at Seth Taylor's remains," Bobby said.

"Why the hell did you do that?" Logan asked.

"We've been friends for a lot of years," Etheridge said, stepping up to Logan's desk. "This young man could see that it was more than some bear or cougar attack and he wanted my opinion."

Logan stood up, put his hands down on his desk and leaned toward the colonel. "You're damn right we've been friends for years. Yet here you are telling me how to do my business. I already told Tucker to leave it alone. Far as I'm concerned, he can give me his badge and gun and get out." Logan was angry, but Josephine saw something else in his eyes—uncertainty and... fear.

"Sheriff, this isn't just about you. If there's someone out there responsible for this, then an investigation needs to be started," Josephine said from behind the other two men.

"We hear from the meddling bank owner. What are you going to do, get me fired? You can't! I'm elected. Two years to the next election, so take a hike, sister." Logan's face had turned a dark red and his breathing was fast and shallow. "A few months ago you meddled in an investigation and look how many people died!" He was looking past the men and directly at Josephine.

"What we did saved this town," she said, meeting his eyes as her anger rose. She hadn't expected anyone to give her a medal, but she did expect a little gratitude from the man whose job they'd been doing when they'd shut down the cult attempting to let who knew what loose in the county.

"By killing the mayor? You didn't hear anyone thanking you, did you?"

"Sheriff—" Bobby started to intervene, but Logan turned on him.

"One word and you're done!"

"You're being a fool," Etheridge said in a strong, flat voice.

"All of this craziness is going to stop now. People talkin' about a monster… We've got a wild animal out there and I'm going to take care of it. I've already called up some of the part-time deputies to patrol the creek bottom out there by the Taylor place." The look on the sheriff's face told them all that he was firmly committed to a policy of denial.

"Sheriff, I'm not going to say that I'm right. All I want is your okay to talk to some folks and open the investigation up a little bit. I won't stir up any trouble. Just let me question a few people. If it doesn't lead to anything, I'll let it drop," Bobby said earnestly.

The sheriff looked at the three of them. Josephine saw his face soften a little, so she resisted the urge to add to what Bobby had said. *Best stop when you're ahead*, she reminded herself.

"If it will get you all out of my office, fine," Logan said. "I'm surprised at you, Sam, listening to these wild stories."

"I saw the body, Tom," Etheridge told him. "Tell your boys to be careful out there on patrol."

"I don't want to read about any crazy theories in the paper," the sheriff said to their backs as they walked out of his office.

"What now?" the colonel asked.

"I'm going to approach this like a regular investigation. Look for anyone who might have wanted Seth dead. That's the easy part. Figuring out how they could have done it is going to be the tricky end of the stick," Bobby said.

"The baron thinks that François, the medium, might be

involved," Josephine said as they left the building.

"Why?" Bobby asked.

"That's a little complicated to go into right now."

Bobby frowned at her, but turned to the colonel. "We'll drop you off back at your house."

Etheridge started to nod, but then stopped halfway to the car. "No. I'm going back in and offer to help with the hunt. I doubt that Logan's told those deputies what they could be getting into."

"I'll be out there tonight too," Bobby said as the colonel walked back up to the building.

"You're going to join Logan's patrol?" Josephine asked.

"I agree with Etheridge. Those guys don't have a clue what they might be facing."

"You don't either."

"You're right about that, but at least I know it's bigger and more dangerous than a black bear. That's probably what Logan has told Willard Paige and the part-timers that'll be working with him."

"I see your point."

"I'll drop you off at your house," Bobby said, opening the car door for Josephine.

"Where are you going now?" she asked.

"After I leave your house, I'm going to the hotel to talk to this medium, whoever the hell he is."

The hotel was on the courthouse square, well within sight of the sheriff's office.

"I'm coming with you," Josephine said, ignoring the open car door and heading toward the hotel.

"I knew you were going to say that," Bobby said and slammed the door.

"Would you please call up to François LeSauvage's room and tell him that Deputy Tucker would like to speak with him?" Bobby asked the stone-faced clerk at the hotel's front desk.

"I don't know about that," the clerk said. "He stays out pretty late. I don't think he'd appreciate getting a call this early."

"It's noon. Make the call," Bobby told him in his best *Don't give me crap* tone.

"Well…"

Bobby was about to tell the clerk that he'd make the call himself if the man was too big of a coward to do it when Josephine tapped him on the arm. He turned to her.

"He's coming down the stairs now," she said without taking her eyes off of François who, in turn, was watching her.

The man was dressed impeccably. "I saw you approaching from my window," he said when he was close enough to talk without shouting.

"How did you know that I was coming to see you?" Josephine asked.

"Let's say I was hoping you were." He gave her a large smile. "And who is your friend?" He turned to Bobby and put out his hand.

"I'm Deputy Robert Tucker. We'd like to have a few words with you about where you were the night before last." Bobby's hand went out and shook François's, seemingly of its own volition.

"Of course. Always a pleasure to meet the local representatives of the law. We can sit in the dining room." He had turned and headed for the door off of the lobby before Josephine or Bobby could protest. "Can I buy you lunch?"

"No. We just need to ask some questions."

"Certainly."

François held out a chair for Josephine, who noticed as the waitress gave François a wide, genuine smile. She came over to the table, patting her hair and brushing down her dress as she walked.

"I'll bring your coffee right out, Mr. LeSauvage. I just made a fresh pot." She never even looked at Josephine or

Bobby.

After the fawning waitress had gone back to the kitchen, Bobby asked François, "If you could tell us where you were and who you were with the night before last, that would be a big help."

"There was a death out in the countryside. I heard about that." He shook his head sadly. "I don't blame you for coming to me. I've traveled most of my life. As a stranger, I've often been questioned by the local constabulary." He paused and turned to Josephine. "I had a rather odd encounter with your cousin last night. He seems to be particularly suspicious of me. Perhaps he's feeling a little... nervous, him being a stranger too."

"The baron is a pretty astute judge of character," Josephine shot back. Everything was all smiles, but she could feel tension growing between them.

"Perhaps in my case he is mistaken," François said and turned to Bobby. "Let us clear this up. I was with a group of people who wanted to contact their loved ones who have passed over. One of them was your friend Alice," he said, turning back to Josephine. "There was also Mr. Copeland, his wife and that poor couple, the MacDonnells."

Josephine and Bobby knew that Guy Copeland was a county commissioner.

"What time of day did this... contacting the dead business start, and when did you all finish up?" Bobby asked.

"We began just before midnight and the séance went on until very early in the morning. I believe around four."

Josephine couldn't help but think that he would have still had time to get out to the Taylor place before dawn.

"And afterward, you came back to your hotel?" Bobby asked.

"Oh no. I was too exhausted. I stayed several hours at the Copeland's house, resting up. I don't think I could have walked back to the hotel without some time to recover," François said with a smile.

Bobby looked at Josephine, who raised her eyebrows

slightly.

"Why are you here in Sumter?" Bobby asked.

"This town seems to have... some rather unusual properties," François said. "I wouldn't expect you to understand. Honestly, I don't fully understand what draws me from one place to another. I often travel across country and stop when I simply feel that the place is right." He gave a small flourish of his hand.

"Would you mind giving me some references from places you've recently stayed?" Bobby asked, taking out a small pad and a pencil.

François hesitated for only a second. "Of course." He proceeded to give Bobby a list of the last four towns he had visited and the names of the hotels where he had stayed. When he finished, he turned to Josephine.

"I think you all have been listening to someone who may have his own secrets to keep." The corners of his mouth lifted in a small smile. "But I will say no more. I am not one to gossip."

"You know the baron?" Josephine asked.

François waved his hand. "It is enough to say I know the type."

"How does this contacting the dead stuff work?" Bobby asked with more than a bit of skepticism. He ignored François's comment about the baron. Bobby had had plenty of experience with suspects who tried to take charge of the interview.

"You should come to a séance. I believe Miss Josephine will vouch for the authenticity of the experience that I provide." He turned once again to Josephine and reached out, putting his hand on hers. "Did you find what your uncle wanted you to have?"

Josephine pulled her hand back politely, yet quickly. "I did." She wasn't going to elaborate.

"It pleases me to have been of some small service to you and your uncle," François said.

Bobby looked back and forth between them. "How could

I arrange to watch one of these séances?"

"There is no watching. Everyone who attends participates. I am letting Mrs. Robertson make all the arrangements. You may contact her. If you will excuse me now. I have a séance scheduled for tonight and I need to rest up." He stood and gave a slight bow. "Let me know if I can be of any service in the future."

"I've got your coffee, Mr. LeSauvage!" The waitress had just come from the back carrying a tray. "I'll be glad to bring it up to your room," she said, sounding a little too enthusiastic.

"Thank you, but I'll not be needing it," François said, taking no notice of the crestfallen expression on the young woman's face.

Josephine and Bobby stood and watched François go back into the lobby and up the stairs, after stopping to have a brief conversation with the desk clerk.

"What'd he want?" Bobby asked the clerk after he'd made sure François was headed to his room.

"Really, Deputy. Our guests have some right to privacy," the clerk said with a stern look. Bobby scowled back at him.

"Do you really want to have this fight?"

The expression on the clerk's face said that he didn't. "He just asked after his mail, for goodness' sake."

"And has he received much mail while he's been here?" Bobby asked.

The clerk looked like he wanted to argue, but he just rolled his eyes. "A couple of letters. Mostly from New York. And there was one from Germany. First letter we've ever gotten from Germany."

"Do you remember who the letters were from?"

"No! I do not! Now if you'll excuse me." He turned and began arranging papers on the table behind the counter.

Josephine and Bobby walked back across the square to his patrol car.

"What was that about your uncle?" Bobby asked.

"At the séance last night, François told me... He was

speaking for... Supposedly speaking for my uncle, and he told me where he'd hidden a letter."

"You found it?"

"Right where he said it would be. The question is, who is *he*? François or my uncle? Finding that letter was certainly... disconcerting."

"Do you think he can really talk to the dead?"

The sun chose that moment to duck behind a cloud and a cold gust of wind blew up, causing Josephine to put her hands in the pockets of her coat. "I don't see how François could have known about that note. An ability to read minds can't be the answer, since I don't think there is a person alive who knew it was in the book."

"When did your uncle die?"

"I was in my teens, but I don't remember much about it. Just some whispers, and my father had to hurry out of town. Uncle Petey died somewhere in Florida. Papa had him brought back here to be buried. I'm not even sure there was a funeral. Uncle Petey was the black sheep of the family and he moved about too much to make many friends."

"Was he that bad?

"Even my grandparents felt he'd let them down. I do remember a couple of times when Papa got into arguments with my grandfather over Petey. He thought that his folks weren't very fair to Petey. As for Grandfather, he was a pick-yourself-up-by-your-bootstraps kind of guy."

"What did the letter say?"

"Just some of Uncle Petey's usual pie-in-the-sky prose. He always believed that the next stone he turned over would yield the gold strike he was dreaming of."

Back at the car, Bobby said, "I can drop you off at your house."

"Where are you going now?"

"I want to go out to Taylor's farm and talk with some of their neighbors. See if anyone knows why Seth was out walking at that hour."

"I'll go along."

"You can't tag along with me all day," Bobby said, a bit exasperated. "I'm going out there to talk to folks as a deputy."

Josephine rolled her eyes. "It's a little late to be making that distinction. You can talk to the men and I'll sit with the women and see what I can get out of them."

"Well…"

"You know that any woman living out there is more likely to gossip about what's going on with me than she would be with you." Josephine opened the car door and got in.

"You're hard to argue with," Bobby said, getting behind the wheel.

"So don't."

CHAPTER EIGHT

There weren't many other homes close to the Taylor and Murphy properties, since the two families owned a combined thousand acres. The only other house near the spot where the body had been found belonged to Mr. and Mrs. Chester and their daughter.

Bobby pulled up in front of the Chesters' wooden clapboard house. Before they were even out of the car, a middle-aged woman came walking around from the side of the house, looking at the car apprehensively.

"Something wrong?" Mrs. Chester asked as she approached them.

"I just wanted to talk to y'all about Seth Taylor's death," Bobby said. The woman looked back and forth between Josephine and Bobby. "I'm Deputy Robert Tucker and this is Miss Josephine Nicholson," Bobby said without further explanation.

"Horrible thing," Mrs. Chester said, shaking her head.

"You're Mrs. Chester?"

"Emma. My husband is out back working on the barn. Matter of fact, he's boarding up some holes in case whatever animal killed Seth comes through here. Come on around," she said, turning and heading back the way she'd come.

Behind the farmhouse was a summer kitchen and a large, unpainted barn. Scattered between the house and barn were several chickens, a clothesline, a tractor and an old Model T. The rapid tapping of a hammer led them to where Mr. Chester was holding a piece of wood in place and trying to nail it to the outside of the barn. Bobby stepped forward and held the wood. The man glanced up, then pounded the piece of wood into place using nails he took from the half dozen he held in his mouth. Finished, he stepped back and looked at Josephine, Bobby and his wife.

"What can we do for you?" he asked in a completely neutral voice after removing the nails from his mouth.

"We want to talk with you about the Taylor boy's death," Bobby told him.

"I heard all kinds of wild rumors."

"Did you go down there?"

"Wasn't none of my business."

"Have you seen signs of any wild animals?"

"Nope. At least nothing that could kill a man."

"Did you know Seth?"

"Momma, you can finish hanging out the laundry to dry," the man said to his wife. She hesitated for just a second before turning toward the clothesline.

"I'll help you," Josephine said, following her.

There were a couple of sheets already hung up on the line, but the laundry basket was still full.

"He don't like to talk about the Taylors and the Murphys," Mrs. Chester said without any prompting from Josephine. She bent down and started picking clothes out of the basket. Determined to help her, Josephine grabbed a handful of wooden clothespins.

"Why's that?" she asked.

"'Cause of the bad blood. He's always wanted us to stay away from them. Said—and it makes some sense to me— that if we got to be friends with one, we'd be seen as an enemy by the other. Best to stay clear."

"I can understand that," Josephine said, managing to put

a clip on the shoulder of a white shirt.

"Mr. Chester doesn't understand that he can't control everything," Mrs. Chester said cryptically. She glanced over toward the barn where Bobby, carrying a plank, was following Mr. Chester around the corner of the building. She turned back and focused her eyes on Josephine. "I got something I can tell you, but I want you to tell me something in return."

"I'll tell you anything I can."

"What I want to know are the details of how Seth died." Her eyes were dark and tinged with sadness.

"You don't want to hear about that," Josephine said without hesitation. The image of Seth's separated appendages rose unbidden before her eyes.

"I got to know."

"Why?"

"I'll tell you afterward." She glanced nervously toward the barn. They couldn't see Bobby or Mr. Chester, but they could hear the sounds of hammering.

"He was torn apart down by the creek. An animal of some sort. Something big. His limbs were ripped from his body," Josephine said, not knowing exactly what information Mrs. Chester was after.

"Did he suffer?"

"I... The attack was so vicious and the creature must have been very strong. I'd think it must have been quick. No. I don't think he suffered," Josephine said and felt that she was being honest. *How long could you suffer if a monster tears your head off?* she wondered.

"That's all right then."

"Why..."

"Our daughter, Molly. She... Her father would have been furious if he'd found out. She was steppin' out with Seth. I told her she was being rebellious. 'Course she didn't listen to me."

"When did they start seeing each other?"

"She went to the fair back in September with some

friends. They met a group of boys. Seth was one of them. Of course she knew who he was. They'd been a grade different in school before he dropped out."

"Was it serious?"

"Who knows with young people. I only found out a month ago. Told her to put an end to it. She wasn't havin' any of it. Said she'd move out before she would break it off with him. I think it would have come to that too, as soon as Mr. Chester found out."

"You're sure he didn't know?"

"Oh yes, ma'am! The whole county would have heard if he'd found out. I told her too. Stubborn." She shook her head.

"You think that's why Seth was out at night?"

"That's right. He was comin' to see her. They used to meet down at our tobacco barn."

"He never met her that night?"

"She waited, but he never showed up."

"Why did you want to know how he died?"

"I got to tell her. She's goin' down and I thought knowin' some of the truth of the matter might help."

"Going down?"

"That's what my mother called it when she'd get the black feelings. The girl hasn't talked for two days. Her daddy is going to know something is wrong and when he gets it out of her, I don't know what's going to happen. Luckily, she's been so squirrelly since she turned sixteen that he hasn't noticed her being any different the last day or two. 'Sides, he's worried about what killed Seth getting our livestock."

Bobby came around the corner before Mrs. Chester could say anything else. She quickly went back to hanging the clothes.

"I think I got what I need," Bobby said, looking back and forth between the two women.

Josephine looked at Mrs. Chester, but the woman wouldn't meet her eyes. "If you need anything, I'll be glad to help in any way I can," Josephine told her.

"What was that all about?" Bobby asked when they were in the car and headed down the dirt road back toward town.

"Seth was on his way to meet their daughter," Josephine said.

Bobby turned and looked at her. "I wouldn't think her father would be too happy about that."

"Mrs. Chester said as much. But she's sure he doesn't know."

"Well, if he did then that would give us a suspect. Not that I can see how he could have pulled off something like that. Besides, he seemed pretty worried about his property."

They stopped at a few more houses without learning anything new. When they got back to Josephine's, Bobby walked her to the door.

"Lock your doors and windows tonight," he told her. "What we *do* know at this point is that whatever we're dealing with is dangerous. Besides, I didn't like the way that François was looking at you."

"I'll be careful. What about you? Are you really going out there tonight?"

"I have to. It wouldn't be right to let those yahoos run around in the woods unsupervised. Of course, Sheriff Logan will be there, but he doesn't seem himself these days."

"Don't take any chances. That's all we'd need is for you to get shot by one of those idiots." She leaned up and gave him an affectionate peck on the cheek. "Call me in the morning."

Blasko woke up with a purpose. His first order of business was to find out what Josephine had discovered during the day. He hurried through his evening routine, which included a few affectionate words for Vasile, who was just waking up and crawling across the ceiling.

Once he was dressed, Blasko went out the inner door that led to the stairs into the main house. Josephine's black cat, Poe, was waiting for him at the foot of the stairs.

"Follow me to the kitchen. I'll fetch you something to eat from Mrs. Durand."

After making sure Anna gave Poe some of the choicest scraps from dinner, Blasko found Josephine in the parlor, a drink in her hand.

"François appears to have a solid alibi for the night that Seth was killed," Josephine told him after she'd filled him in on the day's activities.

"You shouldn't have confronted him."

"I was with Bobby. I wish I could say you're being unreasonable, but there's an aura about the man that's menacing. He hides it well. Still…"

"Exactly. He might just be a rogue, but…" Blasko pondered his impressions of the man. "You're sure that his alibi holds up?"

"I even called Mrs. Copeland when I got home and pressed her. She swears that he held the séance until the small hours of the morning and then was so exhausted they let him sleep for a while in their den. They didn't sleep and they checked on him several times."

"I'm going out with the patrol tonight," Blasko stated.

"Watch out for Bobby. There's also another man who will be there." She went on to describe Colonel Etheridge.

"At least Tucker has some idea of what he's dealing with."

"Don't count the colonel short. Papa always said that if there was trouble, Etheridge would be the man to stand beside."

"I plan on staying in the shadows tonight. But I'll keep a watchful eye."

"There are going to be a dozen or more men stumbling around with weapons," Josephine warned.

"Lock your doors and windows," Blasko said, reiterating what Bobby had told her.

"I saw what was left of Seth. Don't worry, the house will be secured. Anna and Grace are both staying here tonight."

Josephine walked over to her father's gun cabinet and

opened it with a key that was kept on top. There were more than half a dozen shotguns, both side-by-sides and over-and-unders, as well as several hunting rifles.

"Do you know how to use that?" Blasko asked when she brought out a silver inlaid side-by-side with a hand-carved walnut stock.

In answer, Josephine held it under her arm, expertly broke it open and loaded a shell in each chamber before clicking it shut.

"I was out shooting clays and doves when I wasn't much taller than this shotgun," she said.

Blasko bowed ever so slightly.

CHAPTER NINE

An hour later, Blasko went out into the night looking for Matthew. He found him in the shadows of the courthouse.

"That François guy hasn't gone out at all today," Matthew said. He was huddled close to the building both for stealth and protection from the cold north wind. Winter wasn't done with Alabama yet.

"No offense to your powers of observation, but this man strikes me as someone who is good at sneaking out of buildings."

"I hear you." Matthew lifted a pair of binoculars from under his coat. "I'm doing the best I can. I saw Deputy Tucker and Miss Josephine go into the hotel this morning. And I'm doing more than watching. I got a buddy who works in the hotel, keeping an eye out."

"There is a hunting party going out tonight to search for the beast in the woods where the boy was found. I'm going out there to keep an eye on them. If François leaves the hotel, determine where he is headed and let me know if you can. Again, don't confront him."

"I can take care of myself."

"Do you have a weapon?"

Matthew showed Blasko a snubnose revolver. "A friend

loaned it to me once he was convinced I was off the sauce. For backup, I got a boot knife."

Blasko had his own hardware in the form of a Colt 1911 tucked into a shoulder holster. He didn't know what effect it would have on the monster if he met it. The reports he'd read when he was chasing the beast through the mountains back home were mixed. Some said that a bullet could kill a werewolf, while others said it would have little or no effect. Blasko was willing to try anything.

"Have you had any luck procuring a sword?" he asked.

"When was I supposed to do that?" Matthew said, exasperated. "If you want two jobs done at once, you're going to have to double your henchman staff."

"Never mind. I've sent for one," Blasko said, ignoring Matthew's sarcasm and leaving the man wondering if he meant he'd sent for a sword or another henchman.

Blasko walked back to the house and got his car, an enormous 1931 Daimler Double-Six. His driving skills had improved over the last few months, though there were still a few deficiencies. He bumped off of the curb and headed out to the Murphy farm.

He parked the car in a field with several others and got out, standing for a moment in the cold moonlight. The hill provided a perfect spot for his enhanced hearing to distinguish sounds originating from miles away. Not that he needed any special abilities to hear the sounds of a dozen men traipsing through the nearby fields and woods.

Blasko headed down toward the creek where he thought he'd heard Bobby Tucker whisper to another man. After carefully stalking them for half an hour, he approached Bobby close enough to be heard.

"You aren't going to find anything tonight."

Bobby jumped and whirled around, stopping just before he leveled the shotgun he was holding at Blasko's head.

"Damn it! Don't sneak up on people like that. Especially out here tonight. You'll get yourself shot for sure," Bobby chastised him.

"I didn't sneak up on you," Blasko said dryly. "If this mob wasn't making so much noise you might have heard me."

"Tell me about it. From the sound of it, you wouldn't know that all these boys have hunted deer and turkey since they've been able to walk."

"If this creature is what I think it is, then this hunting party isn't going to catch it." Blasko couldn't keep the disdain from his voice.

"I know that. I don't know what we're dealing with, but I know that he, she, it, whatever-the-hell ain't gonna be stalking around here with all this going on. Josephine tell you that your prime suspect has an alibi?"

"I'll admit I might have been too hasty," Blasko allowed, then stopped and turned his head. Placing a finger to his lips, he drifted off into the underbrush. Five seconds later, Colonel Etheridge approached Bobby, moving cautiously on a deer trail.

"Tucker, that you?"

"Yes, Colonel."

"Damn fools are tearing up the underbrush and making a racket. Can't see a darn thing with all these lights on. Told them the full moon was bright enough."

"Sorry, Colonel. They know better. They're just overly excited, not knowing what they're looking for."

"I've been in the brush with their sort. Good way to get yourself killed."

"Colonel Etheridge, I'd like to introduce you to Baron Dragomir Blasko." Bobby couldn't see the man, but he knew he wasn't far away.

Blasko drifted back out of the shadows and the colonel stared at him with lifted eyebrows. "Now there's a man who knows how to move through the woods!" he said, sticking out his hand. "Colonel Samuel Etheridge. Pleased to meet you."

Blasko gave the colonel's hand a quick shake. "Likewise. These idiots are wasting their time."

"Quite agree."

"Folks expect this. Only good thing I can say about it is that it's keeping things under the control of the sheriff's office so no one tries forming their own posse," Bobby grumbled.

"Makes them feel like they're doing something. I can understand that," the colonel said.

The three men talked for a while and listened to the other men moving through the underbrush before the sheriff called a merciful end to the hunt an hour later.

Two weeks passed and the county was growing hopeful that Seth Taylor's death had been a fluke. Every night the sheriff led a group of men into the woods, hunting whatever was the animal of the day. The consensus regarding bear, wolf, coyote and even a rogue alligator changed daily. Fewer men went out as the fear subsided. Meanwhile, Blasko and Matthew kept watch over François, who slept all day and held séances almost every night. More and more of Sumter's upper and middle class had attended one of the séances and no one walked away unimpressed.

"You look awful," Josephine told Bobby one day in late February. He'd come into the bank to make a withdrawal. Josephine pulled him out of the line and into her office.

"Thanks. I'd make the effort to be offended, but I'm too tired."

"How much longer is the sheriff going to keep this up?"

"You mean Sheriff Ahab? I swear he's coming loose at the seams. We haven't even seen a raccoon in over a week. We've scared all the animals away."

"Have you gone back out to the Chester place?"

"I don't want to spook them. I talked to a couple of Molly's friends who knew that she was seeing a boy, but none of them knew who it was."

"You didn't tell them it was Seth, did you?" Josephine asked.

"No, this town doesn't need any more grist for the gossip mill. I just wish I could get Molly out of the house and talk to her alone. No one's seen her since Seth was killed."

"Maybe you're going about it the wrong way," Josephine suggested.

"How's that?"

"Today is Friday. The Chesters come into town every Saturday morning."

"Like most of the farmers around here," Bobby said, realizing where she was going.

"Exactly. I think tomorrow morning would be a good time for Mohammad to go to the mountain."

"Are you inviting yourself along?"

"Are you going back out with Ahab tonight?"

"Do I have a choice? We're mostly down to our part-time deputies. Every time someone drops out, Logan gets crazier."

"Then you may be too tired to drive yourself out to the Chesters'."

"You've got a point," Bobby agreed, and they made arrangements to meet in the morning.

An hour after dusk, Blasko walked into the parlor. Josephine thought he looked as tired as Bobby.

"Good evening," he said morosely. "Can I fix you a drink?"

Josephine held up the glass she'd poured earlier.

"Ah," Blasko said, distracted.

"I saw Bobby today," Josephine told him, hoping to jar him out of his mood. It had grown increasingly dark as the days and nights ticked over without any results from the surveillance of François or the misguided posse roaming the woods.

"I saw him last night. This is ridiculous. They aren't going to catch anyone wandering around in the woods like madmen." Blasko just managed to keep his anger in check.

"Then why are you still going out there?"

"Because if this is anything like the creature that attacked your grandfather's village, then he might turn the tables on that rabble of hunters."

Josephine remembered her grandfather's diary. The monster had killed some of the very men who were hunting him. "I see your point. So you think you might have a chance of catching him when he comes for the hunters?"

"That was my hope. I don't know... Maybe the monster was just moving through the county and there won't be another attack."

Josephine told him that she was going with Bobby in an attempt to talk with the Chester girl in the morning.

"I need blood," Blasko said bluntly.

"You still have some from the last order, don't you?" Josephine asked, though she thought she knew what he was driving at.

"Yes, but what I need is real blood."

"We have an agreement."

"And I've honored it. But now... with the murder and the hunt... I need to drink fresh blood." He was almost pleading with her.

This was an argument they'd had before. She didn't want him taking blood from people, but she hated to see him suffer.

"I don't know. Let me think about it."

Blasko clenched his lips shut to keep from saying something he might regret.

He left the house and, as it had been for the past two weeks, his first stop was to check in with Matthew near the courthouse.

"I think there's something about this guy..." Matthew said.

"Don't fall for his routine. It's all smoke and mirrors," Blasko answered dismissively.

"I've followed him for two weeks now. Every time he holds one of these séances, I see the people afterward. They aren't fools, but they're deeply affected." There was a wistfulness to his voice that Blasko hadn't heard before.

"I tell you, it's all nonsense." The baron was irritated that Matthew seemed to be falling under François's spell.

"But if it *is* true…"

"When a man wants to swindle another man he shows him gold, not lead. Why? Because gold is something men want with a raw passion. This man is using the lure of contacting dead family and friends. Everyone has a lost love they want to talk with one last time. He uses that universal desire."

"What if you're wrong? What if he does have some supernatural ability to contact the dead?"

Blasko looked at Matthew. *Some of his cynicism and pain has been replaced by what… hope? Wonder? Desire?*

"Go to one of his séances, then," Blasko said.

Matthew looked surprised. "But you just said it was all nonsense."

"Exactly, it is. But I can see that the notion has gotten under your skin. So go see for yourself. You want to, don't you?"

"I don't know."

"Bah! Indecision is a crippling disease."

Matthew shrugged. "I'll be here the rest of the night," he said with a curt nod toward François's hotel.

Before Blasko could turn and head back to his car, Matthew uttered an expletive. Blasko turned to see him heading off down the street. Across from the courthouse, Blasko saw François strolling down the sidewalk looking like a man without a care in the world. For a moment Blasko considered following them, but he decided his best course of action was to head to the woods.

Tonight the small hunting party was parked along a dirt road about two miles from the Murphy farm. With each fruitless night, the group had moved out farther away from where Seth's body had been found. *Taking stabs in the dark*, Bobby had called it.

Blasko got out of his car and listened. With fewer men participating, it was harder to tell where they were. But he found their location soon enough and headed into the woods.

"Shame on you," said a voice to Blasko's right. "You should have known I was here."

The baron spun around to find Colonel Etheridge crouched in the underbrush. He stood up. "I've hunted some dangerous predators—man and beast," he said with a crooked grin.

"What are you doing here?" Blasko asked in an attempt to hide his embarrassment at being caught unaware.

"I've never believed we were just hunting an animal. Not around here. I thought it might be a good idea to see if anyone was hunting the hunters."

"And you are smart enough to know that those heavy-footed oxen aren't going to catch anything."

"They might tree a raccoon," Etheridge said with a shrug. "Not much else. I suspect that you and I have some things in common."

"Perhaps."

"Hunters who don't like hunting in a pack."

"I…" Before Blasko could answer, they both heard the sound of a car horn in the distance.

"Here now, what's this?" Etheridge said as the sound got closer, accompanied by the roar of a car engine. Etheridge and Blasko walked the fifty yards back to the road.

A car was careening down the dirt road, its headlights bouncing wildly as the vehicle hit potholes and the driver tried to keep it from swerving in the clay roadbed. The vehicle screeched to a halt just short of Deputy Tucker's patrol car.

"Where's the sheriff?" the man in the car yelled as he threw the door open and half fell out of the roadster. Blasko recognized the man as Claude Elliot, a reporter for the

Sumter Times.

"Slow down. He's leading the hunting party down in the woods," Etheridge said.

"The beast is in town!" the newsman said. "You got to get him, Colonel. There's been an attack at the Handlins' house." Claude was breathing so hard that he might have run all the way to find them instead of driven.

"You find the sheriff. I'll go back to town with this man," the baron said.

Etheridge hesitated for just a moment, then nodded and turned back into the woods.

"Oh, it's you, Baron," the newsman said, having just noticed him.

"I'll follow you." Blasko pushed past him and headed for his car.

Claude hopped back into his own car and they awkwardly turned their vehicles around and raced back toward town.

CHAPTER TEN

There was a crowd outside the home of Timothy and Madilyn Handlin. Lights were on up and down the street and groups of men and women milled about in the yard and on the sidewalk, many carrying lanterns or flashlights.

Blasko could see Dr. McGuire attending to someone on the porch. There were others gathered around him, including Emmett Wolfe, the editor and owner of the *Sumter Times*. Emmett came down to meet them when he saw Blasko and Claude approaching.

"Is the sheriff on his way?" he asked.

"He should be right behind us," Blasko said as he continued toward the house. "What happened?"

"There was an attack. According to McGuire, Mrs. Handlin is dead."

Blasko could smell the blood... a lot of blood. Underneath was the odor of wild animal. He climbed the front porch with Emmett at his heels. Dr. McGuire was tending to wounds on the face of a man in his late thirties, who was sitting in a wicker chair. A woman stood behind the doctor, holding a large flashlight so that he had light to work.

"I need to get you down to my office so I can clean these wounds properly. Several of them are going to require stiches."

"You can do what you have to do right here. I'm not leaving Maddie," Handlin said. His voice held a tremor, but didn't allow for argument.

Dr. McGuire glanced up, cringing as Blasko approached the front door. "No one should go in there," he said. "She's tore up bad."

"Tell me what happened," Blasko said to Handlin, who flinched as Dr. McGuire poured peroxide on a cut across his cheek.

"I... I was upstairs. I heard a noise, sounded like breaking wood and glass. I started down the stairs and heard Madilyn scream. It all happened so fast. When I got to the kitchen the... thing was done with Maddie. I... I couldn't move." He sounded dazed. "The monster looked at me. I've never seen anything like it. Couldn't even imagine such a blasphemous abomination. I think it smiled at me before it reached out and raked me with its claws. It was like it slapped me. For a moment, I thought I was looking at a man in a mask, but... it couldn't have..." His voice trailed off.

"Maybe you were," Dr. McGuire said, putting plaster over a deep cut on Handlin's jawbone.

"That was no man," Handlin murmured.

Blasko heard a ruckus in the street and turned to see half a dozen cars and trucks pull up. It was the posse from the woods. Sheriff Logan came charging out of his car with Bobby Tucker right behind him. Colonel Etheridge and the other men trailed after them. All of them were well armed.

"The animal couldn't have attacked anyone here," Logan said in a voice loud enough to be heard by everyone around the house. "Not in town."

Timothy Handlin tried to stand as the sheriff stomped up the porch steps. "It wasn't any animal I've ever seen," he said, unable to stay on his feet and sinking back down in the chair.

"Bullshit!" the sheriff spat at him. He turned to Dr. McGuire. "Who was hurt?"

"My wife was ripped apart by that thing," Handlin said before the doctor could answer.

The sheriff leaned in and examined Handlin's wounds. "You don't look hurt too bad," he said with a snide smirk on his face. "Watch him," he told Bobby.

The sheriff entered the house, followed by Blasko and Deputy Paige. It was warm inside thanks to the oil heater. The lights were on and everything looked normal except for smears of blood on the wall left by Handlin after his encounter with the creature. The kitchen, however, was a slaughterhouse. Madilyn Handlin's body lay on the floor, with deep gashes across her stomach and chest. From the amount of blood, it was clear she'd bled almost dry.

The odor and sensory input from the blood was almost too much for Blasko to handle. His heart raced as he felt the rich, dark fluid calling to him. The anemic blood that Josephine provided for him was doing little to restore him after spending so many nights in the woods, and now he felt his craving intensely. He took a deep breath and balled his fists, fighting against his nature before he could he speak.

Finally he said, "The animal would have had to be quite large to do this much damage so quickly." He noted that the woman hadn't had time to grab anything to defend herself. Nothing in the kitchen was out of place except for the back door, which hung half off its hinges, the frame busted and window glass shattered.

"Or she knew her attacker. Looks like he used some sort of farm implement or gardening rake," the sheriff said. "Paige, check the back yard for the murder weapon and secure that door. And you, Mr. Baron, need to get the hell out of my crime scene!" After ordering Blasko out, he turned on his heel and marched back to the front of the house.

Blasko glared at his retreating back and followed him.

"I'm taking you into custody," Logan said to Timothy Handlin.

"What the hell do you mean you're arresting me?" Handlin sounded like he was ready to fight. "You need to find the monster that killed my wife!"

Logan ignored him. "Were you having an affair? Never mind. We'll soon discover your motive. Take him to the office and put him in a cell. Drag him, if you have to," he told Bobby, who was frowning and slowly shaking his head. The sheriff saw the look. "You'll do as I tell you." His hand shifted slightly back to rest on the Colt revolver strapped to his side.

"Doc?" Bobby said.

"I'll meet you down at the station. More light there anyway," Dr. McGuire said, and helped Bobby support Handlin as they left the porch.

"What are you looking at?" Logan said as he noticed Blasko staring at him.

"A grave error." Blasko turned and walked back into the night.

He could still smell the animal. If that buffoon of a sheriff had been willing to listen, he could have led a hunt for the creature. Instead, he followed the smell on his own. The scent was stronger behind the house.

"What're you doing back here?" Deputy Paige yelled from the back porch as Blasko stopped to sniff the air.

Blasko ignored the sheriff's toady and followed the scent into a dirt alley that ran behind the house. He could just make out some prints on the ground.

"Mind if I join you?"

Blasko whirled around to see Colonel Etheridge standing behind him, carrying a hunting rifle and a flashlight. Blasko had been so focused on the scent that he hadn't noticed the colonel following him. *A mistake like that could be fatal*, he thought. *That's twice I've let him take me by surprise.*

Shaking off his embarrassment, he pointed to the scuff marks in the dirt. "Tracks."

"Go on, then," the colonel said with a grim smile.

The scent was strong and easy to follow. Blasko was able to track it without making it obvious to Etheridge that he was using his nose to do so. Two blocks from the Handlins' house, the trail led them to the back of one of Sumter's two gas stations. Behind the brick building there was an old hand water pump with a five-gallon tin pail underneath it. Here the odor of blood and animal musk was overwhelming for Blasko.

"Someone's used this within the last hour," Etheridge said, shining his flashlight at the pail.

"The attacker."

Etheridge looked closely at the handle of the water pump. It was wet.

"No animal pumps water," he said as much to himself as to Blasko.

"No natural animal."

"I confronted a beast down in the Belgian Congo back before the Great War," the colonel said thoughtfully. "I hope to heaven this isn't anything like that." Blasko raised his eyebrows, but the colonel did not elaborate.

They spent another half hour trying to pick up the trail before giving up and walking back to the courthouse square. As Etheridge and Blasko neared the sheriff's office, Bobby Tucker was leaning on his patrol car, smoking a cigar in the cool night air.

"We followed the creature's trail to the back of Sam's Service Station where it cleaned itself off at the water pump," Blasko told him.

"Could you tell where he went from there?" Bobby stood up straight, looking like a Labrador Retriever that's just flushed a flock of quail.

"No luck," Etheridge said. "Why do you think Logan flew off the rails like that and locked up Handlin?"

"He's been under a lot of stress," Bobby said, not really wanting to defend the man's action in this case. But Logan had been more than a mentor to him over the years. Now he was watching him break down and he didn't know what to do about it. His job was too important to simply support Logan, regardless of the cost.

"Did Handlin say anything else that could be useful?"

Blasko asked.

"He's too badly hurt. Both physically and emotionally. The doc treated his wounds, but Handlin ain't there. He saw his wife torn up, was attacked himself and then arrested for his wife's murder. I don't think there are many men who'd be in any shape to talk after a night like this." Bobby took a long draw off his cigar.

It was past midnight and quiet, so when the men heard cars heading their way they all looked up. It was Sheriff Logan and Emmett Wolfe. Both cars pulled up to the curb and the sheriff jumped out of his before the engine had stopped coughing.

"Has he confessed?" Logan asked.

"No. The doctor treated his—"

"Then what the hell are you doing out here? We got to keep his feet to the fire." The sheriff was standing close to Bobby, shouting in his face.

"Sheriff, I don't mean to argue with you, but Handlin didn't do this," Bobby said in as submissive a voice as Blasko had ever heard him use.

But it didn't do any good. As soon as the words were out of his mouth, the sheriff's face flushed red and his anger boiled over.

"How dare you? Are you blind? This is nothing more than a copycat murder. Handlin saw an opportunity to kill his wife and make it look like it was done by the same animal that ripped up the Taylor boy. Stupid! 'Cause no wild animal is going to come into town and kill some woman in her kitchen. It's nonsense!"

Logan was out of breath from the tirade, but he wasn't ready to stop. "Now do your job! I swear, if you don't get in there and start putting some heat on the suspect, then you can just hand in that badge." He punctuated his last words by poking at the star pinned to Bobby's chest.

Bobby pursed his lips, but didn't react.

"By George, I'll do it myself!" the sheriff said, spittle flying from his mouth. He wheeled around and started up the steps toward the door of the sheriff's office.

The four men watched his back as he climbed the stairs. His foot had just touched the top step when he faltered. No one had a chance to react as Logan fell forward. Bobby dashed up the steps and managed to catch the sheriff before he slid back down to the sidewalk.

"Help me get him in the car. We've got to take him over to the doc," Bobby said, already half lifting the man up off the steps. Emmett and the colonel took Logan's legs as Blasko and Bobby held his shoulders. Together, they eased him into the back seat of Bobby's car.

Blasko rode with him while the others followed in Emmett's car. They rolled into the doctor's driveway and Bobby laid on his horn. Within minutes, a woman came out of the house.

"What the dickens is going on? Oh, it's you, Deputy Tucker. Dr. McGuire just got to bed," Nurse Wheaton complained.

"The sheriff collapsed," Bobby said, opening the back door of his patrol car to reveal the sheriff lying awkwardly across the seat. The nurse looked in at him.

"I'll get the doctor," she said, and started to turn back to the house. At that moment, the front door opened and Dr. McGuire came out wearing pants, slippers and a nightshirt.

"What's going on?" he asked, and everyone stood back from the car's open door. Without another word, Dr. McGuire leaned in and started unbuttoning the sheriff's shirt.

"Get me a flashlight and my bag," he told the nurse, who hustled back toward the house.

Fifteen minutes later, Dr. McGuire backed out of the car. "We need to get him to the hospital in Montgomery. He's had a stroke."

Without another word, Bobby got back behind the wheel.

"I'll meet you there," the doctor said, heading for his own car.

Blasko, Emmett and the colonel stood watching until

they were the only ones left in Dr. McGuire's front yard.

"Some night," Emmett said. "Y'all need a ride?"

"I'll walk," Blasko said while Etheridge accepted the offer. After watching them drive off, Blasko took his bearings. His goal now was to find Matthew and learn what François had been doing this evening.

Blasko remembered the direction he'd seen Matthew and François heading after the medium left the hotel. He set off at a brisk pace, thinking about the events of the night. What had made the Handlins victims of such an attack?

It took him an hour to find Matthew, who was lying under a sycamore tree about ten feet off the sidewalk in a neighborhood of lavish homes. The area had been built up during the boom years after the Great War. The house across the street from where Matthew was camping out was a Victorian with an excessive amount of gingerbread molding around the eaves, making it look a bit desperate to be noticed.

"He's been in there all evening," Matthew told Blasko, nodding across to the house.

"Are you sure?"

Matthew gave him an irritated look. "If you don't think I can do my job, then fire me. Oh, wait, you don't pay me. I guess you can't fire me."

"I give you money," Blasko said, admitting to himself that it had been a while. "From time to time."

"Yeah, thanks a lot. I'm tellin' you, he walked straight here from the hotel. It looked like they made small talk for a while, had some drinks, then the lights went off and the candles were lit. That lasted for several hours until the lights came on again. Since then, they've been milling about in there. I was just starting to wonder when they're gonna call it quits."

"There was another attack tonight," Blasko told him.

Matthew sat up. "Where?" His voice was tense.

Blasko described the attack on the Handlins.

"Tim Handlin works for the coal delivery company. Nice

guy."

"You know him?"

"When I was still panhandling around town, he gave me a buck now and then. Liked to talk about his father who was in the war. Came back in pretty bad shape. I'm afraid I used the guy as a soft touch. I've seen him around town a couple of times since I got sober, but I've been too embarrassed to say anything to him."

"He'll survive, but Logan's trying to pin the murder of his wife on him."

"Is there a chance the sheriff is right? I mean, it does sound pretty farfetched that an animal killed the Taylor kid and then went after this woman and her husband."

"The pattern, or I should say the lack of pattern, is similar to what happened back in the Carpathians. There the beast seemed to be purposefully wreaking havoc. Like an anarchist who strikes here and there in order to sow panic and terror."

"And you really think this monster is some sort of half-man, half-wolf? The attacks seem motiveless beyond wanting to kill and spread fear." Matthew shook his head. "I'm no detective, but I'd say that a killer like that would be pretty hard to catch."

Blasko looked over at the house where François had held his séance. "I thought I had my suspect," he said wistfully. "I may have to write it off as a coincidence."

"Contrary to what folks say, coincidences *do* happen." Matthew said, standing up. "I hope this means I can stop following the man around."

"For the moment. We're going to have to cast a wider net."

"Fine. You think about it. Can you give me a dollar? I want to head over to the diner before going home."

Reluctantly, Blasko handed over the money and watched Matthew stroll off. Then he turned for home, mulling things over in his mind. François's solid alibi for the most recent attack left him searching for a new suspect.

The lights were still on at Josephine's house, so Blasko bypassed his apartment and entered the house by the back door. He found Josephine in the parlor, curled up on the sofa and reading a well-worn copy of *Melmoth the Wanderer*. When he entered the room, she held up a finger to stop him while she finished a paragraph.

"I decided I'd pull out some of my old Gothic novels. They don't seem as... frightening now that I'm living in one."

"You heard that there was another murder?"

"Evangeline Anderson pounded on my door to tell me about it and to warn me not to answer the door. That woman is crazy. Her account seemed hysterical, even for her," Josephine said, referring to their nosy neighbor.

"Mrs. Handlin was mauled to death in her kitchen. Her husband came in at the end of it and was slashed across the face, but he's going to be all right."

"Now that there's a living witness, is the sheriff finally willing to listen to you and Bobby?"

Blasko sighed. "The sheriff accused Handlin of killing his wife and making it look like a copycat murder. Logan went so far as to order Tucker to arrest and interrogate the man."

"Poor Bobby," Josephine said, then added, "And of course, Mr. Handlin. He must have been distraught."

"That's not the end of the story. Logan had what, according to Dr. McGuire, was a stroke on the steps of the sheriff's office."

Josephine frowned. "That I hadn't heard."

"The sheriff was acting quite irrational before the stroke."

"Is he going to be okay?"

"They took him to the hospital in Montgomery. His condition looked... severe."

"Bobby take him?"

"Followed by McGuire."

"I guess someone told Logan's wife and daughter?"

"I wouldn't know."

"Bobby and I were planning to go back out to the Chesters' farm tomorrow to try talking with the daughter when her parents aren't around."

"On several nights when the hunts were close to their house, I tried to catch a glimpse of her. Her parents seem very protective of her."

"As you certainly would be with a monster creeping around the countryside," Josephine said, not knowing why she was defending them. She had found the father's attitude overbearing.

"You mentioned that her father would have been angry about her courting Seth Taylor. He might have instituted some sort of... isolation for the girl as punishment."

"I'm afraid of that. Or worse. Mrs. Chester seemed scared of her husband. She and her daughter were hiding the fact that she had been seeing Seth, but I don't have much faith that they could keep the secret long if the girl was as upset as her mother said she was."

"You'll be pleased to hear that François was not responsible for the Handlin attack," Blasko said, a smirk on his face.

"I don't know why you insist that I like the man or even believe in his abilities. I just pointed out that it was uncanny how he told me about the note from my uncle. So how do you know that he's innocent?"

"I had Matthew tail him. François was giving another one of his séances tonight."

"I told you it was unlikely that he could have committed the Taylor murder with the number of people who witnessed him at the séance the night Seth was attacked."

Blasko waved his hand. "Still, there is something..."

"He's an odd foreigner. If I was you, I think I'd let that drop," Josephine said with a sly smile.

"I am not..."

"You aren't what... foreign? Odd? I'd say take a look in

the mirror, but that would be a shot below the belt." Josephine was enjoying getting a few barbs in at Blasko's expense, though she had to admit the mirror line was cruel. Blasko had explained to her that he could see his reflection, but only as a disturbing image of his true age.

"Can you think of any other suspects?" he asked, deciding to call off the tit-for-tat exchange.

"If this *is* a monster, then what is the motive?"

"A desire to spread chaos could be the only reason. When your grandfather's village came under attack, I believed that the creature responsible reveled in the murders. If there was a deeper motive, I never discovered it. Here, I don't know." He shrugged.

"The two murders are so different. One in the country, the other in town. A young man and a mature woman."

"The first was in an isolated area where the killer could count on no one interfering, while the second was inside a home where the victim's husband was upstairs and could be counted on to intervene. Is there a reason for the difference?" Blasko asked.

"Looking at the two victims and seeing if they have anything in common would seem like the logical place to start."

Blasko smiled at her. "Exactly."

"Let me guess, that's going to be my assignment."

"You are the one with deep ties in the community. You will be much better able than me to ferret out any connections that might exist below the surface."

"Hmmm, I guess I'd agree with that. I want to talk to Molly Chester first."

"I wouldn't suggest that you go out to the farm by yourself," Blasko said with a stern look.

"If we miss the opportunity tomorrow morning, then we'll have to wait until next Saturday."

"I'll take that as an 'I'm going no matter what you say.' Fine, but if Tucker doesn't show up, please take Matthew with you."

"Matthew wasn't much good last—"

"Do not give him a hard time about that. He has been flagellating himself ever since you two were snatched and held by that cult."

"I was only kidding. He shouldn't blame himself."

"Promise me you won't go out there by yourself," Blasko said, his face earnest.

"You have my word. See, my fingers aren't even crossed." She held up her hands. "Honestly, there was a strange undercurrent to the place that didn't sit well with me."

"If Logan is incapacitated, who will be the chief law enforcement officer in the county?" Blasko still didn't fully understand how local American politics worked.

"Depends on how bad Logan's health is. If he's just going to be out for the short term, then Bobby will probably fill in. But if Logan won't be able to return to duty, then the governor will appoint someone to fill his post. If that happens, it will take a while, possibly a month or more. The governor will seek advice from prominent locals."

"Like you?"

"I might be able to get a word in, but the best way for me to influence the choice would be to put the word out to local politicians who the governor might ask for opinions."

"And because the local politicians need your support, then they would be likely to push your candidate for sheriff when speaking with the governor. This all seems more complicated than is necessary."

"Precisely. But I'm not above using my influence when it will do some good. We shouldn't be talking about this yet. Logan has been pushed over the edge with everything that has gone on in the last six months, but he's a good man. He's a bit... hardnosed, even military, in his approach, but most of the time that's served him well. Less of the good ol' boy and a little more chain of command. I really hope he'll recover."

"Of course," Blasko said noncommittally.

Josephine put down her book. "I need to get some sleep."

Blasko looked at the clock and saw that he had only a few more hours of darkness. He said goodnight and went down to his room to read.

"Vasile, my friend, could I really have been so wrong about this spiritualist?" he asked, gently stroking the bat as it crawled along his arm. "I will only admit it to you, but the truth is, I've been wrong in the past. This time... I'm not so sure that I am. Maybe the man has the power to mesmerize his audience. Make them think they've spent hours with him when in fact they've been sitting there in a stupor while he's been out ravaging people."

Blasko thought about this for a moment. "Could he have put Matthew in a trance when he was across the street? Bah! Even I can't do that."

Blasko decided he'd have to let it go for the moment. He picked up *Murder on the Links*. He liked Holmes better than Poirot, but Christie's stories were much more current.

"Maybe I envy Poirot his little grey cells," he suggested to Vasile before settling into the book.

CHAPTER ELEVEN

Despite her late night, Josephine was up early on Saturday morning. If Bobby made it back to town in time, she wanted to be ready. She couldn't shake the feeling that talking with Molly Chester could answer some important questions.

"I can't be goin' out at night no more," Grace said as soon as Josephine came down the stairs. "And you shouldn't either."

"So you heard about the attack last night."

"Everybody in this town has heard about it. First that boy was killed and now this. There's a monster loose, for sure. Does the baron have any idea who's doin' these horrible things?"

"Right now, everyone is in the dark."

"People are sayin' that the sheriff was attacked too. They took him to the hospital in Montgomery," Grace continued as Josephine made her way to the kitchen and the promise of coffee.

"He wasn't attacked. Sheriff Logan had a stroke. At least that's what the doctor thought it was last night."

"What is this town gonna do now?" Grace said, shaking her head and following Josephine into the kitchen.

"Don't spread rumors. The truth in this case is bad

enough." Josephine grabbed the coffee that Anna held out to her.

"My husband won't let me come home in the dark either."

"Okay, no one has to go out at night. Grace, you have your room upstairs. No reason for you to go out. And Anna, we can take our meals at five and Grace and I will clean up." Josephine thought Grace might object to taking on some of Anna's work, but apparently the current crisis was enough to mitigate any concerns about domestic responsibilities.

"You get home and lock your doors before it gets dark," Grace told Anna.

"That woman was attacked in her own kitchen," Anna said, making it sound like the worst part of the crime was that it had been committed in the kitchen.

Before anyone could say anything else, there was a light tap on the back door. Josephine looked out and saw a very rumpled Bobby Tucker standing on the porch.

"I didn't want to disturb anyone if you weren't up yet," he explained as he came inside.

"I'm up. But I'm amazed that you are after driving to Montgomery and back."

"I just stayed until Mrs. Logan and Jessie got there. I managed to get a couple hours' sleep."

"I'm glad you're here. I didn't want to miss our window of opportunity." Josephine finished her coffee and, in a very un-ladylike manner, gulped a fist-size piece of apple fritter that Anna had made.

Ten minutes later they were in Bobby's car, driving slowly through Sumter's business district, looking for the Chesters' truck.

"I think that's it," Josephine said, pointing to a black truck that looked like most of the other black trucks parked along the street.

"How can you tell?"

"I noticed the crack in the back window when we were out at the farm."

"You need to learn to be more observant," Bobby joked with a shake of his head. He put his foot down on the gas pedal and they rumbled out of town toward the Chesters' place.

"Looks like you were right," Bobby said, studying the farm from the road as they drove up. "Though that doesn't mean Mrs. Chester isn't home."

"Or that Molly is," Josephine said as Bobby pulled through the farm gate and up beside the house.

"Maybe you should wait in the car," he said.

"That's not going to happen. We're talking about a young woman. I'll have a better chance of talking with her than you will."

Josephine opened her door and felt a strange sense of dread as she stepped out of the car. The farm didn't look much different than it had when they'd been out there before, but it *felt* different. She noted that Bobby's hand was hovering over the gun that rode in a leather holster on his belt.

"Front door or back door?" Bobby asked.

"If she's up in her room, she's more likely to hear us at the front door." Josephine looked up at the two sets of second-story windows. White curtains hung in one set while the other appeared to have boards behind the curtains. "That's strange."

Bobby followed her gaze. "Let's try the door," he said with a frown.

The steps up to the porch creaked as they walked up to the front door, which was in need of a coat of paint. Bobby rapped on the door, waited and rapped again. Nothing. He reached down and tried the knob. It turned, which surprised him only a little. Not many people bothered to lock their doors out in the country. At least they hadn't before the killings.

"In for a penny, in for a pound," Josephine encouraged him.

Bobby pushed the door open and the smell of old

tobacco and musty furniture wafted out.

"Hello to the house! Anyone home?" Bobby shouted into the semi-darkness. No sound answered his call. He looked back at Josephine.

"In for—"

"I heard you the first time." Bobby stepped over the threshold, continuing to call without getting any response.

"Is it me or is there something... off about this house?" Josephine said, looking around warily.

"Come on, let's see if she's here. I wouldn't want to be in Mr. Chester's house when he comes home," Bobby said, and quickly checked the four main rooms that made up the downstairs. Finding nothing, he said, "I'm coming up," as he put a foot on the bottom stair.

"This seemed like such a good idea yesterday," Josephine said, following close behind him.

On the second floor, which was laid out in the same four-room pattern as the first, only one of the four doors was open. They checked that room first, but it was empty.

"Molly, it's Josephine Nicholson. We're just checking to make sure you're okay," Josephine said, trying to keep the nervous quiver out of her voice. The house was too quiet for a place that didn't feel empty.

They checked the first closed door and found that it opened into a room full of old clothes and furniture that had been made in the last century.

"Looks like these might have belonged to Molly's grandparents," Josephine suggested.

The next door led to one of the front rooms. Bobby tried the door, but it was locked. He knocked gently and Josephine called Molly's name again. Still nothing. They left it for the moment and looked in the last room, which appeared to be a seldom-used guestroom. Bobby went back to the locked door, reaching up and feeling along the ledge just above the door frame.

"Clever boy," Josephine said when he revealed the key he found.

"Molly, if you're in there, we're going to open the door. We just want to make sure you're okay," Bobby said to the closed door before inserting the key in the lock. He twisted it and the door started to swing open as soon as the bolt was clicked back.

The room was a mess, but not filthy, and the wooden-frame bed looked slept in. Only slices of light coming through the boards illuminated the dark room.

"Why did they board up the windows?" Josephine asked.

"Because of the monster," came a hoarse whisper from the far side of the bed, making both Bobby's and Josephine's hearts skip a beat. Josephine moved around the bed and saw a young woman crouched down low, hugging her knees. Josephine couldn't make out her features in the dim light.

"Molly?" she asked and saw a slight nod of the girl's head.

"I'm going to turn on the light," Bobby said.

"Is that okay with you?" Josephine asked and received another small nod.

Bobby flipped the light switch and the single electric bulb clicked on, casting the room in a dull yellow glow. With the light, Josephine got a clearer look at the girl. There were dark circles under her eyes and her shoulder-length blonde hair was uncombed and tangled. To Josephine, Molly looked like she hadn't slept since her boyfriend had been killed. *Her eyes look haunted*, she thought, instinctively crouching down beside the girl.

"Molly, this is Deputy Tucker. We'd like to talk to you."

"You shouldn't be here."

"Did your father lock you in here?" Bobby asked.

In response, Molly gave an odd little giggle.

Josephine gently reached out and examined the girl's arm and face to see if there were any marks or bruises, but she didn't see anything that a bath wouldn't remove.

"Has anyone hurt you?" Josephine asked and Molly answered with another strange laugh.

"It killed him," she said, looking at the boarded windows.

"Were you there?" Bobby asked, coming closer and kneeling down beside Josephine.

"It was horrible. When I woke up, I thought I'd had a nightmare. Then... then... I heard about Seth."

"Did you go out to meet him that morning?" Bobby said.

Molly's eyes grew wide and her lower lip trembled.

"It's okay," Josephine said, taking the girl's hand. "Can you tell us who killed Seth?"

"A monster. It was awful. Blood everywhere. Wolf. A great wolf. Standing up." She started to shake and cry. Awkwardly, Josephine hugged the girl and held her, trying to calm her down. She looked up at Bobby, who shook his head sadly.

"Do you know of anyone who was angry with you or Seth?" Bobby asked after a minute.

"I..." Molly went quiet and looked lost in thought.

"Did either of you have an ex-boyfriend or girlfriend who might have been jealous?"

"Tom. Tom wasn't happy when I quit steppin' out with him. I just didn't love him." Her eyes were still unfocused.

"Tom who?" Bobby pressed.

"Bradford."

"Luke Bradford's son?"

"That's right," Molly said. "But the *monster* killed Seth."

"The monster," Bobby repeated with a sigh.

Josephine looked at the helpless young woman. *How can we just get up and leave her?* she thought. She hadn't realized until that moment that they hadn't developed an exit plan. How could they leave this poor girl in this condition? What were they going to tell the Chesters if they came home while she and Bobby were still in the house? And, anyway, Molly was likely to let the Chesters know they'd been there. *I need to work harder at thinking my plans through*, Josephine chastised herself.

"Is there anything we can do to help you?" Josephine asked the girl.

"I want to die," she moaned.

"I know you do. I understand the impulse, but you can't give in to it," Josephine said, hugging the girl to her.

Then they heard the sound of a truck pulling up outside.

"Hell," Bobby said under his breath.

Within minutes, heavy boots stomped onto the front porch. "I don't know who you are, but you better make yourself known quick-like!" came a shout from downstairs.

Bobby opened the door. "It's Deputy Tucker, Mr. Chester. We just come by to—" Bobby tried to explain, but Chester was already pounding up the stairs.

"What? Break into my house? Damn you!"

Bobby was standing in the doorway and could see the shotgun that Mr. Chester was carrying.

"We were concerned for your daughter," Bobby said, keeping an eye on the shotgun and ready to move if Mr. Chester looked like he planned to use it. Bobby remembered the advice Sheriff Logan had given him years earlier: *Try to keep an eye on the end of the barrel and the man's trigger finger. You'll know you're in trouble if the barrel starts to point toward you or if the man puts his finger on the trigger.*

"Who asked for your help?"

"No one has seen her for days. Not since the Taylor boy was killed," Bobby said, trying to make it sound reasonable that they'd come out and entered the Chesters' house uninvited.

"You mean since her beau was killed. That's what you mean. Sure, I know about it," Mr. Chester growled.

"When did you find out they were seeing each other?" Bobby said, trying to take control of the confrontation.

Mr. Chester glowered. "You think I tore that boy up?"

"I bet you have quite a temper when you feel like you've been betrayed."

"I'll show you what kind of temper I got," Mr. Chester said, clutching the shotgun in his hand. Then he took a deep breath and slowly relaxed. "You aren't goin' to trick me. Sure I was angry when I found out, but I didn't know nothin' about what those two were gettin' up to until a few days after the boy was killed. Ask my wife. She knows when I found out."

"You can count on me asking her. What are you doing for your daughter? She needs to get some help," Bobby pressed him.

"My family is my business. I told you I haven't broken no laws. So you don't have any right to be here."

"I'm investigating the murder of a young man. One who was on his way to see your daughter against your wishes. Seems like I got a good reason to be here."

Mrs. Chester came up the stairs behind her husband. "Where's Molly? Is she okay?" she asked, her eyes hooded and sad.

"She's as good as she was when we got here," Bobby said.

"Stay out of this," her husband told her, but she kept coming up the stairs.

Bobby wondered if Mr. Chester would try to block her way, but when she got to him he didn't move as she edged around him. Bobby moved out of the doorway so she could get into her daughter's bedroom.

"It's all right now, Molly, we're here," her mother said, stroking her hair lovingly. Mrs. Chester looked at Josephine. "She's gotten worse."

"She told us she saw Seth get killed," Josephine said.

"I don't know if she did or not. I told her about how they found him. I swear I thought it was the right thing to do. Now I don't know." She pulled her daughter to her.

"You should get Dr. McGuire to come out and see her."

In response, Josephine saw a look in the woman's eyes that she had become very familiar with. *We can't afford it.*

"Would there be a problem if I asked him to check on her?"

Josephine saw more hesitation. *We don't take charity.*

"If she did see the attack on Seth, then she's a witness and the county might need her to testify. They'd need her to be strong and will pick up the cost of any medical bills."

Josephine didn't know if that was true, but it didn't matter. She'd talk to Dr. McGuire and pay for any costs.

"That'd be good." Mrs. Chester nodded.

Josephine stood up.

"We should go," Bobby said from the doorway as Mr. Chester pushed past him.

Josephine and Bobby didn't speak until they had put a few miles between them and the Chester farm.

"We were lucky to get out of there without someone getting hurt," Bobby finally said, turning to Josephine.

"That poor girl." Josephine couldn't get the image of Molly's haunted eyes out of her mind.

"When we found her, I thought her father had beat her, or worse," Bobby said.

"He's a hard man, but I don't think he's mean."

"Whatever or whoever killed Seth did a hell of a lot of damage to Molly too. I'd guess she was lucky to escape it that night." Bobby shook his head. "Man or beast. Or maybe part man and part beast. I know how to hunt down a man, and I'd have a good idea how to go about hunting down a beast, but something that's both and not all of either? How the hell do we deal with something like that?"

"I guess you're in charge right now."

"Until we know more about Sheriff Logan's condition. I feel like we weren't being very fair to him. Making decisions when you don't even know what's doing the killing isn't easy. I can't come out and tell everyone that we're after some werebeast. I'd be thrown off my high horse in a second. Of course, if Logan really is bad off, then the governor will appoint somebody. That happens and we could have a real mess on our hands with somebody who's not from around here coming in and trying to make sense of things that... don't really make sense." Bobby's voice was tired.

"I've got my own thoughts on that," Josephine said as they approached town.

"Don't go off half-cocked," Bobby warned.

"That's why I don't want to tell you about it right now. Let me think on it."

He dropped her off at her house and promised to go home and get some more sleep. However, when he left, she saw him head toward the sheriff's office.

Josephine decided to take her own advice. *I'll lie down for just half an hour or so*, she told herself, heading upstairs to her bedroom.

CHAPTER TWELVE

Three hours later, she opened her eyes. She'd dressed and started back down the stairs when she heard someone at the front door. Squinting against the afternoon sun streaming through the front windows, Josephine answered the slow, steady knock that came from the other side of the oak door.

"Have boxes for Baron," said a short, grey-haired man when she opened the door. He had a full beard and was grasping his cap to his chest with both hands. Josephine could see two wooden crates behind him. One was about three feet long and two feet high and just as wide, while the other was the size of a hatbox. Both looked overbuilt and had strong iron straps.

"Who are they from?" Josephine asked.

The man looked puzzled by the question. He spoke with a strong accent and Josephine suspected he had come with the boxes.

"I have boxes for Baron," he said again, turning and pointing at them.

Josephine thought the man looked like a garden gnome with his beard and cap. "I understood the part about the boxes. Who are you?"

Apparently this was a question he understood because he

smiled and said, "Anton Lacob."

"Okay, bring in your boxes, Anton Lacob."

It was late afternoon, so Blasko would be up in a couple of hours. The man had no trouble bringing the longer box into the house, but when he went to lift the other one, he bent at the knees and there was a lot of huffing and puffing as he struggled to raise it off the porch and carry it into the house.

Once the boxes were in the hallway, Josephine fetched a five-dollar bill and handed it to the man. He looked at it oddly.

"Thank you. I'll see that the baron gets them," she said, holding the door open.

The man suddenly seemed to understand what she was saying. He handed her back the five dollars and sat down on the larger box.

"No, no. Give them to the baron," he said.

"No. I'll give them to the baron," Josephine told him in her most commanding voice.

But the man just shook his head slowly back and forth, defying her.

"What's in the boxes?" Josephine decided to try a different tack.

"For the baron."

"I know who they're for. This is my house and I want to know what's inside them." Josephine had already figured out that they'd most likely been sent in response to Blasko's telegram, but she was not going to have this man drag them in and then plunk himself down like it wasn't her house he was squatting in.

"Baron." The man was becoming more monosyllabic.

"I think you know English better than you're letting on," she said, staring at him with her hands on her hips. "You know that I could call the police and have you thrown out?"

"Baron."

"You sure know how to get on my nerves." She looked up at the grandfather clock. "You've got a couple of hours to wait for the baron." He just stared straight ahead as though he hadn't heard her. "Fine, you stupid oaf, have it your way," she told him and stomped off to the kitchen.

"We have a… I wouldn't call him a guest since I just tried to kick him out. Let's call him a squatter, sitting in the front hall on some boxes that he's delivering to the baron. Take him a sandwich and a glass of milk," Josephine told Anna. "And tell him I hope he chokes on it."

She needed to make a phone call, but the phone was in the hallway and she wasn't sure if she wanted to make the call if there was going to be a life-size garden gnome listening in. Finally, she decided she'd have to ignore him. Blasko would be up once the sun went down, then he could take possession of his boxes and get rid of the rude deliveryman. She walked back into the hall where the man was calmly eating his sandwich and taking gulps of milk.

"Hope you're comfortable," she mumbled, picking up the phone and turning the crank. In a few minutes, Dolly the operator had connected her with Dr. McGuire. She told him about their visit to the Chester farm and Molly's condition.

"They should have called me in sooner," he grumbled. "I'll go out there this evening."

"Have you heard anything more about Sheriff Logan?"

"He's had a very severe stroke. It's going to take a long time to recover. If he recovers," the doctor said with the grim but matter-of-fact way of a person used to delivering bad news.

Josephine hung up the phone and looked at her unwanted houseguest. He'd finished his snack and appeared to be taking a nap with his chin resting on his chest. She shook her head and went to find Grace, who didn't deal well with surprises. Finding a strange old man sitting on boxes in the hallway would certainly qualify as a surprise.

Josephine was waiting at the baron's door when he came out shortly after sunset.

"You have a visitor," she said in a tone designed to let him know she wasn't happy about it.

"I see," Blasko said. "And they are?"

"A gnome named Anton Lacob," she told him with a narrow-eyed stare.

"Excellent!" he said, edging past her and taking the steps two at a time. "I hope he has brought the things I asked for."

"He's got some suspicious-looking boxes with him," she shouted at Blasko's back.

"Anton, I am pleased to see you," Blasko said when he reached the entry hall. He stopped in front of the man, who bowed his head.

"*It is good to see you too, Baron,*" Anton said in Rusyn, the language of the Carpathian villages.

"*Have you brought me what I asked for?*" the baron responded in the same language.

"*Yes, Baron.*" The man stepped back, indicating the boxes. "*As you ordered.*"

"English, please," Josephine said as she walked up to them.

"Anton's English is not very good."

"You can speak Romanian or whatever you like in private. But when you're in the company of others, I'd prefer that you speak English."

"Of course." In Rusyn, he said to Anton, "*Bah! She insists that we stumble along in English.*"

"I saw you roll your eyes," Josephine said, understanding his tone if not the words.

Blasko bowed slightly toward her. He wanted to avoid an argument so he could get the boxes into his apartment and open them up.

He reached down and picked up the smaller box. "I'll come back and help you with the other one."

"No. I bring," Anton said and hefted the box up on his back.

Josephine scowled at the two of them as they made their

way down to the basement. She would've liked to know what was in the boxes, yet even she had to admit she didn't have the right to demand that packages coming for Blasko had to be opened in her presence. *Even those delivered by strange little foreign men*, she thought.

Back in his apartment, Blasko looked at the two boxes while Anton stood back with his eyes cast down at the floor.

"It must have been a long journey for you," Blasko said, kneeling down next to the smaller box, which he assumed held the gold he'd requested.

"The world is much bigger than I ever imagined," Anton said. *"And so strange."*

"You didn't go to the Great War?"

"No. I was already too old and someone other than the women needed to stay home and tend the fields."

"How did you come to be the courier for my boxes?" Blasko asked as he pried the lid off of the box of gold. The coins, ranging across hundreds of years and many countries, had been covered in wax to keep them from rattling and shifting while they were being transported. From the weight, Blasko was sure they had sent the full amount he'd asked for.

"The bandit leader came to me. He said he didn't have a single man he could spare or that he trusted for such a responsibility. I have no family left, but I am not too old and still quite strong from working the fields." The man shrugged.

"He chose wisely." Blasko set the box of gold to the side. He'd have to melt the wax off, but that could wait. He turned his attention to the larger box.

"I thought I wanted to see the world. Now… I'm not so sure. So much to take in." Anton shook his head.

"New experiences are what life is about," Blasko advised him as he began to pull the lid off the box. The nails screeched as they came free of the wood. Inside, wrapped in red velvet, was his sword. He'd had it made over four hundred years earlier by a man reputed to have been the best sword-maker in Europe. The broadsword was a fair testament to his skill. Blasko had never found another blade that was as well

balanced or held a better edge. He'd sliced through lesser swords as though they were made of wood.

He lifted it out of the box, wondering how he could have left his fortress in the Carpathians without it. Pulling it out of the tooled leather sheath, he held it fondly in his hands. The room was not wide enough for him to swing it, but the heft alone was enough to convey a renewed sense of strength.

Beneath the sword were three leather-bound books. He lifted the one he'd been most anxious to get his hands on and gently thumbed through the pages. It was Captain Jean Baptiste Duhamel's privately published book on his campaign against the Beast of Gévaudan. Blasko set the book on the end table between two wingback chairs. He'd start studying it tonight. The other two were more common books on werewolves, one written by a German and the other by an Englishman.

Finished unpacking, he turned to Anton. "*Sit.*" He pointed to one of the chairs.

The old man looked uncomfortable perched on the edge of the chair. "*Relax,*" Blasko told him, taking the chair across from him. "*Most of the villagers fear me. Why not you?*"

"*Many blamed you for the attacks on the village that occurred when I was just a baby. But not my family. My cousin saw the beast when he attacked the third girl. When he told my grandfather, he defended you. You see, his father, Stefan Lacob, was captain of your guard back when the little Frenchman was marching across Europe.*"

"*Stefan Lacob. I remember him. A small man who combined strength with speed. One of the best swordsmen I ever met. He was wounded during an attack on the castle,*" Blasko mused. So many memories. They were organized more by how vivid they were than by their chronology. Memories of battles always seemed the most intense and therefore the most lasting.

"*After that, you granted my family our land. Why would we turn on you, my lord?*"

"*We are in America now. You don't need to call me lord. Baron will do,*" Blasko said with what he assumed was grace, but the uncharitable would have labeled as bombast.

"*Yes, Baron.*"

"*I assume you don't have a place to stay.*"

"*No, Baron. But it is no matter. The weather is mild. I can find a place to rest. I left my luggage at the depot.*"

"*We will go get it,*" Blasko told him. What he really wanted was to begin reading through Duhamel's book, but the old man had traveled thousands of miles. The least Blasko could do was to see that he was comfortable for the night. "*There is a small storage area down here. You may fix it up for your use while you're here.*"

Blasko showed him the spot next to the door that led from the basement directly outside, then they headed for the depot. As they walked, he pointed out a few highlights of the town and explained some of the more peculiar American customs to Anton.

"*As in our land, these are a proud people. I've been impressed with their resolve,*" Blasko told him. "*And like our people, most are farmers. Even though their people have only been here a few generations, they have a strong affinity for the land.*"

"*If it is not too impertinent to ask, Baron, why did you call for your sword?*"

"*The beast that once besieged our village, or something very similar, has staked out this county as its hunting ground,*" Blasko told him and Anton crossed himself.

After retrieving his satchel from the depot, Blasko took Anton to meet Matthew, who was relaxing on the porch of the boarding house, glad to be relieved of his spiritualist stalker duty at least for a while.

"You all may work together," Blasko told them. Neither of the men looked comfortable with the concept. After the introductions, Matthew pulled Blasko aside.

"I'm not really looking for a partner. I don't even really like working with you," he said with a grunt.

"With the work ahead, you may be glad of two extra hands," Blasko told him.

"How old is that guy?"

"Don't underestimate a mountain peasant. He had no

trouble getting here with the items I sent for." Blasko took a gold coin out of his pocket. He would have to clean and sort the coins at home, but with the addition to his account, he didn't mind paying Matthew some back wages. "For your trouble," he said, pressing the coin into Matthew's hand.

Matthew looked at it, nodded and placed it carefully in his coat pocket. "I've found a few people who claim to have heard the creature last night, before and after the attack. Some of them are the usual suspects. Blowhards and the look-at-me crowd. But there were a couple in the mix I'd call reliable."

"Did anyone see anything?"

"One guy said he saw an enormous dog. Not sure if he's credible. Wears glasses and has a tendency to tell tall tales. On the other hand, he looked… I'd call it cowed."

"Where was this?"

"About a block from the Handlin house. The guy went out to the alley to put some garbage in his burn can. Saw this thing coming down the alley. Maybe half an hour before the murder. Said it would go from standing upright to walking on all fours. He thought it looked… confused. What I find confusing is that the guy saw this monster and then just turned and went back in his house."

"What was his explanation for his actions?"

"Lack of action, you mean. He said he didn't really believe he saw it. He claims he's never had a hallucination in his life, but he figured that's what it must have been, so he ignored it and went back inside to listen to the Grand Ole Opry on the radio."

"Which way was it traveling?"

"Toward the Handlins' house. At least in that general direction. It would've had to turn at the end of the alley and go two blocks north before turning back east. It's also in line with the garage where you said the monster cleaned up."

Blasko thanked him. When he turned to look for Anton, he saw him sitting on a bench, slightly slouched with his head down and snoring. *The man did have a long day*, Blasko told himself before going over and nudging him. Matthew watched with a frown, shaking his head.

Back at the house, Blasko saw that Anton got settled, then pointed at the ceiling. "*Breakfast will be served upstairs.*"

Blasko went searching for Josephine, but didn't find her in the parlor, library or kitchen. He wanted to talk to her about the sheriff and what had transpired during the day, so he went up to her bedroom to see if she'd retired already, though it was still hours before her usual bedtime.

For some reason, he found himself walking more softly than usual up the stairs. At her door he hesitated, listening. With his enhanced senses, he could hear as she turned the pages of a book. She also had a habit of occasionally mumbling words aloud as she read, and she was doing it now. He felt ashamed for eavesdropping on her and stepped forward to knock on the door.

"Are you alone or is your gnome with you?" she called through the door.

"Quite alone," he answered and opened the door without waiting for a reply.

She was sitting on her chaise lounge by the window with a Gothic novel in her hands. She closed the book, and her fingers slipping over the pages made a distinct sound that was quite different from the one he'd heard through the door. The book she was holding was not the one she'd been reading before he knocked.

"Did you get everything you requested?" she asked.

"I did, actually," he said, moving over to where she was sitting. "Did you meet with the Taylor boy's girlfriend?"

She proceeded to tell him about the visit to the Chester farm.

"When the beast was stalking my village, there were several people who witnessed attacks. I don't believe that any of them were ever completely whole again," Blasko said, edging closer to the chaise lounge. It was near the wall and

Blasko could just make out the edge of a leather-bound book stuck between it and the wall.

"I should probably get ready for bed," Josephine said, standing up. When she did, he swept in and pulled out the book. After one look at the cover, he dropped it like it was on fire.

"That book! Where did you get that thing?" he said in disgust. "Don't tell me. Franklin Carter sent you this abomination."

Josephine stood her ground. "And what if he did?" Josephine and Blasko didn't see eye to eye on her cousin, though she had to admit the baron had good reason since Carter had attempted to kill him during his last visit.

"The Reverend Thaddeus Moriah was an evil man who relished torture. What could you hope to learn from him?"

"Maybe a way to break this… bond that ties us together, but that also… keeps us apart." She was angry that he would question her, angry that he'd found the book and angry that it hadn't held any simple answers.

Ever since she'd bitten him in self-defense when Blasko had attacked her during their first meeting, they had shared a blood bond. It made it impossible for them to be separated for long distances and, according to Blasko, also impossible for them to pursue a more intimate relationship. Josephine found the situation both frustrating and confusing.

"Did you read the chapter where he explained how to break the bond? It's so simple." Blasko's voice was furious and his accent became stronger as he spoke. "All you need to do is strap me down where the sunlight can burn my body and soul into ashes. He goes on to explain that you will feel great pain, but as the vampire is… Let me get this correct… 'Rendered unto ash with soul scorched and sent to the hinterlands to burn amongst the damned until the trumpets of Gabriel sound from the heavens.' At that point the victim—that would be you—will be free, your soul unchained from the vermin of the night. Vermin—that would be me."

"I'll admit that the solution it offers doesn't seem practical," Josephine said without backing down.

"Trust. You have never fully trusted me. You believed that I hunted your grandfather and his family. And you think I'm lying to you when I say that there is no way for us to break this bond."

"You don't make it easy to trust you."

"Nonsense. You don't *want* to trust me. Maybe you *can't* trust me. Is that it? Is there something that makes you unable to trust me?"

"Wait a minute. I'm not the one who came in here snooping around. How did you know the book was behind my lounge? You positively pounced on it," she shot back.

"You didn't fool me by holding up that other book."

"But how did you know it wasn't the one I'd been reading?" She detected a chink in his self-righteous armor and pressed her advantage.

"I... could tell," he faltered.

"How?"

"I heard you turning the pages from the hall. Not the pages of that decoy." He pointed at the book she'd pretended to be reading.

"You were eavesdropping on me. Admit it."

"I... can't help that my hearing is superior. Bah! How many times do we have to go over this? There is no way out of our dilemma. Unless you want to burn me alive."

"I can't be trapped like this," Josephine said, voicing her frustration. "What kind of life do I have if I'm hobbled to you?" She said it too harshly, but at that moment it was how she felt. If he wouldn't let her have a relationship with him, then who else could she find who'd be willing to forever share their life with a strange man in the basement?

"What about me?! Do you think I enjoy drinking that moldy blood you supply for me?"

"I go to great expense to get that for you."

"We can't keep having the same argument over and over. You are being unreasonable. You've lived a privileged life and just can't accept that you've run into a situation you can't buy your way out of!" he said, punctuating each word with his anger.

They stood a foot apart and glared at each other.

"Get out!" Josephine said coldly.

"Delighted." Blasko turned on his heel and strode to the door. He opened it with dramatic flair and stepped through, closing it behind him with exaggerated care.

Josephine threw herself onto the bed and buried her face in her pillow to muffle her screams of anger and exasperation.

CHAPTER THIRTEEN

Blasko turned to see Grace step quickly into the bathroom.

"Y'all don't need to be fightin' when that wolf-thing is prowlin' our town," Grace said as he walked by the open bathroom door. To hide her eavesdropping, she was collecting the laundry, a task she usually did in the morning.

Blasko was going to walk on by, but thought better of it and stopped. "What have you heard about the creature?"

In the time that he'd spent in Sumter, he'd learned that there were two distinct communities, separated by a color line he didn't fully understand. But he'd learned that the men and women of the black community often held knowledge that wasn't available to the white folks.

"I got a cousin who seen it," she said, putting the dirty clothes in a wicker basket.

"Last night when the Handlins were attacked?"

"That's right. Funny thing, he said he seen that thing go behind the garage, but it never come out from back there," she said, lifting the basket.

"Did he see anyone else around the same time?"

"I'd have to think about that. 'Course I'd think a might better if I wasn't carryin' this heavy basket," she said with a coy smile.

Blasko bristled, but took the basket from her.

"What exactly did your cousin see?" Blasko asked as he tried to navigate the stairs while carrying the basket.

"He said he saw a monster go 'round back of the garage, and when he went to look and see what it was doin', he saw an Indian walkin' away."

"An Indian?"

"That's what he said."

"I didn't know there were any Natives in this area."

"My grandmother was part Creek. There's a lot of folk got some Indian in them. Not many full-blooded, though. Most of them were taken out west a long time ago," Grace explained.

"I'd like to talk to this relative."

"George. He lives a block east of my place. You can go by my place and my brother Ronnie will take you over to George's house."

Blasko set the basket down at the foot of the stairs and headed for Grace's house.

Josephine heard the front door open and close. She looked out the window to see Blasko strolling toward the street. Once she was sure he was gone, she headed downstairs and straight to the kitchen to fix a bowl of Anna's blackberry cobbler. Every summer, Anna canned bushels of blackberries for use during the winter months. For Josephine, they were a comfort food that reminded her of summer breezes and warm rains.

"I see you stuffin' yourself with cobbler," Grace said, coming into the kitchen. She took the opportunity to give Josephine her own scolding. "You and the baron don't need to be fightin' when there's a monster tearin' this town apart."

"You know I had an argu... a discussion with the baron, and you see me eating cobbler, but you came in to give me a hard time anyway?"

"With your father gone to a better place, you need

someone to speak gospel to you," Grace said, getting a bowl of her own from the sideboard.

"And you think you're the right person to take on that job?"

"Who else you got? I guess you got a bunch of friends I don't know about hidin' under the table that know all about you and the baron?" Grace said mockingly, looking under the table before filling her bowl with a hearty portion of cobbler.

"You didn't even want the baron in the house when he first came here," Josephine reminded her.

"I might've mistook his strange ways for the devil's ways. Maybe they are, but he helped me and he helped Ronnie. My preacher talks about hypocrites about every other Sunday. I won't be one of them."

"Our relationship is... complicated," Josephine allowed.

Grace broke into a hearty laugh that almost had her choking on the cobbler. "Lord almighty, I ain't never seen a relationship between a man and a woman that wasn't."

"Didn't you want me to marry Bobby Tucker?"

"No sense standin' on the platform wavin' to a train that left the station yesterday."

"I can't marry the baron."

"There's bein' married and there's bein' together."

"I think you're seeing a relationship that isn't really there."

"You either don't know me or you don't know yourself. I've seen you and the baron." Grace shook her head and took another bite of the cobbler.

"You've heard us too. Everybody in this house eavesdrops on everyone else. Do you really think we are going to get together?"

"Every woman, and pretty near every man, has felt trapped by their husbands, wives or lovers. You know why?" Grace said with a thoughtful tilt of her head.

Josephine felt like she was hearing Grace for the first time. Not her servant, not a paid companion, but the woman, Grace.

"Why?"

"'Cause you *are* trapped. That's what love is. A big ol' bear trap."

"That's a lovely image," Josephine said with a smile. "With an attitude like that, I can see why you haven't married."

"You don't know everything about me, Miss Josephine. I might not have gotten tied down, but I've stepped out with two gentlemen and one of them had my heart," Grace said, suddenly very serious. "Just 'cause you're trapped doesn't mean you can't be happy. The man I loved didn't trap me. I was free to go and it made me miserable. I wanted him to want to hold onto me as much as I wanted to hold onto him."

"I see your point. Who was this lost love of yours?" Josephine asked, curious to know more about Grace's life. She felt guilty that she'd been so involved in her own life that a woman she'd spent more time with than anyone outside of family was a stranger to her in many ways. The events of the past year had broken down the barriers between them, but there was a lot she didn't know.

"I don't think you'd know him. He's gone off to New Orleans anyhow. I 'spect I won't see him again. He seen himself as a musician. His name was Gunner Henderson."

"Where'd you meet him?"

"He worked with Ronnie back when Ronnie was working for the railroad. I was eighteen and he was almost twenty-seven. We went out a couple of times, then Daddy heard him talkin' about us goin' down by the river to the juke joint and the two of them almost got in a fight. Gunner didn't come 'round much after that and, about a month later, he went down to New Orleans and I haven't heard from him since. A cousin told me he was playin' regular at a few clubs down in the French Quarter."

Josephine did the math and figured out that it had been almost twenty years since Grace had seen her musician, yet there was still an almost visible tie that bound her to him. She looked at Grace and caught her eye.

"When we put an end to this monster, maybe we'll take a trip down to New Orleans. I haven't been there since Papa and I went ten years ago."

Grace dropped her eyes down to her cobbler, but Josephine thought she saw a slight smile raise the corners of her mouth. "Guess I'd need to go to keep you company."

"Question is, would we dare leave the baron at home alone?" Josephine said and smiled herself. Then she remembered the pain of separation caused by their blood bond and some of her irritation came rising right back to the surface.

"What are they gonna do about the sheriff?" Grace asked. Josephine suspected that she'd seen the cloud settle over her again and changed the subject in order to keep Josephine from dwelling on the fight.

"I've got an idea how to handle it. I'll just need everybody to cooperate." *I'm going to have to use some of the political skills that Papa tried to instill in me to pull it off*, she thought.

"Mr. Bobby could do the job fine," Grace said.

"I don't think the governor will appoint Bobby to serve out Logan's term. He's going to be looking for someone with more gravitas."

"You mean a big man. I guess you're right. You got someone in mind?"

"I do. Someone we could count on."

"Who?" Grace wasn't going to let it go.

"Colonel Etheridge."

"Ohhhh, that man scares me. I went with my aunt once to clean his house. There were animals on the wall and under glass bowls that I'd never seen. Now, though, I will say he's got the guns. That's for sure."

"The colonel's a good man. Plus, he understands what we're dealing with."

"He'll listen to you. You're his goddaughter." That

seemed to settle the question for Grace.

Josephine wasn't so sure that would be enough to persuade him. Etheridge didn't like dealing with politicians and bureaucrats. He'd had enough of that in his former life. If he had to do any elbow-rubbing to get the job, he'd most likely refuse.

Blasko stood for a moment outside of Grace's house before knocking on the door. Her brother Ronnie and his family had been living there since he'd lost his job and been picking up piecework when he could get it. Blasko had helped him out of a tight spot when Ronnie had been suspected of killing a man.

"Baron, what are you doin' here? Is Grace okay?" Ronnie asked when he opened the door.

"Grace is fine. I want to talk with her cousin George. She said you can take me over to his house."

"Sure! What do you want... Oh, you must have heard he seen the monster. He's been tellin' everyone he meets about it. I'll just get my coat and hat."

As they walked through the cool night air, the streets were deserted. Fear of more attacks had everyone staying indoors. Blasko noticed that faces would occasionally appear at the windows of houses as they passed. One of the silhouettes was holding a shotgun, while another had a baseball bat.

"Are you not afraid to be out here with the monster?" Blasko asked Ronnie.

"Scared enough. I'm waitin' at Cousin George's house and walkin' back with you."

"If this creature is what I think it is, then you have reason to be cautious." Blasko wondered if the rest of the town was this empty. It might be telling to see who was and wasn't afraid to be out and about. Was François still walking to his séances?

"This is it," Ronnie said and opened a gate that swung

awkwardly on a bent hinge. They walked up the dirt path to the porch. No sooner had Ronnie put his weight on the wooden steps than a voice came bellowing out of the house.

"Who's out there?"

"It's Ronnie, Cousin George."

"What the darn fool you doin' outside?" George said, but stopped when he opened the door and saw Blasko's shadowy figure standing behind Ronnie. "Who dat?" he asked, alarmed again.

"This is the baron who lives at Miss Josephine's. Grace told him about you seein' the monster."

George seemed to consider whether he wanted to talk with the stranger.

"George, he helped get me out of jail."

"I remember that. I guess y'all can come in," he said, holding the door open. "Your sister should learn not to talk so much," he muttered under his breath as they walked past him.

The house was shotgun-style, like most in the neighborhood. George offered them a seat on a sofa in the front room. A walnut radio the size of a footlocker sat on the floor, softly playing jazz music. George clicked the radio off and sat down across from them.

"I saw it, sure 'nough," he said as though someone had claimed he hadn't. George had a broad face and dark eyes that seemed to challenge them to argue with him. His bear-paw-size hands clasped the arms of his chair.

"I want you to tell me everything you saw," Blasko said.

"You won't believe me," George said, sticking out his chin.

"Perhaps I will."

"I warned you," the man said, before taking a deep breath and plunging into his story. "I was walkin' home from my job at the grocery store. Used to have a good job drivin' a truck. Best I can do now is workin' at the grocer's when he needs a truck unloaded. He lets me drive a truck sometimes, but—"

"George, he doesn't want to hear about your troubles," Ronnie chided him.

"Yeah, yeah, okay. I was walkin' home from the grocery when I get near the garage. I always kinda look in their yard to see what they're workin' on. That's when I seen this… thing creepin' alongside the garage lookin'…strange, real strange. Like an animal, but not. One minute I thought it might be a dog. Like that big ol' dog the Benders got. But it weren't no dog. The thing was as big as a man, and it went from walkin' like a dog to standin' up.

"I thought I was seein' things. Maybe I'd eaten some rotten food or somethin'. Leaned against the electric pole and just watched it ease up past the corner of the building. I didn't know what to do, I was sort of frozen. Finally, I convinced myself I hadn't seen anythin'. I started walkin' again. I tried to keep my eyes on the road, but my head kept turnin' to look at the garage. That's when I saw a man at that water pump they got 'round back. He stood up straight and started walkin' away. All he had on was a cloth around his middle, like an Indian. His hair might have been a little long too."

"What color was he?"

"He wasn't black. Could have been brown. Light brown or white, hard to tell. I wasn't gettin' no closer with that beast around. It was funny, seein' that man after just seein' the dog thing. Either one of them would have been enough freaky stuff for one night, but seein' both almost at the same time… Maybe I did imagine him up. I know I'm not goin' to no police with that story. They'd have me locked up for somethin'. I've had enough trouble with the law. For sure."

"George got arrested for stealin' cigars when he was in high school," Ronnie explained.

"The woman said I done that was crazy. She couldn't tell one black person from another. I'd been in her damn store one time when Momma needed some eggs. Didn't touch her old cigar. Wasn't anywhere near there that afternoon," George grumbled, rubbing his arm nervously.

"Do you have any idea who the man might have been?" Blasko asked.

"No sir, I don't. I wouldn't know any man that would go walkin' around nearly naked in the middle of the night."

"Which way did he go after leaving the garage?"

"He headed east. I know 'cause I wanted to make sure he wasn't headed toward my house. I felt kinda bad not warnin' him about the monster, but I figured he wouldn't believe me anyhow."

"Was he tall or short, fat, skinny?" Blasko asked, disappointed at the lack of information.

"Medium all around, I'd say."

"How old do you think he was?"

"Guess middle-aged. Maybe forty. Something like that."

It didn't sound like François LeSauvage. Blasko spent another twenty minutes probing George for answers before finally giving up.

He walked with Ronnie back to his house, then headed over to the boarding house. He found Matthew on the front porch, this time with the usual group of codgers who lived at the house. They spent most of their waking hours sitting on the porch giving a running commentary of everything that went on in the county, state and country. All of it was colored by their six decades or more of experience.

"What you hear about the sheriff?" one of the old men asked Blasko. They all knew that he lived in the basement of Josephine's house, giving him the opportunity to be privy to a lot of information about the community.

"The sheriff had a stroke and is at the hospital in Montgomery," Blasko said, humoring them.

"We know that. Is he gonna recover?"

"I haven't heard anything," Blasko said.

"You need bigger ears," the scrawniest of the old men said after he removed the wooden pipe from his mouth.

Blasko ignored him as Matthew smiled and came down the steps.

"What work are you doin' for the baron tonight?"

mumbled a man with a rather cumbersome potbelly.

"Daft old curmudgeons," Blasko muttered when they were out of earshot.

"I thought you were done with me tonight," Matthew grumbled, then asked, "How *is* the sheriff?"

"I haven't heard." Blasko had intended to ask Josephine about Logan until they'd become embroiled in their argument.

"Seems like it's goin' to be harder to catch this thing if leadership at the sheriff's office is all up in the air," Matthew said.

"We'll find Tucker and ask him," Blasko said, making the decision on the fly.

"He'll most likely be over in the Handlins' neighborhood or the area nearby. There was a big outcry from the folks livin' there. Our faithful old friends on the front porch were tellin' me about it before you showed up. Seems there were a about a dozen families at the sheriff's office demanding patrols on their streets. The old guys said that everyone who's ever been a deputy or part-time deputy has been called up to help."

CHAPTER FOURTEEN

As Blasko and Matthew drew closer to the neighborhood, they saw several occupied cars parked on the side of the road, or driving aimlessly down the street. Twice they were asked to stop and identify themselves. The second time it was by Deputy Willard Paige, who reluctantly told them that Bobby had been at the Handlins' house the last time he'd seen him.

Bobby's car was backed into the driveway when they arrived. Blasko looked up at the porch, then put his hand on Matthew's chest and stopped him, holding his finger to his lips and walking up to the porch alone. When he got to the foot of the steps, he stomped his foot loudly. Bobby, who had been sitting in a wicker chair pushed back in the shadows, jumped to his feet, holding his lever-action Winchester at the ready.

"What the hell?" he said when he saw Blasko.

"You shouldn't sleep on sentry duty," the baron said with the hint of a smile in his voice.

"And you shouldn't be a smartass," Bobby said grumpily. "I haven't had a lot of sleep in the past twenty-four hours."

"How's Sheriff Logan?"

"They say they aren't sure yet. But I got the impression

talking to his daughter that they don't think he'll make a full recovery." Bobby's hand clutched the rifle more tightly. "Which means that, right now, it feels like no one's in charge."

"Aren't you the senior deputy?"

"Most of the time, when the sheriff went out of town or was sick, he placed me in charge, but... not always. Everyone's going along with me giving orders for the moment. That's not likely to continue past a few days."

"Someone spotted the monster last night after the attack on the Handlins," Blasko said.

"Who?" Bobby asked, coming down the stairs.

"A cousin of Grace's. He didn't see much. The colonel and I told you how we tracked the beast to the garage. This man saw it go there and leave. Leave as a man."

"I want to talk to him."

"He doesn't care much for lawmen."

"Doesn't matter what he thinks of me. I need to hear his description of this man... or whatever it is."

"Average, around forty, naked except for something he was wearing around his waist."

Bobby considered this. "Someone has to know something. If your husband comes home naked, you're gonna notice."

"He might not be married."

"Doesn't matter. Around this town, a neighbor or relative or *someone* is going to notice a guy walking around naked. Which way did he go from the garage?"

"East."

"Let's go."

Bobby started for the car, then said to Matthew, "You stay here and tell anyone looking for me where I went. We should be back in less than an hour."

"What do you expect to find? He's not likely to still be walking around naked," Blasko said as Bobby steered his car into the road.

"I just want to see the area. Maybe he was close to home

at that point. That makes sense. Otherwise, someone would have come forward with a report of a naked man."

"Maybe." Blasko was unconvinced.

"Besides, I'm tired of sittin' on my ass doin' nothing. We aren't gonna catch the beast by patrolling an area where he's already killed. That's what we did the first time around and what did that get us?"

"I'm not going to argue with you. That was the sheriff's idea."

"When he thought it was a wild animal."

"So why did you order the patrols tonight?"

Bobby sighed. "We can't ignore public opinion. There was a crowd at the office this afternoon and it got pretty ugly. If I hadn't told them we'd have deputies out patrolling their neighborhoods, they'd've taken it upon themselves to do it. Which is not what we need right now." He paused for a moment, then asked, "So why attack a boy out in the county and now a woman in the middle of town?"

"I suspect to sow fear. I encountered a beast like this back in my homeland and that's what it did. Created an atmosphere of terror and took advantage when people made mistakes."

"Mistakes?"

"One woman was killed when her son didn't come home from his work before dark. She was so scared something had happened to him that she went out looking for him and was attacked by the beast. If she hadn't been so worried, she'd have realized that her son had the good sense to stay with a friend when they were late unloading the hay. He knew better than to walk home in the dark. Fear was what drove the woman to make a foolish mistake that cost her her life. You were lucky no one was killed when Logan had that posse wandering around in the woods."

"I said the same. So where will he strike next?"

"I don't think we have enough pieces of the puzzle to make an educated guess."

They rounded a corner and Bobby pointed. "There's the

garage."

"Park here," Blasko instructed. For a moment he thought Bobby was going to argue with him, but instead he pulled the car to the curb. The two men got out and walked to the water pump.

"So he washed up here. East is that direction," Bobby said, pointing. He retrieved his flashlight from the car and turned it on as he walked, looking at the ground for clues.

"Since he was naked, I doubt anything fell out of his pockets," Blasko said, irritated with the flashlight, which interfered with his night vision.

"You search your way, I'll search mine."

Blasko strode down the road to get ahead of the glow of the flashlight. He couldn't decide whether he wanted to look along the ground for footprints or scan the neighborhood to see if there was something to indicate why the man came this way. He settled on the latter since Bobby was tending to the former.

The homes were modest and middle-class. Most of them looked like they'd been built in the post-war boom.

"Here!" Bobby said.

His light shone on a spot a foot in front of him, where sand had blown up and collected against the curb. Blasko looked at it closely and saw the print of an adult foot.

"I wouldn't think there are too many people walking around barefoot in this neighborhood," Bobby said.

"Can you make a cast or something?" Blasko was a little vague on the forensic capabilities of local law enforcement. He didn't think this would be as easy as taking a cast from the mud along the creek.

"Not in this sand. It's so soft and fine that a cast won't work. I've got a tape measure back in the car. At least we'll know what size foot our suspect has." Bobby looked at Blasko expectantly.

Blasko stared back at him then asked, "Would you like me to hold the flashlight?"

"I was actually thinking you could go to my car and get

the tape measure," Bobby said, looking back at the print.

For the second time that evening, Blasko found himself performing what he considered a menial task. He found the tape measure after going through several canvas bags in the back seat of the car. Grumbling internally over the waste of his talents, he started back to where Bobby stood over the print. Then he smelled something on the wind—a faint animal scent, but not that of dogs, cats, squirrels or raccoons that usually permeated the town.

He kept walking, but raised his head to get a better whiff of the breeze. A slight wind was coming from in front of him. He homed in on the odor and was sure now that it was the beast. *Where is it?* he asked himself with a sense of urgency. With every step he took, the scent became stronger.

Blasko stared into the night ahead of him and past where Bobby, unaware of the creature's presence, knelt beside the footprint. Two desires warred within Blasko. One wanted to catch the beast at all costs, but the other counseled caution. If this monster was anything like the one he'd confronted in the past, it was capable of killing both him and Bobby if it got the jump on them.

He was still fifty yards from Bobby. If he shouted a warning, the creature might get spooked or might decide to attack. Blasko knew that even if he had the ability to defeat the monster, at this distance he could never reach Bobby in time to save him. There was nothing to do but keep walking and scanning the area.

Blasko caught movement out of the corner of his eye. A moment later, an orange tomcat started across the street. Then the cat hesitated in midstride and suddenly bounded back the way it had come. *The cat caught wind of our lurker in the bushes*, Blasko thought.

When he was twenty paces from Bobby, he saw eyes peering out of the bushes across the street. They had caught the light from the flashlight and, for just a moment, reflected red in the darkness.

"Come on. I'm getting a cramp in my leg," Bobby said,

turning to look at Blasko. Something in the baron's posture or expression must have clued him in to the danger, because Blasko saw him stiffen and look around, rising slowly to his feet.

Blasko was now close enough to speak softly. "Our friend is across the street in the bushes on the right side of that brick house." His voice was calm and measured.

Bobby reached back and slowly lifted his Colt 1911 automatic from its holster before letting it ease down along the side of his leg. "I can't see it."

Blasko thought this was a good idea and was glad he'd thought to don his own shoulder holster and pistol before he left the house. "It's there watching us. I can smell it and I saw its eyes."

Both men were pretending to look down at the print while actually scanning the opposite side of the street for any movement. Blasko caught sight of something just beyond where he had seen the eyes of the beast. At the house on the left, the door opened, a light came on and a figure walked out onto the porch. A man shouted over to them.

"Hey, what y'all doin' over there? I'll call the police on—" Before he could finish, there was a great roar from the side of the house and the dark figure of the beast rushed toward the man, who turned and froze.

Blasko and Bobby broke into a run, reaching the other side of the street just as the monster grabbed the man and hurled him in their direction. The man screamed as he flew thirty feet through the air to land just in front of them. He hit the ground with a sickening thud and crack. Bobby stopped at the fallen man while Blasko ran past him and toward the dark shadows where the creature had disappeared.

Blasko quickly found himself outdistanced, but he was close enough to confirm his suspicions. It was definitely a werewolf. Fleet of foot, the creature cleared fences and other obstacles easily while Blasko struggled to get over or through them. Soon, he only had his ears and nose to guide him as he followed the beast. Lights were coming on in houses throughout the neighborhood as they passed and Blasko hoped none of the residents would take a shot at him.

For ten minutes Blasko followed the scent, but luck wasn't with him. The werewolf reached a lake just north of town a good three minutes ahead of him. By the time Blasko reached the shore of the lake, he could see the water rippling but no sign of the monster, and the scent was fading.

He spent half an hour trying to pick up the trail, but he knew what had happened. The werewolf had plunged into the water, transformed back into its human form and emerged without the smell of the beast to give him away.

At last, Blasko had no choice but to give up and start the long walk back to where he'd left Bobby and the creature's victim. Along the way, he encountered a dozen people who'd heard the commotion and come out of their homes with their guns loaded.

"I'm with Deputy Tucker," Blasko told them all. "The creature was sighted in this area. Go back in your house."

Most just muttered and complied, but a couple tried to argue with Blasko.

"Bah! Then go stumble around in the dark and get torn apart. Dr. McGuire will come by and pick up the pieces in the morning," he told them.

CHAPTER FIFTEEN

Blasko found Bobby on the ground, using strips of cloth torn from his shirt in an attempt to staunch the blood from the man's many wounds.

"He's got broken bones and he's bleeding badly. One of the neighbors is trying to get ahold of the doctor, but I'm not sure if it will do any good." Bobby sounded frustrated and angry.

"I followed him as far as a lake. The werewolf must have gone into the water and changed back into his human form, because I couldn't get any hint of his trail beyond the lake."

"Must be Cypress Lake. Werewolf, you call it? Even after everything we saw out at Mrs. Rosehill's, that's hard to swallow. But now that I've seen it, or at least seen what it can do, I'd be a fool to doubt you."

"How much did you see?"

"The thing was in the shadows most of the time, but I could tell it wasn't human. Or any kind of normal animal." Bobby looked around. There were people standing on their porches, but none of them were close enough to hear what they were saying. "Can you check his house? I'd assume that if anyone else lived there, they would have come out by now, but you should probably check."

As Blasko stood up, a man came from across the street.

"Doc McGuire is on his way. I called the sheriff's office too, like you told me. They're going to hunt up some deputies and send them out here." The man looked down at his neighbor. "That's Calvin Nash."

"Does he have any family nearby?"

"He's got a wife, but she's staying with her sister's family down in Mobile. They've been having some problems. I think money, mostly. Her brother-in-law is out of work and…" The man quit talking when he realized that, in the face of the dying Calvin Nash, the story of his brother-in-law's unemployment wasn't really important.

The road was soon blocked with several cars, including the doctor's.

"He's in bad shape. His back in broken." Dr. McGuire opened one of Nash's eyes and shined a light in it. He moved the light to the other eye and repeated the process. "His skull is fractured, and there's most likely bleeding under the skull. This man is not going to live. I'd suggest you find a backboard and we'll move him into his house."

Dr. McGuire made up a syringe of morphine and gave it to Nash while a group of men assembled a makeshift stretcher from a couple of fence boards. Colonel Etheridge showed up just as they lifted the man and carried him back into his house.

"You saw what attacked him?" Etheridge had pulled Bobby and Blasko aside out of earshot of the rest of the group.

"I saw enough. Two hundred pounds at least. Stood up on its hind feet and tossed that man more than twenty feet through the air. With force. I've never seen anything like it."

"I saw it clearly. It was a werewolf," Blasko said. "It looked very similar to a creature I had to deal with back in my country."

"How did you kill it?" Etheridge asked.

"I never did. Every time I thought I had it trapped, the creature managed to escape. Remember, this is a monster with the abilities of an animal and the cunning of a man."

"As I mentioned, I had an experience in Africa. A witchdoctor who could seemingly turn himself into a tiger. We hunted him for three months until the villagers found where the witchdoctor was hiding and set a fire to trap him. My small contingent arrived just as the fire reached the compound. The screams were unimaginable."

"I don't think burning it out is an option," Bobby said.

"No, probably not," Etheridge muttered.

"Removing its head is the surest way," Blasko said.

"Hmmm, an axe then. I'm afraid the only swords I have are ceremonial," Etheridge said.

"Getting close enough to use a sword on that thing would be risky," Bobby said.

"I wouldn't suggest that anyone but me attempt it," Blasko said. "I sent for my old broadsword. It arrived today." Etheridge and Bobby weren't sure if Blasko was kidding or not.

"We have guns," Bobby reminded him.

"A large enough caliber could stop it or slow it down. But if you think getting close to it with a sword is difficult, I promise you that hitting it with a well-placed shot will be nearly impossible."

"Shotguns with slugs are our best chance," Bobby said. "Question is, how do we prepare the other deputies for what we're dealing with without sounding crazy?"

"Rabid bear," Etheridge stated firmly. "Tell them that a grizzly bear escaped from a zoo train and is believed to be infected with rabies."

"A rabid grizzly isn't a bad description of what I saw," Bobby admitted.

They were silent for a few minutes as each man thought about the dangers of confronting the creature.

"You know, those villagers in Africa might have had the right idea," Etheridge said. "The best plan might be to hunt him like any other human killer. Catching him in his human form is going to be safer and easier than when he's out and about mauling people."

"Which was our original plan," Bobby interjected. "Look for someone who has a motive or find someone acting suspicious."

"Right, and that way we can deal with him when he's human. Human... It all sounds mighty crazy." Etheridge shook his head.

"This animal must be brought down. In the mountains back home, the creature that hunted there killed over fifty people. There was a werewolf in France that slaughtered hundreds," Blasko told them.

"We'll kill it or capture it," Bobby said with determination, looking at the house where a dozen people were gathered around the door, standing vigil over the dying man.

Etheridge asked about the sheriff and Bobby explained the situation as he understood it.

"Sad news, but we don't have time to be sentimental. If Logan is going to be laid up for a while, the governor needs to find a replacement. This town is going to need leadership," Etheridge said.

"We better hope some idiot isn't appointed to fill out his term as sheriff. For now, I'm going to proceed with our plan. I'll question Handlin in the morning and see if there's anyone who might have a reason to target his wife." Bobby paused and looked at Blasko. "Man or beast. In your experience, do you think he is acting with human motivations when he kills?"

"If he's committing random assaults then we don't have much chance of catching him, so we'd better hope he has human motivation. For now, I think it's best if we assume that the attacks on Seth Taylor and Mrs. Handlin had some reason. Of course, tonight he was in beast form, became enraged when he was discovered and struck out at whoever was nearby. But I don't think it was a coincidence that he was stalking us tonight."

"I saw that in Africa. The witchdoctor was able to

channel his beast self for his human motivations, but at times the animal seemed to take over."

"With my sword, I also received a book that might have more answers," Blasko told them. "It was written by the man who was tasked with hunting the werewolf that stalked the French countryside in the 1700s."

"I'd like to get a look at that myself," Etheridge said.

"You're welcome anytime." Blasko gave a slight bow.

"You said that you planned to question Handlin. Are you still holding him?" Etheridge asked Bobby.

"I told him that I would keep him at the jail for another night or two for his own safety. People are so riled up, I'm glad I did. With him in jail, no one can blame this attack on him."

They agreed to meet again the next night. Etheridge volunteered to stay awhile and help organize a team of deputies to search the area around Cypress Lake. Even if they didn't find anything, it would help keep the deputies busy and prove to the community that the sheriff's office was actively searching for the killer.

Bobby stayed behind at Nash's house, sending for Emmett Wolfe to photograph the man's injuries. He was going to have to treat this like a normal crime scene, even though this murder would probably never go to trial. He could just imagine being on the witness stand and testifying that he had seen a monster attack Nash. He doubted he'd be able to keep his job after that.

Blasko, feeling drained from chasing the creature, headed home. He was eager to start his research. They needed to know everything they could about the beast.

He'd only gone a couple of blocks when he saw Matthew walking toward him.

"I noticed all the cars heading this way and figured the monster had been sighted. I didn't see any point in hanging out at the Handlin house."

Blasko told him about the evening's events.

"Is this the same creature you were hunting in Romania?"

"I don't know. It would seem unlikely."

"But how many monsters like this can there be?"

"You said you saw one during your time in France."

"Two. I've thought about that."

"Maybe they are like other creatures of the night. Some are evil and others are, at heart, good." *Even if Josephine doesn't believe I'm one of them*, Blasko thought bitterly.

"This one would definitely fall into the evil category."

"Agreed."

Matthew walked with Blasko back to the boarding house. "What do you need me to do?" he asked.

"Listen. If you hear of anyone acting oddly or who has disappeared for a day or two, make a note of it. It seems odd that this creature just emerged out of thin air. He had to have come from somewhere. Are there any other strangers in town?"

"None that I've heard of. I'll keep an eye on the medium."

Blasko nodded. He was just about to part ways with Matthew when he asked, "Who is the worst person you know of in town?"

Matthew narrowed his eyes. "Why?"

"A whim," Blasko lied.

"Guy I hate the most is a creep by the name of Gene Hawkins. He lives four blocks off of the courthouse square."

"What makes you hate him?"

"He's a loan shark."

"A what?"

"He makes loans at ridiculous rates that no one can repay. When they default, he kicks them out of their house, or takes their car, whatever he can. I've seen him boot a family of five to the curb for a debt that started out as ten dollars and was a thousand by the time he had them evicted. But he always stays just inside the law."

"I see." Blasko needed fresh blood and, after his most recent fight with Josephine, he didn't feel overly bound by their agreement. "He must live in an impressive home."

Matthew looked Blasko dead in the eye. "He lives on Texas Street. The house is brick with green trim."

"I will see you tomorrow," Blasko said and left Matthew staring at his back.

He found Gene Hawkins's house with little difficulty. His watch said it was three in the morning when he climbed the steps onto the small porch and rang the bell. It took five minutes for a very irritated man to come to the door.

"This better be worth getting your knees capped!" Hawkins hollered from inside the house. When he opened the door, one hand was shoved deep in the pocket of his robe. Blasko was sure he was holding a gun.

"What the hell do you want?" the tall man asked.

Blasko held up a gold coin to catch the light from the bulb above the door. "I think you will be very interested in a deal I can offer you," he said.

Hawkins looked Blasko up and down, taking in the quality of his clothes and shoes. "You better have a good reason why you couldn't have pitched it to me at a decent hour," he said, but his eyes were already following the coin in Blasko's fingers as it sparkled in the light.

"This coin and many others like it can be yours if you give me a few moments of your time. Look at the superb quality of the minting."

Hawkins's jaw hung slack as he looked at the coin.

"This is business better conducted inside," Blasko instructed him, and Hawkins moved back to let him enter.

When Blasko left half an hour later, he was feeling reinvigorated while Gene Hawkins would feel weak for several days. After he recovered, he'd learn that the mere idea of offering a predatory loan would make him violently ill.

When Blasko arrived back at Josephine's house, he looked up at the large Victorian. There were no lights on inside. *Good*, he said to himself. He wasn't in the mood to talk with her tonight. The wounds were too raw. What was she thinking? He'd explained a dozen times now that their options were limited. The bond that bound them together could only be broken by death. And death for either of them would mean pain and suffering for the other. Josephine was going to have to accept their fate. Of course, there was one other way... but he wouldn't consider it.

Blasko wouldn't admit it even to himself, but he was already feeling ashamed of breaking his promise to her by feeding on Hawkins. Which was another reason he was glad that she was asleep.

He entered his apartment to find Poe waiting for him. He'd had a carpenter install a cat door for the animal's use once Poe had become more accepting of Vasile and Blasko was convinced that he would not harm the bat. Now the two mostly ignored each other.

"Where's our flying friend tonight?" Blasko asked Poe, who sat by a food dish looking expectant. "He must be out enjoying the warmer weather."

Blasko opened a tin of canned meat and put some of it in the cat's bowl. He could hear snoring coming from the alcove he'd shown Anton for his sleeping quarters. "Have you met our guest?" he asked the cat, who was purring softly as he ate his food. "I don't know how long he will be staying, but he seems to irritate your mistress and that is somewhat satisfying." Blasko chuckled.

Then he sat down in one of his wingback chairs with the book by Captain Duhamel. The attacks in the south of France had been underway for months when the captain and his troop of dragoons had been sent to the Gévaudan region. Blasko read about the captain's first engagements with the beast, who always managed to slip away. Baffled by the creature's ability to escape his troops, Duhamel began to listen to some of the locals that he'd originally dismissed as superstitious peasants.

The peasants told him that the beast was able to shift from human to animal form at will. As insane as it sounded, Duhamel came to believe in the beast's supernatural abilities after several close encounters in which the monster seemed to vanish when Duhamel's troops were sure they had him surrounded.

Blasko, his attention riveted, read until the first tinge of blue showed on the horizon.

CHAPTER SIXTEEN

"There was another attack last night," Bobby told Josephine. He'd come over as soon he received the message she'd left with the sheriff's office that morning. "What'd you want to talk to me about?"

"First tell me what happened," Josephine said, surprised that there had been another killing so soon.

Bobby told her what he'd seen. "And in all of that, I lost the chance to get a picture of the footprint. By the time I got back to it, some of the gawkers had walked through it."

"It's not like you could compare it to the cast you collected where the Taylor boy was attacked."

"You got a point there. I sent the plaster cast over to the zoology department at the University of Alabama. Their best guess is that it was a deformed Mackenzie Valley wolf, which is ridiculous. It lives out west. The professor also suggested that it might be a dire wolf, but they went extinct eleven thousand years ago. I think he was joking."

"Did you tell them what Dragomir suggested?"

"I'm trying *not* to get tossed into a loony bin. Now, what did you want to talk about?"

"I think I can get the governor to appoint Colonel Etheridge to the position of sheriff."

Bobby thought about it for a minute. "That wouldn't be the worst solution. Will he do it?"

"If you and I both ask him to, I think he might. I thought we'd go talk to him and then drive over to Montgomery. We can visit Logan. After that, I'll speak to the governor."

"Can you get to see him that fast?"

"Money talks. I've spoken to Ray Butler on the bank's board of directors. He was a state representative until two years ago and knows the governor well. He's already gotten me a write-in on the governor's schedule."

Bobby stood there and looked at Josephine in awe for a moment. "On a Sunday? I should never underestimate you."

"Damn straight," she said with a smile.

"I'll need to check in at the office and let them know I'll be out of touch for a while."

"And I need to dress the part. Pick me up in an hour."

Bobby left detailed instructions with Deputy Paige that could have been summed up simply as: *Don't do anything stupid*, then headed back over to Josephine's. He got out of the car and started toward the front door, only to stop short when he saw her. Josephine stood on the porch wearing a stunning sapphire-blue day dress, black gloves and snappy black heels. Her honey-brown hair was elegantly styled and topped with an impressive black hat sporting several ostrich plumes.

"Are you looking for a marriage proposal from the governor?" Bobby asked with a wide smile.

"I thought I better bring out the big guns," Josephine responded, walking carefully down the steps in heels that were an inch taller than she was used to.

The talk with Etheridge wasn't difficult. He wasn't about to be left out of the hunt for this creature and, with his experience, he had no qualms about being the person in charge. Bobby and Josephine were soon on their way to Montgomery.

"That was depressing," Josephine said as they were leaving the hospital. "I'm glad Papa was able to die at home."

"The doctor said Logan will recover enough to be released."

"I remember when Mr. Norris had his stroke. His left side didn't improve much."

"Some people who've had strokes can get better. Logan has his wife. She'll see him through it, if anyone can." Bobby was reluctant to give up on the man who had guided him through his entire career.

Josephine grew quiet as they drove to the governor's mansion. She felt like she was betraying a sick man by pulling the job out from under Logan so quickly. *If it wasn't for these murders, we could give him time,* she told herself.

Governor Benjamin Miller met her in the back garden. It was a bright day and pleasant for late winter. Farther south the azaleas had started to bloom, but here they would have to wait almost another month before the bushes would be covered in pink, purple and red blossoms.

Bobby had agreed that it would be best for him to stay out with the car. They didn't want it to look like this had anything to do with internal politics at the sheriff's office.

"Miss Nicolson, it's a delight to see you," the governor said. "I still appreciate the advice I got from your father and your bank manager when I was considering that bank holiday last year."

"You were eight days ahead of Roosevelt's declaration."

"I think we saved a lot of people from rack and ruin."

"You certainly saved a lot of banks. Since it was at your order, it didn't look like an act of desperation when the banks closed their doors."

"A cooling-off period can make all the difference. Especially where money is concerned. Now you didn't drive all this way to talk about banking." He waved her toward a white wrought-iron table and chairs on the brick patio.

"Did you hear about our sheriff?" Josephine asked once they were settled. "He had a stroke and the prognosis is not good."

"Yes," the governor said solemnly.

"I don't know if you're familiar with our current difficulties. There have been several violent deaths in Semmes County."

"I did read something about that in the *Montgomery Advertiser*. A bear attack or something?" he said with raised eyebrows.

"Or something. Trouble is, people are all worked up about it. Now the sheriff can't fulfill his duties, so there's a... power vacuum."

Governor Miller leaned forward with a smile. "Just like we were saying. When people get all worked up, trouble follows."

"Exactly, Governor Miller. I knew you would understand our situation," Josephine said, layering on the butter.

"I can assure you that I will expedite the matter. I'll get my secretary to look into qualified candidates and, as soon as we sort through them, I'll appoint someone to fill the position."

"I don't mean to be presumptuous, but there is a candidate who is ready-made to step in."

"Appointing a sheriff is a big decision." The governor hesitated, recognizing Josephine's pull in Semmes County. "Who do you have in mind?" he asked carefully.

"I think you know him. Colonel Samuel Etheridge. He served as the adjutant general of the state militia for several years and has a laundry list of other qualifications."

"And why are you so anxious to see him appointed sheriff?" he asked, genuinely intrigued.

"He has already been involved in the hunt for the killer, so there wouldn't be any loss of time with a new person trying to get up to speed. Honestly, I think the county is on edge. The people need some stability."

"I see. Yes, I do remember Colonel Etheridge. He struck me as a very forthright individual. Very professional. Hmmmm." The governor was lost in thought as he went over the pros and cons. Josephine wanted to push him a little more. *Don't do it*, she advised herself.

Finally he said, "I'll have my secretary dig into his background a bit more and, if nothing seems amiss, I don't see why I wouldn't make the appointment."

Josephine sat back in her chair, relieved. She spent the next half hour talking to the governor about issues that he thought would be of interest to a woman. Truth was, she had little knowledge of gardens or popular movie stars, but she smiled and agreed with his opinions until he excused himself to attend to state business.

In the large circular drive, Bobby was leaning against the car like a taxi driver. He stood up when he saw her coming and opened her door.

"I think we hit the bull's-eye," Josephine told him as she slid into the car.

It was late afternoon by the time they got back to Sumter. Bobby had offered to buy her dinner before dropping her off, but she was tired and ready to get out of her fancy clothes and into something more comfortable. Plus, she wanted time to consider how she and Blasko could breach the crack in their relationship. *However crazy the relationship is*, she thought.

"I'm going to grab something at the diner," Bobby said, "then I may come back for the baron. I'd like to question some suspects this evening, and having him along might come in handy. I'll stop by and let Etheridge know that his appointment is in the works."

Josephine thanked him and went into the house, where Grace met her at the front door.

"You look rode hard and put up wet," Grace told her, taking in Josephine's rumpled dress and drooping ostrich feathers. "Anna's fixed a pot roast. Mr. Bobby didn't stay?"

"I thought you'd given up on matching me up with Bobby?"

"I just worry that the man don't ever eat enough," Grace said with sincerity.

"He said he's going to the diner."

Grace huffed. "That food ain't fit for man nor beast. You should have made him come in and get something."

Blasko rose ten minutes after the sun dropped below the trees. It had become his favorite time of day. If he timed it right, he could just catch some light coming through the small windows high on one wall of his parlor. He received a not unpleasant warmth from the diffused sunlight. On the other hand, he never tried to catch the first light of morning before he slept. There was too great a risk of something happening to leave him fully exposed to the sun's burning rays.

As he stood in the pale fading light, he decided to make amends with Josephine for his eavesdropping and accusations. *I must realize that she has not lived with this for centuries as I have,* he reminded himself. What he didn't acknowledge was the guilt he was feeling from feeding on Hawkins the loan shark.

After he dressed, Blasko opened the door that led to the staircase and found Anton sitting on the bottom step, apparently waiting for the baron to rise. Blasko didn't want to admit that he'd forgotten about the man.

"*Ah, Anton, there you are,*" he said, clearing his throat and greeting the man in Rusyn.

"*Yes, Baron. Forgive me. I did not know what you wished me to do. So I waited.*"

"*Excellent,*" he said distractedly. "*When do you plan to return to the mountains?*" Blasko realized that he didn't have a need for a manservant.

"*I am at your disposal. I sold my farm to my cousin. I have no home to go home to.*"

"*I see,*" Blasko said, thinking that he should have quizzed the man more closely the day before.

"*I am still strong. I can do whatever you need.*"

Then again, he might come in handy, Blasko thought.

"*Did you go upstairs to eat?*"

"*No,*" Anton said, as though he had failed in some great test of character.

"*You must eat. Come. I'll take you upstairs and introduce you to the other servants.*"

Upstairs, Blasko took Anton into the kitchen and introduced him to Anna. At first, the two looked as nervous as ten-year-olds at their first school dance. But after Anna offered him a heaping plate of potatoes, roast and bread, they began to work out the language barrier. Anna's mother was French, but had also taught her a fair amount of German. After a few false starts, Anton and Anna worked out a mix of German and English words that they both knew. Soon they were communicating in a mix of languages that Blasko didn't even try to understand.

Leaving the two new friends in the kitchen, he found Josephine in the parlor.

"Is that man still here?" she asked. The tone wasn't at all what she'd planned when she'd been considering how to reconcile with Blasko.

"He is my guest," the baron shot back, more harshly than he'd intended.

"In my house!" Josephine responded. "No, I didn't mean that," she backpedaled quickly.

"And I should have asked if you minded him staying," Blasko admitted with a slight nod of his head.

They looked at each other, feeling a distance that separated them more like diplomats than friends or lovers.

We have to deal with my feelings, was what Josephine wanted to say. Instead, "I went to see the governor today."

You have to come to terms with the situation as it is and then bury it, Blasko wanted to tell her. Instead, "Who will replace Logan?"

Josephine told Blasko about her day.

"I think the colonel will be an excellent choice."

"That man is still here!" Grace said, coming into the room and pointing back toward the kitchen.

"He's going to be staying down in the baron's apartment

for a little while," Josephine said.

"You can use Anton for any work you feel is appropriate," Blasko told Grace generously.

Grace seemed to consider this for a moment. "You mean I can ask him to do somethin' around here and he'll do it?"

"I'll instruct him to be available during the day."

Grace tried hard to hide her excitement. She had never in her life supervised another person. The thought made her straighten her back. "Yes, sir!" she said and returned to the kitchen to inspect her underling.

"Do you have any idea what you just did to poor Anton?" Josephine smiled and then downed half the glass of wine she'd been holding.

Bobby Tucker came by an hour later.

"Baron, I was hoping you'd go with me to talk with some suspects in the Handlin case. I had one of the deputies put together a list."

"Of course."

"I'll stay here. Not that I was invited," Josephine said playfully.

"You are—" Bobby started.

"No. Really, I'm quite tired," she told him. "However, I would be interested in seeing the list."

Bobby pulled it out of his pocket. "Five names. Three of them were given to us by Mr. Handlin. The other two came from talking to the immediate neighbors." He held the paper out to Josephine, who took it and ran down the names.

"I know Silas Palmer. That old goat is a thorn under the community's saddle." Josephine frowned.

"He and Mr. Handlin had an argument a couple of weeks ago over a bill for a load of coal. Handlin works as the manager for the All Alabama Coal company. They delivered a ton of coal to Silas's house and he claimed they shorted him. Silas went so far as to pull his truck up in the coal yard and got his son to start shoveling coal into it. Handlin went out to talk to them. Long story short, Silas personally threatened Handlin before driving off."

"What is Charlie Parsons's name doing on this list? He's the nicest guy in town," Josephine said.

"A story from one of the neighbors suggests that Charlie was a little too nice to Mrs. Handlin," Bobby said. Josephine was amused to see him blush.

"I don't know Benny Byron or Lee Brooks."

"Benny is a neighbor they played bridge with once a week until about six months ago, when he accused the Handlins of cheating."

"What about Lee Brooks?"

"He works at the bakery. Makes deliveries. Apparently, Mrs. Handlin thought he was looking at her funny one day and said something to the owner. I know Brooks. He's a little slow, but a good guy. One of our deputies went and talked to both of them at the time. Bottom line was, the only person who thought there was anything funny going on was Mrs. Handlin. Deputy Olson told the owner to just have Brooks go in the back whenever Mrs. Handlin came in."

"Okay, this last one has to be a joke. Daniel Robertson? *My* Daniel Robertson?"

"According to Handlin, Robertson threatened them over a mortgage payment that Handlin said they made and the bank had no record of."

"Daniel has never threatened anyone," Josephine said with a dismissive wave.

"There must be some bad blood between them for Handlin to make the claim," Bobby said, looking at his watch. "We need to get going if we're to have a chance of questioning everyone this evening."

Josephine watched Blasko and Bobby leave, fascinated by the strange twists of fate that had brought them all together. She thought of the note that her cousin Franklin Carter had placed inside the book that had so angered Blasko.

Dear Cousin Josie,

Of course I cannot send the Necronomicon, *but until I can return, I'm sending this book instead. Read it carefully. There are errors throughout, but I can vouch for the major themes. No vampire can be trusted. If you need further help, call me. I feel that I will soon be drawn back to Semmes County. Fate is drawing all of us closer.*

Yours,
Franklin

Josephine had just turned from the door when there was a knock. Thinking that Bobby had forgotten something, she swung the door open again. She was surprised to see Matthew Hodge standing on the porch.

"The baron just left with Deputy Tucker," she told him, expecting him to turn and go.

"I know. I wanted to talk to you." His voice was almost too soft for her to hear.

"Certainly. Come in," she said. "Let's go to the parlor. Can I get you something to drink?"

"Water would be nice."

"I didn't mean to offer you a… Everyone is impressed with how you've maintained your sobriety," Josephine said, getting a glass of water for both of them.

"It's okay, you can drink in front of me," Matthew said with a small smile for her kindness.

"Sit." She offered the chair across from the sofa. "What can I do for you?" She hoped that it wouldn't be about money. There had been more than one friend and neighbor who had misunderstood her relationship with the bank.

"I was hoping you'd introduce me to François LeSauvage."

"But you've been following him for weeks," she said with a laugh, baffled by the request.

"I'd like to try one of his séances."

"You could just ask him. He seems to be open to letting anyone join in. No charge," Josephine said, still not understanding why he wanted her help.

"I would feel… odd. I *have* been following him. I was just hoping you could take me to one."

Josephine stopped herself from pushing him to go by

himself. She could see that he was embarrassed to be asking her for a favor. If he had felt comfortable going to a séance alone, he already would have. He was obviously nervous about it and this was the least she could do for him after what they had already been through together.

"Okay. What do you hope to accomplish by going to one?"

"I'm not any different than a million other guys. I've got a few ghosts from the war that I'd like to put to rest. I've heard that, at these séances, if someone… on the other side needs to contact you, they will. I just thought I'd give a few of my old buddies a chance. In case there's something I can do for them or… if they think I owe them something." This last was said so softly it was almost a whisper.

"I'm sure you don't owe anyone anything."

"*I'm* not so sure."

She waited, but he didn't say anything else. "I'll make the arrangements. What day would be best for you?"

Matthew looked surprised that she thought he had a calendar to check. "Any day would be great. Best if you didn't tell the baron. He doesn't seem to like that guy much."

Josephine told him she'd send word to his boarding house when she had a date and time, then walked him to the door. Watching him walk away, Josephine reflected on the influence Blasko had had on the county. Little more than six months ago, Matthew had been the town drunk, ignored by those who didn't openly despise him. *No, Franklin is wrong. There is more good than bad in Dragomir.*

CHAPTER SEVENTEEN

"You pick a name from the list. 'Cause I don't know how to decide which of them is most likely to turn into a wolf," Bobby told Blasko.

Blasko looked at the names and remembered what Bobby had said about each of them. "Maybe we should use age. The witness who saw the man walk away from the garage thought he was in his late thirties or forties."

"That leaves Silas out. He's sixty-something if he's a day and looks like he's been living rough the whole time. Your witness didn't think he was black, so that would leave Brooks off the short list. Daniel is also outside the age range. That leaves us with Benny Byron, the card player, and Charlie Parsons, who might be playing other kinds of games. Both of them live in the right direction from the garage. Benny's house comes up first."

Five minutes later, they pulled into the Byrons' driveway. The house was nothing special—a small clapboard structure—but the property boasted an impressive ancient live oak whose massive branches spread the width of the entire front yard. There were lights on in the house and a face peeked out from behind the front curtains as Blasko and Bobby made their way up the stone walk to the small porch.

When Bobby knocked, they heard the sound of kids shouting to their parents that there were two strangers at the front door. A woman yelled at them to stay away from the windows.

"Who is it?" a male voice asked from the other side of the door.

"Deputy Tucker."

"How do I know you're a deputy?"

Bobby pulled out his star and held it up to the small window at the top of the door. He tapped it on the glass to get the man's attention. After what sounded like furniture being pulled across the floor, the door opened.

Blasko looked the man up and down, trying to judge how well he fit George's description. It was a slight stretch to call the man's build average as he was a bit stocky, but there was nothing that would completely rule him out.

"We'd like to ask you some questions about the murder of Mrs. Handlin," Bobby said.

"You should be out there looking for the animal or crazy man that did it," Benny said, waving at the darkness behind them.

"We just have a few questions for you," Bobby said and started to walk forward.

Obligingly, Benny stepped back so they could enter the house. Mrs. Byron was standing in the living room with her hand up to her mouth, looking baffled at the evening's turn of events.

A young boy and girl peered into the living room from the hallway, spurring Mrs. Byron into action.

"You two get back down to your room," she said, shooing them in that direction.

"I don't know what I can tell you," Benny said.

"I understand you accused the Handlins of cheating at cards," Bobby said. In an instant, Benny's face turned red and angry.

"They *were* cheating! I know they were. But Pete kicked *us* out of the card circle. What was that..." His voice suddenly trailed off. "You don't think... I would... it was just cards."

After watching Benny's outburst, Blasko raised his eyebrows at this.

"Where were you the night before last?" Bobby asked.

"Here. I'm always here in the evening if Mittens and I aren't going out to play cards or go to a movie," Benny said, his face all open innocence now.

"Did you make any threats against the Handlins?"

Benny's face went from innocent to flustered. "Threats? Like what? I was angry. I might have said something in the heat of the moment."

"When Pete asked you and your wife to leave the card circle, he said you told him that the Handlins would pay a price for cheating." Bobby waited, giving Benny time to squirm.

"I might have. Like I said, I was really angry... but not that angry. I was upset. I might have said that," he finished lamely.

"Don't mind Benny," his wife said, walking back into the room and putting her hand on his shoulder. "He gets upset all the time. Dr. McGuire has warned him not to get so worked up, but..." She paused, then added, "Benny was here with us the night before last. We had pork chops. A real treat. Didn't we, Benny?" Benny nodded. "I think we listened to *Tarzan* and then a music show out of Atlanta," she continued, waving at the radio.

Bobby tried a few more questions without any luck. Mittens had formed a fortress around her husband and wasn't going to let Bobby or Blasko breach it.

"She would lie for her husband every day through Sunday," Bobby said as they left the house. "I know the type. She'd make the perfect gun moll."

"I remember a battle once. We'd broken through the enemy's main line and were approaching their camp. A woman came out of a large cooking tent with a cleaver in one hand and a butcher knife in the other. As one, our victorious soldiers stopped and watched the woman. She would stab and slice at anyone who made a move toward her camp kitchen. We made much fun of her, but she was still there with her tent, kettles and pans when we moved on."

Bobby gave Blasko a sideways glance. He knew that there was something not quite natural about him, but he didn't know Blasko's true nature or his history. Hearing the baron talk about the battle as though he'd been there yesterday struck him as very odd.

"Yeah, exactly," Bobby said, not knowing how to respond. "Charlie Parsons lives just a couple of blocks over."

Their reception at Charlie's house stood in stark contrast to the one they'd received at Benny's.

"Come in. I am devastated by Mrs. Handlin's murder." He looked it. Charlie's eyes were red and underlined by dark shadows, as though he'd been crying recently. "That sounds so trite." He shook his head and waved them into his living room.

"How well did you know the Handlins?" Bobby didn't want to tip his hand.

"I manage the local office of the Southern Alabama Dairy Company. I've been doing that for a year. Before that, I was making deliveries myself and the Handlins were on my route."

Bobby wondered if the rumors of an affair stemmed from the trope of the randy milkman. "So you had an opportunity to talk to the Handlins on more than one occasion?"

"I talked to all my customers. I was good at my job. Knowing your route and the folks on it is what the job is all about. I remind my drivers of that every week. To remember that we don't just make deliveries; we're salesmen too. There are occasions when you have to know what your customer needs, even if they don't."

"Milk delivery business aside, how well did you know Mrs. Handlin?" As soon as he asked the question, he saw Charlie's mask slip a little. Bobby knew then that there was some truth in the rumors.

"I don't know what you're implying," Charlie said unconvincingly.

"Yes, you do. By saying that, you just proved to me that you're stalling. We know you had a relationship with Mrs. Handlin." They didn't know any such thing, but Bobby decided to go for the gold ring.

"I did not," Charlie said firmly. Bobby's gamble had fallen short.

"Are you married, Mr. Parsons?" Blasko asked. He'd gotten up and was walking around the small living room. It was furnished with a mix of furniture that wasn't very valuable, but was sturdy and well made.

"No."

"A girlfriend perhaps?"

"Not at the moment. I don't know—" Charlie stopped when he saw Blasko reach under a man's coat on the hall tree and pull out a scarf. A woman's scarf. Blasko sniffed it.

"Whose scarf is this?" Blasko said, holding it toward Charlie, who looked like a fish lying on the dock. "I think Mr. Handlin might recognize this scarf," Blasko finished with a wicked smile that even Bobby found unnerving.

In the blink of an eye, Charlie Parsons's face told them he'd surrendered.

"Yes, the scarf belongs to Maddie."

"Madilyn Handlin?" Bobby pressed.

"Yes, yes," Charlie blurted, then began to cry.

"You were having an affair with Mrs. Handlin." Bobby made it a statement and Charlie, still crying, nodded his head.

"I was in love… We were in love with each other," Charlie managed to say as he tried to get his sobbing under control.

"Maybe she rejected you."

"No, no, it wasn't like that."

"She was happily married."

"Not hardly."

"So you went there with the intention to kill her

husband?"

"No, I didn't go there at all."

A car came roaring down the road and they heard it bump over the curb outside.

"Find out who that is," Bobby said to Blasko, who was already moving toward the door. Before he got there, boots pounded on the concrete outside. Blasko opened the door to a frantic deputy whose hand was raised, ready to knock.

"Where's Tucker? We've been looking all over town for him!" the man yelled, trying to look past Blasko into the house.

"Olson, what's going on?" Bobby said, coming to the door.

"It's a bloody mess. Something awful. You got to come now," Deputy Olson spat out.

"Settle down. What's going on?"

"There's been another attack. Out at the Chester place." Olson was shifting from foot to foot like he was running in place. "You got to see it."

"Okay," Bobby said as Blasko pushed past him on his way to the car. Bobby flashed a look back at Charlie Parsons to let him know the interview wasn't over, then he followed the others out the door.

CHAPTER EIGHTEEN

They followed Deputy Olson's truck at breakneck speed through the streets of Sumter and then across the washboard roads of the county until they pulled up into the driveway of the Chesters' farmhouse. Cars and trucks were parked all around the yard, while men with guns and lanterns wandered about between them.

"Damn it, Paige, get everyone off the property!" Bobby yelled when he saw Willard Paige standing on the front porch. Paige grumbled, but began talking to the men and getting them to move their vehicles.

As Bobby walked up onto the porch, a part-time deputy came out of the house carrying a biscuit.

"Where'd you get that?" Bobby growled.

"There's a basket full of them in the kitchen."

"Put it back where you found it. This is a crime scene, for Pete's sake! Ignoramus." This last comment was muttered after the man had gone back into the house. "Everyone out of the house!" Bobby shouted.

A stream of half a dozen people walked past Bobby and Blasko. Some were part-time deputies while others were just curious neighbors. Bobby noted that none of them were Taylors or Murphys.

When the biscuit thief came out looking chastised, Bobby grabbed his arm. "Has anyone told Colonel Etheridge about this?"

"Not that I know of."

"If you think you can get there without stopping for more food, go and tell him about this and drive him back here if he wants you to."

"Sure, boss," the man said, hustling out to his car.

"And one of you dunderheads go and get the doc... Also Emmett Wolfe, and tell him to bring his camera," Bobby yelled to the men who were now milling about by the road.

With the yard and the house finally cleared, Bobby and Blasko began to walk through the scene. Downstairs, everything appeared normal. The kitchen looked like it was in between lunch and dinner. There were dishes left to dry by the sink, biscuits that looked freshly made on the table and a pot of stew still warm on the back of the stove.

But before they even started up the stairs, they noticed the blood stains on the steps.

"It's going to be impossible to tell how much blood was tracked by our killer and what was left by all the knuckleheads traipsing through the house," Bobby grumbled.

For Blasko, the smell of blood was overwhelming. Even though he had fed recently, the craving was still strong. The warm iron scent of new blood only intensified his thirst.

"What in the name of—" Bobby said when he had gone far enough up the staircase to see the second floor. Blasko saw him put his hand up to his mouth to stifle his gag reflex, but was impressed when Bobby continued up the stairs.

"Who... What would do this?" Bobby mumbled to himself.

Blasko stood beside him at the top of the stairs and looked at the bloody chaos around them. Mrs. Chester was sprawled in the hallway outside Molly's room. Her internal organs were strewn around the walls, floor and doorway. There were claw marks across her face and chest.

"Savaged," Blasko said. The sight of the poor woman tempered his own bloodlust. When he was younger, his empathy for the dead wouldn't have been enough to override his need for blood. Back then, he might have fallen to his knees and drank from the rivulets flowing across the floor. The image caused a wave of self-loathing for his behavior in those early days of his affliction.

"This is fresh," Bobby said as he looked at the blood still trickling off of Mrs. Chester's body.

There was just room for them to make their way around the fallen woman without stepping in any pools of blood. The scene in Molly's bedroom was even more horrific. The walls were literally sprayed with blood. Mr. Chester had been torn apart as though he'd been drawn and quartered.

"Oh man," Bobby said, and turned and closed his eyes. He took half a dozen long, deep breaths.

"Impressive," Blasko said as he looked at the carnage.

"Damn it!" Bobby said, turning back to the room. "Where's the girl?" He looked left and right, trying to find some trace of her before entering the room and looking in the corner beside the bed where they'd found her crouched down the day he and Josephine had visited. There was no sign of her.

Blasko could discern three distinct blood smells in the room. "A third person was injured in this room. Her blood is here. A fair amount of it."

"How the hell can you tell one puddle of blood from another?"

"You'll have to trust me," Blasko said, following the scent to the bed. "The blood on the bed belongs to the girl."

The comforter was soaked with blood.

"That doesn't look good," Bobby said sadly.

"There is something else here," Blasko said, kneeling down.

On the floor beside the bed was a piece of skin that appeared to have been cut from someone. It was roughly eight inches in diameter with a red scar in the middle.

"This just gets better and better," Bobby said sarcastically. "What is that?"

Blasko peered closely at it, careful not to disturb the evidence before Emmett had a chance to photograph it. "A piece of skin with some type of scar or tattoo," he said with a detachment born of many battlefields.

"Gruesome. Was it ripped off?"

"I think it was cut off with that." Blasko pointed to a butcher knife with a nine-inch blade half hidden under the bed. The knife was covered in blood and pieces of tissue.

"What the hell happened in here? And where is the poor girl?" Bobby asked, walking to the window that had previously been boarded over, but was now shattered with pieces of board scattered on the floor. "Whatever was in here left through this window. It must have taken the girl with it. Let's leave this for Wolfe to document. I need to get some of these goons searching for the girl."

Blasko took another look around the room, wondering what ghastly narrative had played out there.

Bobby organized a few of the more trustworthy onlookers into a search party and put Paige in charge.

"You understand that the girl could be lying out in the woods bleeding to death. Be quiet and listen for any sounds. Also, you men saw what this killer did. Be careful, but don't shoot each other," Bobby advised the group. There was a lot of nodding as the men solemnly spread out to look for Molly.

Blasko watched them while sniffing the air, trying to get a scent of the killer. He could smell it and, as with the Taylor boy, the trail led down toward the creek. Even in animal form, the creature had enough sense to head for water to wash off. Blasko didn't see the point in following the trail to another dead end. Besides, several of the men were headed that way.

Two more cars roared up to the house. One of them carried Colonel Etheridge and the other was Dr. McGuire.

"What's going on?" Etheridge said, walking over to

Blasko and Bobby.

"Two people were slaughtered and their daughter is missing," Bobby told him.

"Didn't you say that the girl witnessed the attack on the Seth Taylor?"

"That's what she told us," Bobby said.

"So maybe the murderer came back for her. Either she was the original target and Taylor got in the way, or the killer wanted to eliminate a witness to his first murder," Etheridge said.

"Both are possibilities," Bobby agreed.

"The fact that he took the girl would indicate that it was the former. If she'd just been a witness that he wanted to eliminate, then he would have killed her and been gone," Blasko pointed out.

"Good point," Etheridge said and turned to Bobby. "Have you initiated a search?"

"I've got Paige heading up a group of men working out from the house," he said and received an approving nod from Etheridge.

The doctor walked up next to them.

"You won't need your bag," Bobby told him. "The Chesters are in pieces. I just wanted you to see them as they are for the inquest." Dr. McGuire also served as the county coroner.

"There is one thing you should pay particular attention to," Blasko interjected. "There is a piece of skin lying by the bed that has been cut off of someone. Your opinion would be valuable."

"He's got a point. See if it came from either of the two victims upstairs," Bobby instructed the doctor.

"This is quite the circus," said a voice from behind them. Everyone turned to see Emmett Wolfe approaching.

"Emmett," Colonel Etheridge said, sticking out his hand.

"Colonel. Rumor has it that you're the new sheriff in town."

"Unconfirmed," Etheridge said.

"Another attack?" Emmett asked.

"Two dead. And the details on this one need to be kept quiet if you want to keep your role as our photographer of record," Bobby said.

"You know I can be counted on. I've never printed anything about a murder scene without permission."

"This one's worse than most," Bobby said.

"I'll need assistance with my equipment."

"Take any one of those boys," Bobby said, pointing to three part-timers that he had standing at the front fence, keeping everyone back. The number of gawkers was increasing as word spread about the attacks.

"I'll go in with you too," Etheridge offered.

After they'd gone in the house, Bobby pulled Blasko to the side. "Give me your thoughts."

"There are no signs of forced entry and the rest of the house was undisturbed. That seems curious," Blasko said with raised eyebrows.

Bobby thought about this. "I see what you mean. A crazed beast breaks in, goes upstairs to get the girl, parents go to protect her and are killed. Monster grabs girl and escapes by crashing through the window. Why wouldn't there be more evidence downstairs? The door was open, or at least unlocked. Most doors are out here, though not so much since the attacks. Plus, Mr. Chester was probably taking extra precautions after Josephine and I came by uninvited."

"Let's be clear. We're talking about a werewolf. He has the power to change, perhaps at will. Maybe he changed after he was in the house. He might even be someone that the Chesters trusted, and they let him into the house. Once inside, he could have morphed into the monster we saw the other night. Then killed the parents and absconded with the girl." Blasko paused. "Through the window... I want to go back inside and check the window."

Dr. McGuire came back onto the porch. "The deaths happened about two hours ago. Who discovered the bodies?"

"A friend of Mrs. Chester's. They were supposed to ride to church together. When the Chesters didn't come by her place, she walked over here. Lives about a mile down the road. According to Paige, the woman ran all the way home. Come to think of it, you might want to check in on her. She may be in shock," Bobby said.

"I'll do that. I collected the piece of skin and I'll examine it at my office. Nothing more I can do here. Have Connelly lay the bodies out at his place. I'll come over there to do the autopsies. When I piece them together, I'll be able to say definitively if the piece of skin came from either one of them. If I'd've known how many autopsies I was going to have to do for the county, I'd have insisted on being paid by the body rather than take a salary," Dr. McGuire grumbled and headed back to his car.

"I'm going to make sure Paige is on top of the search for Molly," Bobby said. "Not that I have much hope she's alive."

"He took her rather than tearing her apart, so there's still hope," Blasko assured him.

Once Bobby had gone, Blasko went back into the house. Emmett was still photographing the bloody smears on the stairs. Blasko carefully went around him and worked at avoiding contact with any evidence as he made his way back to Molly's room.

Etheridge was standing in the middle of the room with his eyes closed.

"Wait one minute," he said without opening his eyes. He turned his head slightly, then opened his eyes. Blasko was fascinated as he watched the man count to thirty while staring at one corner of the room. When he reached thirty, he closed his eyes again. Another minute passed, after which Etheridge opened his eyes and turned.

"Oh, it's you, Baron. I was employing a technique that a fellow in Africa taught me. Quite effective, really. You take mental pictures of the room. By concentrating for thirty seconds on a particular section of the scene, it allows you to really see the details. After which, you close your eyes and think about what you've seen for a full minute or so. That embeds the memory and again forces you to think about the items you saw in that one snapshot."

"Fascinating," Blasko said and meant it. "I wanted to take a closer look at the broken window."

He walked to the window with Etheridge looking over his shoulder. "We're thinking that the beast took the daughter and left through this window," Blasko said, looking at the busted glass and wood.

The window was a double-sash affair. While all the glass in the window was cracked or broken, it was clear that the creature had gone out through the bottom part. There were just a few jagged pieces of glass stuck in the frame, with smears of blood on the glass. Blasko looked closely and saw some hairs that looked like they might have come from Molly. There were other hairs as well, shorter and more animal-like.

"Interesting," Etheridge said.

Blasko sniffed the blood and hairs. He could only smell one type of blood. It came from the same person whose blood covered the bed. As he knew it didn't belong to either of the adult Chesters, he assumed it could only be Molly's.

Blasko looked at the smashed window and put his upper body carefully through the hole. He could smell and see blood on the tin roof of the front porch where the beast must have landed after jumping from the window. Satisfied, he pulled his head back into the room.

"Not a very large opening to jump through carrying a woman," Etheridge observed.

"Exactly, Colonel."

"Perhaps the girl escaped down the stairs while her parents were fighting with the beast. Then it broke free and jumped out of the window."

"There *is* blood on the staircase," Blasko agreed. "I'm going to look around outside."

He left Etheridge to take more mental pictures. Emmett was on the landing, photographing what was left of Mrs. Chester. Blasko made his way around the man and back down the stairs. Through the front windows, he could see lights moving around in the darkness a hundred yards from the house as the men searched for any signs of Molly.

He went onto the front porch and tried to find the spot where the beast had landed after coming off of the roof.

"Curses!" he muttered at the dozens of footprints in front of the house. He wasn't even sure why he was interested in where the creature had landed. He already knew the direction it had taken away from the farmhouse. *Aha! Think backward*, he told himself.

Blasko drew a mental line from the trail that he had smelled earlier back to the front of the house. There he found a deep impression where one of the beast's feet had landed in the soft earth.

An hour later, he was watching Etheridge pour plaster over the print. Bobby had assembled the necessary materials and had been ready to take the cast when the colonel had offered to take over. It turned out that collecting prints in Africa had been one of his many hobbies.

"Better than I could have done," Bobby admitted when the colonel had finished.

"It's a skill that improves with practice," Etheridge said. "Except for it being a right foot rather than a left, I'd say that, to my eye, this print looks similar to the one you collected at the creek."

"I agree. Though I don't know what good collecting prints is going to be," Bobby said.

"If Molly Chester was the original target when the boy was murdered, then we need to focus on people who were obsessed with Molly. She had an old boyfriend. I think it's time to look a lot harder at him," Blasko suggested.

"We'll need to show some results soon. After this," Etheridge tilted his head toward the house, "the county will go crazy."

Bobby nodded solemnly.

Blasko left them an hour before sunrise. He caught a ride back to town with Deputy Olson, who was going for coffee and pastries. The searchers hadn't turned up anything, but were going to renew their efforts after the sun came up.

CHAPTER NINETEEN

Josephine opened her eyes to a sunny day. She was happy with what she had accomplished on Sunday and was looking forward to a day spent tending to bank business.

When she got down to the kitchen she found Anna, Grace and Anton discussing the overnight murders in animated detail.

"What happened?" she asked, realizing that the bank's business would probably be taking a back seat again today.

"That thing killed a family out by where the Taylor boy was murdered," Grace said.

Josephine felt a sinking feeling in her gut. "Which family?"

"My husband did work for them a couple of years ago. The Chesters," Anna said.

"The whole family was killed?" Josephine was stunned.

"They're still looking for the daughter," Grace said.

"Looking for her?"

"Did you know them?" Grace asked, having realized that the look on Josephine's face was more than the usual shock of a distant tragedy.

"I met them twice. The girl was Seth Taylor's girlfriend." Josephine's mind was a confused jumble of conflicting thoughts and emotions. "You said they're looking for the girl?"

"That's right. When I stopped by the market this morning, everyone was talking about volunteers out at the farmhouse," Anna said.

Josephine turned around and started out of the kitchen.

"What about your breakfast, Miss Josephine?"

"Make me a bagged lunch and I'll grab a biscuit and sausage when I come back down. I'm going out to the house." She turned around. "On second thought, please pack up a box of food that I can take out to the searchers."

Josephine changed into pants and an old shirt and jacket suitable for the woods and came back down. Anton helped her carry the box of food that Anna had prepared out to the car.

"I put cheese, bread and lots of canned fruit in there," Anna told her.

There were cars and trucks lining the road leading to the Chesters' farmhouse. Men were coming and going with dogs and guns by their sides. Everyone looked grim. As soon as she pulled up, she spotted Colonel Etheridge and Bobby standing in front of the house, organizing groups to go out in search of Molly. Both of them looked exhausted. Bobby broke away from the group when he saw Josephine walking up.

"Is it bad?" she asked him.

"Worse," he said, leading her off to a quiet corner of the yard. Only a few feet away, she could see the clothesline where she'd talked to Mrs. Chester. Josephine felt the weight of recent events settle on her shoulders, along with a firm determination to do whatever she had to do to take this creature down.

"Molly is missing?"

"Yes. Her mother was killed outside her bedroom and her father was ripped apart inside the room. But so far, we haven't found any sign of Molly."

"Do you think she could still be alive?"

"According to the baron, she lost a lot of blood upstairs, so it's hard to say. How the hell can he tell one person's blood from another?"

Josephine stared at Bobby. Beyond the fatigue he was obviously feeling from the long night, his usually boyish face looked like he'd aged five years in the last month.

"You need to get some rest," she said, deflecting the question of Blasko's abilities.

"That's not going to happen for a while. I'll say this, though. You made a good call with Etheridge. He's going to make an excellent sheriff."

"Hopefully the governor will agree and make a decision soon. If this goes on much longer, some folks are going to be looking for people to blame. You and Etheridge are the face of the sheriff's office right now."

"I see your point."

"I'll make some calls if we haven't heard anything in a couple of days. Right now, I've got food in the car and I'm here to help search."

"What we could really use is your organizational skills. I don't know how long we're going to be out here. If you could get us some tents, and maybe some ladies to put together a cook tent to provide the searchers with hot food. They're saying that a late cold front is going to blow through. If we're still out here in the morning, it's gonna be chilly."

Josephine wanted to go out into the woods and search for Molly herself, but she saw the wisdom in what Bobby was saying. With her pull and connections through the bank, she was in a unique position to get resources out to the farmhouse quickly.

"I'll head into town and come back when I've organized it all," she said, putting her hand on his arm. "Take care of yourself."

Bobby put his hand on hers. "We'll find her."

By the end of the day, they had found nothing but some articles of clothing that might have belonged to Molly. They had searched as far as two miles from the house without any clear indication of which way the monster had gone after going down to the creek.

"We don't even have a family member to ask if the pieces of cloth belong to her," Bobby said, pointing to three pieces of flowered print fabric lying on a table in the yard where they'd been placed after the search teams had turned them in.

"That looks very similar to the dress she was wearing when we talked to her," Josephine said, pointing to the largest piece.

"That's something," Bobby said. He bent over another table where a map was laid out and pointed to a spot on the paper. "It was found here. So maybe we'll concentrate the search in that direction."

"Are you going to search through the night?"

"No. For two reasons. We don't want anyone lost, and we don't want anyone killed by the beast."

Two days later, Josephine, Bobby, Blasko and Colonel Etheridge were in Josephine's parlor, trying to figure out where the search and investigation had led them.

"There's been no sign of Molly since we found the piece of cloth that might be from her clothing. We had no choice but to scale back the search," Etheridge told them.

"I can't stand the thought of her being out there somewhere, possibly hurt," Josephine said. She tilted her glass back and finished the two fingers of whiskey.

"Everyone feels horrible about it, but the search wasn't getting anywhere," Bobby said.

"I'm not blaming anyone for calling it off," Josephine said.

"We're still looking. We've just stopped combing the woods. We've got volunteers driving every back road in that part of the county daily, looking for signs of her. Tomorrow we've got a fellow with a plane who's going to fly over the whole area," Etheridge said, sounding as tired as everyone else.

"We have to focus on the creature. He is human and cunning. He might have even taken the girl so that we would spend time and resources looking for her," Blasko said.

"My problem is that I just can't get my mind around a monster that's this vicious and still human," Bobby said.

"He's very human. At least part of the time. But even in his animal shape, he's able to reason."

"Why has he chosen two different parts of the county for his attacks?" Josephine asked. "It just seems odd that there would be a set of attacks around the Taylor and Murphy farms, while a second set of attacks have occurred in a twenty-block area of town. And the victims in the two locations seem to have nothing in common."

"Smart woman," Etheridge said and raised his whiskey glass in salute. "What is the connection between those two areas? Or, I should say, *who* has connections with those two areas?"

"Someone who lives in the country and works in town? Or who works out there and lives in town?" Bobby said.

"Or perhaps someone who has a childhood connection to the rural area, but lives in town now," Etheridge suggested.

"That could help us build a suspect list. We should check the suspects we already have and see if any have a foot in both areas where the attacks have occurred," Josphine said.

"I still need to talk with Tom Bradford, Molly's ex," Bobby said.

"And we never finished our visit with Charlie Parsons," Blasko reminded him.

"That's right. He had just admitted to having an affair with Mrs. Handlin," Bobby remembered.

"How did this creature come to be?" the colonel asked. "The shapeshifters in Africa were witchdoctors who chose to take on animal forms, usually to seek revenge or to enact some play for power."

"Ah," Blasko said. "I've been doing some research.

According to Captain Duhamel, who fought the infamous French werewolf in Gévaudan, the beasts can originate by several different methods. The first is, as you've suggested, a person who performs ceremonies with the intent of becoming a werewolf. Duhamel was vague about the details of these rituals. He pointed toward gypsies dancing naked in the moonlight, certain herbs, blood rituals. I don't think he ever received any firsthand knowledge. The second method is to be bitten by a werewolf. If you aren't killed, then you will become a werewolf yourself. Unlike the first type of werewolf, Duhamel says these people cannot control when they change. He claims to have observed several who had been captured and taken to sanitariums."

"Lycanthropy *is* listed as a psychological condition," Etheridge said.

"You said there were three ways?" Josephine asked.

"The last is very special. Duhamel swears in his book that he met one of these last types. According to him, there are people who are born werewolves. They inherit the condition from one or more of their ancestors. Their early life can be completely normal, but during late puberty they begin to experience episodes where their wolf nature will present itself. With training, they can learn to control the beast until they are able to change at will. The werewolf he met explained that they belong to clans throughout the world. The different clans have different philosophies about their role in the world of humans. Since most of them have relatives that are fully human, most of the clans are sympathetic to humans."

"Big of them," Etheridge said. "Much of that sounds like poppycock to me. Did he have any useful information on how to hunt and kill one?"

"He came to the same conclusion that we have—track and confront it when in human form."

"Which puts us back at square one," Bobby said.

"He also says that chopping off the creature's head is the only way to guarantee death," Blasko added.

"Aren't werewolves supposed to attack during full moons?" Josephine asked.

"Duhamel addresses that. He says that the first type perform their rituals under the light of a full moon, which means there are often werewolf attacks at that time of the month. With the second group, those bitten are out of control and can change at any time. Anger or pain is often what causes them to change. The full moon can aggravate their condition. Again, think about patients in a sanitarium."

"You said the last group, those born to it, can change at will?" Bobby said. Josephine could see how hard he was trying to be open-minded. His years as a hardnosed deputy were making it difficult to adapt to the strange new world that had suddenly come upon their small Alabama community.

"That's right. Which, if Duhamel is to be believed, means we're dealing with the bitten or the true-born werewolf. Our murders have occurred at different times in the lunar cycle," Blasko said.

"How does that help us?" Etheridge asked.

"As far as I know, we've never had a murder like these in our county," Josephine said, "A werewolf has moved into the area. Someone who's been bitten or who was born a werewolf. Someone new."

"Duhamel did say that a very old and powerful warlock might be capable of changing at will. But, again, your point is taken. It's not likely to be someone who has lived in this county all their lives," Blasko said.

"We've looked at the strangers in town. François, our resident medium, being the most prominent. I think Blasko can speak to his guilt or innocence," Bobby said.

"I don't trust him. However, he had a solid alibi for the attack on Seth Taylor and he was not guilty of the Handlin murder. I had Matthew keeping an eye on him at the time the Handlins were attacked."

"But you don't trust him?" Etheridge questioned.

"Call it intuition if you like. The man is up to something."

"I've been to one of his séances. They are unnerving. And… strangely compelling." The mention of Matthew and the séances reminded Josephine of her promise to take him to a séance. "I'd be willing to participate in another one, if it would help get more information about François."

The three men looked at her, considering the offer.

"I don't see that it could hurt," Etheridge said. "You might possibly learn more about this man and his methods."

"I advise caution," Blasko said to the group.

"Anyone else who should be under observation?" Etheridge asked.

"While it makes sense from the viewpoint of Duhamel, I don't think we can stick to the stranger theory," Blasko said to nods all around.

"Let's go back to Charlie Parsons and do an interview with Tom Bradford. Also, we'll look for anyone who has a connection to both areas of the county," Bobby said.

"Forgive my ignorance of American politics," Blasko said with a slight bow, "but is Colonel Etheridge officially the sheriff?"

"I haven't been notified if I am."

"I'll reach out to some of my contacts in the governor's office and see if he's made it official," Josephine said.

"I'm going to see Tom Bradford now," Bobby said, grabbing his hat from the rack by the parlor door.

"I'll go along if you'd like," Blasko offered and Bobby nodded.

"I'll work out a grid flight plan for the plane we've got coming in tomorrow. We'll need to have a couple of teams follow up on the ground if the pilot and his lookout see anything," Etheridge said.

They thanked Josephine and she escorted them to the door. The first thing she did after seeing them out was to call Alice Robertson.

"Of course I can arrange another séance. I saw François downtown this afternoon and he asked about you."

"I'd like to bring a friend along."

"Of course. Anyone I know?" Alice asked.

Josephine weighed her options. She was pretty sure that Alice knew of Matthew from his years as the town drunk. Should she tell her now or spring him on her? She decided to play it safe.

"You may be surprised. The baron has taken Matthew Hodge on as a project. The man was a war hero and he's been sober for months now." Josephine reeled this off at a speed she hoped would bedazzle Alice.

"Oh my. I should be scandalized. However, I saw him just a couple of weeks ago. I was positively amazed at how he's cleaned himself up. You know, I remember when he came back from the war. Everyone made quite the fuss about him. I thought at the time how hard that must have been for him. Of course you can bring him. I'll talk to François tomorrow and make all the arrangements."

With that chore taken care of, Josephine went up to her room and took out the book that had angered Blasko so much. She hadn't looked at it since the night they had argued. Why had he been so angry? Though she did have to admit that the book was pretty much a vampire hunter's guide. The title was *Particulars of the Black Forest Nosferatu*. It was a 1768 translation by an Englishman who, according to the foreward, had found the information in the book invaluable during a vampire outbreak along the Scottish border.

Josephine opened the book and started reading from where she'd left off.

CHAPTER TWENTY

"My question for you is, why is there a werewolf hunting in Semmes County?" Bobby asked as he and Blasko motored out of town to meet with Molly's ex-boyfriend.

"For the same reason that a group of town elders tried to open a pit to hell here a few months ago. There is some eldritch power at work drawing dark forces to this place."

"This all started shortly after you arrived," Bobby said.

Blasko couldn't tell if this was an accusation or just an observation. "I have wondered if the same force drew me here," he admitted.

"Then are you a dark force too?"

"I hope that my actions have proved otherwise."

"So far," Bobby said noncommittally. "Bradford's place is about a mile down this next road." He slowed to make the turn onto a narrow dirt road that ran through rows of pine trees. "His family collects turpentine."

The road ended at an old cracker shack surrounded by pine trees that reached up to a starry sky.

"Why is this called a cracker house?" Blasko asked, looking at the glow coming from the windows of the pine-board house that sat a foot off the ground on stone columns.

"Back in the day, ranchers let their cattle roam free in the longleaf pine forests so they could eat the wiregrass. The men who herded them carried long bullwhips that they cracked in the air above the cows to move them around. They became known as crackers. They built houses like this all around the Gulf Coast. This one is probably a hundred years old," Bobby said, stepping up onto the porch. "Hello in the house!" he yelled.

"And the purpose in that?" Blasko asked.

"Out here at night, you're more likely to have a critter on your porch than a man. Best to let the man inside know you're here."

"Who are you?" came a gruff voice from inside.

"Deputy Bobby Tucker. I want to talk to you."

"What about?"

"Open the door and we can talk a bit easier."

"Stand back," the voice called. After a couple of beats, the door cracked open a few inches. "Shift over to the right so's you're in the light from the window."

Dutifully, Bobby and Blasko moved to the right.

"Who's the other fella?"

"He's helping me. We're trying to find Molly Chester."

"She ain't here."

"We just want to talk to you."

Reluctantly, the door opened all the way. "Get in here quick," the man said, waving them in. He held a double-barreled shotgun in his left hand.

"What are you scared of?" Bobby asked.

The man looked at him with narrowed eyes. "I ain't scared of nothin'. Sometimes it pays a man to be careful."

"You always this... careful?" Bobby asked, trying not to sound too judgmental.

"I heard about the killin's."

"What else have you heard?"

"Things," Bradford said cryptically. "A couple days ago, there was something out in the woods."

"You see it?"

"Sort of. Enough. I seen the eyes reflecting my lantern.

Damn near pissed myself."

Blasko looked at the man. He was older than he'd expected. Molly was still in her teens, yet this man appeared to be near thirty. He was wiry with a narrow face, a strong jaw and soft eyes. He was good looking in a country sort of way.

"Have you seen the thing in the last couple of days?" Bobby asked.

"I haven't heard it. Of course, I ain't gone out at night lookin' for it neither."

"You and Molly went out together?"

"Yep. I don't know nothin' about her disappearance. I went out with my dad and rode all of our property to see if we could find her. 'Course, we've got almost five hundred acres. She could be under any of the palmettos. All you can do is check the roads and trails."

"Why'd you all break up?"

"We didn't exactly break up, 'cause all we done was go out to a dance and a couple of movies. I don't care much for movies, but Molly did."

"So why didn't you keep seeing each other?" Bobby said, a little put off by the man's attitude.

"'Cause her daddy liked me. Least, that's what I think. She wanted someone her dad wouldn't like her seein'. I don't claim to know what goes on in women's heads, but she would talk about her brother who died a lot. I think there was some odd thing goin' on. Kind of a love/hate thing with her father."

"What do you mean?" Blasko asked. He'd been walking around the small cabin, which consisted of the main room, two bedrooms and a small kitchen at the back.

"She told me that her brother was her daddy's favorite. After he drowned, Mr. Chester blamed Molly since her and her brother were together at the pond that day. 'Course, that was crazy. Molly was only ten at the time, while her brother was fourteen. But the way she talked, I took it that she blamed herself too."

"I guess you were pretty upset when she stopped seeing you," Bobby said.

"Nah, she talked too much. Always wantin' to go to the movies and to dinner and such. All that costs money. What's wrong, I said, with sittin' on the porch swing? Not for that girl."

"You seeing anyone now?"

"Beth Mills. Good woman. Knows how to cook and spends most of her time at church. Doesn't get after me with too much churchy stuff either, so I like that." Bradford nodded his head, agreeing with himself.

"Have you been bitten by an animal in the last month?" Blasko asked him.

"What kind of crazy question is that?"

"Just answer it," Bobby pushed.

"No."

"You spend much time in town?" Blasko asked.

"I try never to go into town. Told you, that's one of the things I didn't like about Molly. Always wanted to go where there were people."

"You ever lived in town?" Bobby asked.

"Ha! Not likely."

"Family live there?"

"Nope."

Blasko and Bobby looked at each other. Bobby shrugged and Blasko gave a small nod.

"I'd keep your doors and windows closed and your shotgun close by your side," Blasko told him as they walked out the door.

"You don't got to tell me that."

When they were back in the car, Bobby looked at Blasko. "What'd you think?"

"I wouldn't let him marry a relative of mine, but I don't think he had anything to do with the attacks on the Chesters," Blasko said with a sigh.

"Me neither. What about his story of the eyes in the woods? You think he really saw something?"

"Maybe. Might even be the same thing that attacked the Chesters. There is a connection between him and the family. Then again, everyone around here is probably seeing and hearing things in the woods."

"You got that right." Bobby started the car and they headed back to town to talk with Charlie Parsons.

When Charlie let them in this time, he looked agitated.

"You doin' okay?" Bobby asked him. The man's face was flushed and they could see beads of sweat around his temples.

"Not sure why you all came back," he said, clipping off each word as though he were in pain.

"Mr. Parsons, the fact that you were having an affair with a married woman who was murdered makes you a pretty interesting fella for someone investigating the case."

"I loved her. It was some monster that killed her."

"Who said anything about a monster?" Bobby asked.

"All the rumors going around town say she was torn apart. They're saying her husband even saw the beast." Charlie spoke fast, as though he was trying to convince them that what he was saying was true.

"We don't know what killed Mrs. Handlin yet. So we're going to go about this right and talk to everyone who had a motive," Bobby explained.

"Can't you understand? I loved her!" Charlie shouted. "And you don't have permission to go snooping around my house." This was directed at Blasko, who was making his way around the room and looking down the hallway.

"You got something to hide?" Bobby asked.

"No," Charlie said very softly.

"So can I look around the house?" Bobby asked.

"No." Charlie spoke louder this time.

"If you don't have anything to hide, then what can it hurt?"

"I didn't do anything. I've got a right to my privacy."

"Come on, Charlie, admit it. You *did* do something. You were romancing another man's wife. In most religions, that's a sin. In fact, adultery is against the law."

"You... you wouldn't."

"In my country, you would be hanged," Blasko said flatly.

"We won't hang you, but I darn sure wouldn't mind taking you into jail if you aren't going to help find the murderer of the woman you were taking advantage of," Bobby said.

"We loved each other," Charlie said, staring down at the floor.

"Then help us find the monster that killed her."

"How can I help you? I didn't do it!"

"I'm getting real tired of this merry-go-round. Let us look through your house. That way, we can eliminate you as a suspect. Deal?" Bobby said.

"I don't understand any of this," Charlie muttered.

"Yes or no? Let us search, or find yourself spending the night in jail. On top of that, I'll let Claude Elliot know why you're spending the night in jail. Think that's going to help your milk company if it makes the front page of the *Sumter Times*?"

"Fine! Look! Go on!" Charlie shouted, dropping into a chair and putting his hands over his face.

"First, you got any family that lives down by the Chesters' farm?"

"No. My family is all from Georgia."

"When'd you move here?"

"Ten years ago, after my wife died."

"What'd she die of?"

"Pneumonia," Charlie said. He kept his hands over his face as he answered Bobby's questions. "Just look around the house and get out of here."

Blasko and Bobby started at the back of the house. Two bedrooms and a small bathroom were down the main hall. The first of the rooms was used for storage. Crates and boxes of old books, papers and clothes were stacked against the walls. They picked at some of the items, but there was a patina of dust covering everything.

"Doesn't look like he's been in here in months," Bobby said.

In the bathroom, everything seemed normal if a bit unhygienic. In the other bedroom, there were clothes lying around on the floor and the bed was unmade.

"I guess she stayed over on occasion," Bobby said. There were two dresses in the wardrobe alongside Charlie's suits and shirts.

The last room they checked was the long, narrow kitchen. As soon as they were in the room, Blasko caught the smell of blood. He followed it to a trashcan by the back door. Toward the bottom of the can, he found a piece of cloth that was stained with blood. He held it up to his nose and smelled it.

"Here," he said, holding the cloth out to Bobby.

"Not much blood, but it's something."

They went back into the living room where Bobby held the bloody cloth out to Charlie.

"Whose blood is this?"

"Mine. I cut myself right before you came." He held up a finger, showing a tiny cut in the skin where a small amount of blood still oozed. It was possible it could have generated enough blood to account for the stain on the cloth.

Blasko pulled Bobby aside and leaned in close. "He's lying."

"About what?"

"The blood. The blood on the cloth is days' old. It didn't come from that cut on his finger." Blasko didn't tell Bobby that if Charlie had had a fresh cut on his finger when they'd arrived, he would have been able to smell it.

Bobby looked at the brown stain on the cloth. "Does look old. Why do you think he's lying about it?"

"The blood on the cloth is his."

"How can you know that?" Bobby asked. "Never mind. Let's say you're right. That would mean he doesn't want us to ask about some other wound on his body."

"Like a bite mark," Blasko said.

Bobby's face turned red and, before Blasko could stop him, he whirled around to confront Charlie.

"This isn't from your finger." Bobby held out the cloth. "We want the truth."

"Get out of my house!" Charlie groaned, holding his hands up to the sides of his head.

"Not until we get some answers."

"I want you out now!" Charlie screamed. He leaped up out of the chair with such speed and ferocity that Bobby stumbled backward.

A roar came from Charlie's throat and, in a matter of seconds, he transformed into a wolfish creature that stood close to six feet tall. There were bear-like claws on the ends of his hairy, muscular arms and his face was a bizarre caricature of a wolf's, with a protruding snout and four-inch-long canines. The eyes were golden and appeared to glow with an internal heat.

The werewolf swiped at Bobby, who was fortunate to have stumbled backward when Charlie first jumped up from the chair. Unfortunately, he was off balance and the swipe of the claws, while missing him, caused him to fall onto the floor.

Even though he'd thought that something like this was possible, Blasko was still stunned to have actually witnessed the transformation. While the creature was focused on Bobby, Blasko pulled his Colt 1911 from his shoulder holster, but the monster saw the movement out of the corner of its eye and, with a quick and powerful swipe, sent the gun flying out of Blasko's hand.

Now unarmed, Blasko realized that a single snap of the beast's jaws or a swing of its claws could end Bobby's life. Seeing no other option, he threw himself onto its back. As he did so, the creature let out a tremendous roar that was heard blocks away and had residents nervously locking their doors and checking their guns.

While the creature began to flail in an effort to dislodge Blasko, who was clinging to the monster's neck with all of his strength, Bobby rolled out of reach of its teeth and claws and reached for his pistol. But he was in an awkward position, giving the creature time to rise up, Blasko still clinging to its back, and leap for the window at the front of the house. Afraid of hitting the baron, Bobby couldn't get a clear shot. In a fraction of a second, Blasko and the creature went crashing through the window.

Blasko sensed that the beast was attempting to flee and let go, slamming down onto the porch as the werewolf bounded off. A silence fell as Blasko and Bobby both lay in their respective places and tried to assess what had just happened.

Bobby managed to get up first and hurried to the window, his gun held out in front of him. "Are you all right?" he shouted to Blasko.

"Except for my dignity, I'm fine," Blasko said, getting to his feet. They could hear doors opening and closing and neighbors shouting to one another for blocks around.

"He transformed in seconds. How is that possible?" Bobby asked.

"According to the reading I've done, when a werewolf changes you see its true nature. The trick is not that it changes, but rather that the beast is able to disguise itself most of the time. That's why, when you push a werewolf who doesn't have control, he can change without wanting to."

"At least we've found the monster. It can't hide amongst us anymore."

"I hope that's true."

"Stay here and watch the house. I need to get word out to the other deputies to pick up Charlie Parsons."

"Warn them."

"I'll do my best. I'm not sure anyone else is going to believe that a suspect might turn into a six-foot wolf beast from hell. I'll bring men back to board up the house."

"And I'll search the house for clues to where he might go to ground."

Bobby and his posse spent the rest of the night searching for Charlie, but there was no sign of the man or the beast.

CHAPTER TWENTY-ONE

First thing the next morning, Josephine called Ray Butler, the friend who'd set up her meeting with the governor.

"Miss Nicolson, all I can say is that the governor has received several other suggestions about who to appoint as sheriff in Semmes County." He sounded almost embarrassed to tell her.

"Who was suggested and who did the suggesting?"

"Well, now, I don't think that's my place to say."

"My father was a good friend to your family," Josephine said in a slightly menacing voice.

"Now that isn't fair."

"I need to know what's going on," Josephine pressured him.

"He's received several calls from people, prominent people, that he should look internally for a replacement for Sheriff Logan."

"Internally? Tucker?"

"Who?"

"Deputy Robert Tucker. Is that who people are suggesting?"

"No, it's a Deputy Paige."

"What?!" Josephine was shocked. She knew that Willard

Paige had some family connections. His grandfather had owned a large cotton gin serving three counties and some of the family had considerable assets. But Paige's father hadn't been the pride of the family, running off to Florida to make his fortune in real estate only to come back with his tail between his legs. Could someone in the family have been pulling strings to get him the appointment? Bigger strings than hers?

Josephine got busy making a list of who else might be calling the governor. She was going to get to the bottom of this. The thought of Willard Paige becoming the sheriff was too galling.

There was a knock at the door, but she ignored it and let Grace answer.

"Mrs. Robertson is in the parlor," Grace told her, and Josephine reluctantly got up to meet her.

"Josie! It's wonderful to see you. Isn't this weather beautiful? Gonna be an early spring. Terrible about the wild animal attacks," Alice said.

Josephine just smiled and let her prattle on. Eventually she'd get to the point of her visit. *It'll just slow the process down if you actually answer her*, Josephine told herself.

"I figured I'd stop by and let you know that we're scheduled for another séance tonight. I am so looking forward to it. Did you ever look up that book your uncle told you about?" Alice stopped and Josephine knew she'd have to answer the question.

"I did. I admit I was surprised by everything that happened that evening."

"Everyone is just enthralled with François's powers. I know some folks have been going to him for advice."

"Really? I'm not sure I'd go that far."

"He is in touch with the spirit world," Alice said as though it was a proven point. "He's bound to be privy to facts that the rest of us aren't. And he has such a deep understanding of the world."

Josephine gave Alice her full attention for the first time.

Was she that much under the sway of this man? She was talking about him like he was some sort of miracle worker. The look Josephine saw in Alice's eyes worried her. The woman looked like a religious zealot talking about her leader.

"I know that the mayor and some of the county commissioners are going to him when they want advice. Almost all of them, or at least their wives, have sat in on a séance," Alice went on, not understanding the effect she was having on Josephine.

"Are any of these men part of François's inner circle?" Josephine asked, showing Alice the list of influential people she'd been drawing up.

"Why, yes, most of them," Alice said with a smile.

"Daniel hasn't been consulting François concerning bank business, has he?" Josephine asked with concern, holding her breath until Alice answered.

"No. I've been telling him he should, but he's so pigheaded. I bet if you talked to him, he would," Alice said.

Josephine was appalled that Alice thought she'd want some swami giving her bank manager advice on investments. "How many séances have you been to?"

"A dozen, at least. François calls me his ambassador to Semmes County."

Josephine was now sure where the suggestion that Paige should become sheriff was coming from and she could guess why. Few men would be easier to manipulate than Paige. He was a nice enough guy and, when watched closely, he was a competent deputy. However, if he was put in the big chair he'd be flailing around until someone propped him up. Josephine wasn't sure if this was an effort by one of the powerbrokers to gain more control or if François himself was trying to make a power play. The latter would be very worrisome and point toward Blasko being right about the man.

"I'm really looking forward to tonight's séance," Josephine told Alice and began to walk toward the door, hoping Alice would take the hint. Alice was gregarious, but not one to overstay her welcome. She allowed Josephine to escort her to the door.

"Anton!" Josephine yelled as soon as Alice was gone.

The man appeared so suddenly behind her that she almost bumped into him.

"Yes, please?" the little man said, looking down at the floor.

"I have a chore for you to run." She made sure he knew where Matthew lived and sent him to the boarding house with a note telling Matthew to meet her at the Robertsons' house that night.

An hour later, she found Bobby Tucker still at Charlie Parsons's house.

"Took me forever to find you. Most of the folks I asked weren't sure where you were," Josephine told him while her eyes took in the boarded-up window at the front of the house. "What happened here?"

"Good question. I'm still not sure that what I saw actually happened."

"What?"

Bobby sighed. "Last night, Blasko and I confronted Parsons. We found, actually the baron found, a piece of cloth with blood on it. He was sure that it was Parsons's blood and... I guess we got it in our heads that it might be from a bite. I said as much and Parsons went... wolf." There was no humor in Bobby's words.

"Went wolf? You mean he changed? In front of you?"

"Damn straight! I..." He ran his hand over the top of his head, a tell for when he didn't have a good answer for something. "I don't know. Craziest thing I've ever seen."

"Crazier than the tentacled monster crawling out of the pit beneath Mrs. Rosehill's?" Josephine found that hard to believe.

"Yes, in its own way. To watch a person transform from a human into a werewolf? I don't know." He shook his head. "Needless to say, I haven't broadcast what I saw beyond Etheridge, Blasko and you. I've been telling the deputies and the public that Parsons had been keeping a giant wolf hybrid that escaped with him. Both are to be considered dangerous."

"Speaking of Etheridge, we might have a problem." Josephine told him what she'd learned that morning and what she suspected about François.

"Willard Paige? That can't happen. I'd quit before I'd work for that clodhopper," Bobby said with resolve.

"I'm going to a séance tonight. My plan is to find out what François's game is."

"I don't think that's very wise."

"I'll have Matthew with me."

"Still doesn't sound like a great idea."

"I'll be safe enough. I just hope I can pierce François's suave veneer."

"I got through Parsons's veneer last night and he turned into a wolf. You need to be careful and keep us informed of where you are and what's going on," Bobby insisted.

"No word on Molly?"

"Not yet. I think the options are all bad. Either she's been killed by Parsons or she's somehow involved."

"Involved? How?"

"I'm just sayin'. She either was taken or ran off. Why else would she run off if she wasn't involved?"

"Scared, delirious. You saw her. She was half out of her mind from fear the day we met her. If she saw her mother and father killed, how much worse would she be?"

"You have a point there," Bobby agreed.

"Could Parsons have killed Taylor and the Chesters?"

"I will swear to the fact that he has the means. But motive and opportunity, I don't know. I was just finishing going through all of his papers when you showed up. Want to go along with me while I talk to some of his friends and co-workers?"

"Ready when you are, Sherlock."

"Let's swing by the jail first. I think I can let Mr. Handlin go free."

"Should he go home with Parsons running loose?"

"No. I'll suggest that he leave town until Parsons is captured," Bobby said, locking the door of the house and ushering Josephine out to his car. "I'll follow you to your house, and you can drop off your car."

At the jail, Bobby had Timothy Handlin brought into an interrogation room. He looked even worse than the last time Bobby had seen him. His bruises had turned yellow and purple, making him look like some half human vegetable.

"Charlie Parsons was having an affair with your wife," Bobby told him, seeing no way to sugarcoat the information.

"No," Handlin said, shaking his head emphatically.

"I'm sorry. There were articles of her clothing in his house and he admitted to seeing her."

Without saying a word, Handlin put his head down on the table.

"Did you see any signs of their relationship?"

"Maybe. She was gone sometimes in the afternoon and, when I'd ask her where she'd been, her answers didn't always make much sense," he said without lifting up his head.

"You didn't press her on it?"

"I didn't want to be one of those jerks who has to know what his wife is doing every second of the day. I wanted her to feel like she could take some time to herself. I sometimes just drive out into the country and sit in the car and smoke a cigarette. You know?"

"Did you ever see Parsons?"

"Sometimes. We had a few parties at the house. Charlie would bring the booze. What are you saying? Charlie didn't do this. It was some sort of creature. I saw it!" He looked up.

"You were badly injured. We think that Parsons wore a costume of some sort when he broke into your house and killed your wife and attacked you," Bobby lied. "We think the motive for the murder could be that your wife was going to break off the affair."

Josephine looked hard at Bobby. He didn't know any such thing. He was just throwing the poor man a bone, something he'd be able to cling to in the long days that were to come. Handlin would be able to think that, in the end, his wife was going to come back to him.

"Do you know if Charlie Parsons knew the Taylor or Chester families?"

"The other people that were attacked?"

"Yes. Did he ever mention them?"

A thought occurred to Josephine and she spoke up for the first time: "Did the dairy get milk from local farmers?"

Handlin nodded. "Sure. Charlie talked about the supply and some of the troubles they had. Particularly when the banks were failing and milk prices crashed. Farmers didn't want to deliver the milk. Some of them would pour it out on the ground rather than sell it to Charlie's company at the prices they were paying. He bragged that one of the reasons he got the promotion to manager was his idea of forming relationships with some of the smaller dairy farmers so that the company wasn't beholden to just a few of the largest dairies. He said it also kept the small farms from undercutting their prices."

"Taylor has a herd of dairy cows," Bobby said.

No matter what they tried, they couldn't get Handlin to remember Charlie Parsons ever talking about Seth Taylor or Molly Chester.

"We'll walk you out," Bobby finally told him. "Do you need a ride home?"

"After being cooped up in here for days, I'm looking forward to stretching my legs."

"Go home and get what you need, but until we catch Parsons, you need to leave town."

Handlin looked at them with sad eyes and nodded.

"Where to now?" Josephine asked once they were back in Bobby's car.

"The Taylors' farm. I want to see if any of them remember Parsons ever mentioning Molly."

Josephine and Bobby received a cold welcome from Elroy Taylor.

"Where's the murderer of my son?" he asked as soon as Bobby and Josephine got out of the car. He'd been preparing the soil in a garden plot beside the house when they drove up. As soon as he saw them, he'd tossed the reins of the mule over the fence and walked up to them.

"I confronted a man who might have been involved last night," Bobby said.

"Involved? What kind of word is that? Did he kill him or not?"

"Possibly."

"Who?"

"Charlie Parsons."

"The guy from Southern Alabama Dairy? That fella? What sense does that make?" Elroy was shaking his head, looking like he couldn't decide whether to be angry or confused.

"We think he might have been interested in Molly Chester."

Elroy deflated before their eyes and leaned against Bobby's car. Even though the air was cool, sweat formed on his brow.

"Why don't we go up and sit on the porch?" Josephine suggested. She gave Elroy a smile and a nod toward the porch as encouragement.

"Of course." Looking even older than his years, he led them through the gate and up to the porch. There were several rocking chairs and a swing. Josephine took the swing while the men sat in the rockers.

"I didn't know that Seth was seeing the Chester girl and I don't know how I feel about it. Now Chester and his wife are dead. It's too much. My missus wants us to sell up and move. But who's goin' to buy a farm now?"

"Did Parsons come out here very often?"

"I don't think he came more than once or twice. First time was to give us a sales pitch about how much money we could save lettin' Southern Alabama do all the sellin' and deliverin'. He said all we'd have to do is fill up the milk cans and have them ready for his trucks to pick up. Guess he was as good as his word. Only once did I have to go in and talk to him. The driver, when he picked up, didn't count one of the cans. I knew 'cause it'd been the same amount every time."

"You went in and questioned them? Did you talk to Parsons himself?"

"He was the one who sold me on them, so, yeah, I went to talk with him. Can't say a bad word about him. He looked at all the old invoices and then corrected the one that'd been wrong. Gave me my money right there. Now you're telling me that he killed my son?"

"We think so. We know that he killed Mrs. Handlin."

"Heard about that. Everyone sayin' it was the same animal that killed Seth, but that don't make no sense. What kind of animal ranges that far and kills one man out in a field and then some woman in town? No sense." He shook his head.

"Did you ever hear anyone, your son, Charlie Parsons, anyone, mention Molly Chester?"

"Nope. I'd hardly heard of the girl till my son was killed and people were sayin' they stepped out together. Now, my wife, she did know Molly. The Chesters went to church at Broad Creek Baptist, same as us."

"Could we talk to your wife?"

"I'll check. She had a sick headache earlier. Been gettin' a lot of them since Seth was killed. Her sister comes by regular. Doesn't seem to help. She doted on that boy." He got up slowly and went into the house, letting the screen door close with a bang.

The woman that came back with Elroy was thin and sad-eyed. She wore a housedress and fidgeted with her clothes.

"Vera, they just want to ask you a few questions," Elroy told her. Bobby had stood up as soon as she came out of the house.

"I'm Deputy Tucker and this is Josephine Nicolson. Go ahead and have a seat."

"I don't know what I can tell you," she said, sitting on the edge of one of the rockers.

"Did you know that your son was seeing Molly Chester?" Bobby asked and saw her glance up quickly at her husband, who was standing across from her.

"I thought he might be sweet on her," she said softly.

"Why was that?"

"He was goin' to church. Seth quit goin' when he was ten, then all of a sudden he's gettin' dressed up to go to church again. I seen them makin' eyes at each other a couple times." She looked down, not meeting the look her husband was giving her.

"Do you know Charlie Parsons?" Bobby asked.

Vera looked up at him, confused. "Who?"

"Charlie Parsons. He ran the dairy that processed and distributed your farm's milk."

"I don't have anything to do with the milk." She shook her head.

"Never heard Seth mention him?"

"No."

"How well did you know Molly?"

"I didn't hardly know her at all. I knew her mother a little. Horrible, horrible what happened to them." Tears formed in the corners of her eyes and she wiped them away. "Our church is reaching out to their family in Birmingham. And Molly, where is that poor girl? Killed, I'd expect." She wiped more tears. "What's happening to our town?" she said, looking at Josephine and Bobby.

"There is evil loose in the county and I promise you we'll track it down," Bobby said.

"You need to get on with it," Elroy said sadly. He stepped forward and put his hand on his wife's shoulder and she reached up to clutch it. "We've buried our son. Now I'd like to see his killer buried."

They left the couple looking forlorn on the front porch.

"We didn't prove much," Bobby said.

"We know that Parsons was visiting local farms. It's

possible he could have met Molly."

"He was already seeing a married woman. Why would he suddenly go after Molly?"

"Maybe he had some sort of grudge against Seth."

"Back to Seth being the intended target. Then why go after Molly and her family?"

"Because she saw something that would lead back to him."

"Molly eliminated as a witness. That makes more sense to me than Molly as a love interest."

"Now only Molly and Parsons know the truth," Josephine said, "assuming Molly is still alive."

"Finding either one is going to take a stroke of luck."

Bobby drove them back to Charlie Parsons's house.

"I want to walk through the house," Josephine said.

"Sure. I've been through everything, but another pair of eyes won't hurt." Bobby shrugged.

Inside, Josephine examined the wreckage in the living room. "I'm glad you weren't hurt."

"The baron was quite the sight, riding on the back of that thing. I owe him. Ever since he came to town, the world seems to have flipped on its head. On one hand, I want to blame him for it, but we've come through the worst of it because of him." Bobby shook his head.

"The older I get, the more I believe in fate. I believe that we can shape our destiny, but we can't avoid it," Josephine said.

"You think this insanity is our destiny?"

"Since we are living it, I do." She turned and started down the hall. In the master bedroom, all the dresser drawers had been turned out.

"I didn't do the neatest job," Bobby apologized.

She picked up a cardboard photo album. Opening it, she found black pages with pictures glued neatly in place. All of the pictures were of Madilyn Handlin. Charlie Parsons was in some of them, but most of them were just her. Many had been taken outdoors, and Madilyn was smiling in all of them.

Her white teeth gleamed and, even in the black-and-white photos, Josephine thought she could see a twinkle in the woman's eye.

"She looks so happy."

"So does he. But being a deputy, I've learned that love can change to hate in a very short time. You mix in a husband and, well…"

"I see your point." She looked at some of the other items Bobby had uncovered, then picked up a small cedar box full of trinkets. Inside were tickets, cards and letters. All of them were from Madilyn.

"They're well worn. Looks like he took them out and read them often," Josephine said.

"I looked through a few of them. Pure mush. She was clearly in love with Parsons."

"Anything about her husband?"

"Just regrets. When she mentions him, it's in comparison to Parsons and Handlin doesn't fare will. Nothing nasty, though. I was talking to a deputy who knows the Handlins. He said that they married when they were both sixteen. Guess the love just didn't last."

"That was sweet of you to tell him she was planning to give up the affair."

"I hope he never sees these letters."

"Think Madilyn had a similar box?"

"If so, I hope she hid it well." Bobby was quiet for a moment, then asked, "You ever think about us?"

"What do you mean?"

"What would have happened if we'd… you know, gotten married," Bobby said, looking at her with a solemn expression.

Josephine sighed. "I used to… Bobby Tucker, you are a good man. I think in the right situation, you could be a great man. But together, I never felt like we raised each other up. I think you are better without me. We make great friends. I don't even mind that I feel a spark of… something once in a while. But a real relationship between us, I think, would lessen each of us."

When she saw the hangdog look in his eyes, her heart ached for him. There had been times when she had tried to force her heart to care more for him than it did. Those days were part of her youth now, and she wasn't going to revisit them.

"I think I understand. Maybe you're right. If so, then I'm glad you were strong enough to resist. I wouldn't have been."

Josephine reached out and took his hand and, together, they walked out of the house.

CHAPTER TWENTY-TWO

Josephine found Grace and Anna in the kitchen.

"I'll be going out this evening, so I'd like to eat early," she told them. Hearing the sound of snoring, she turned to find Anton Lacob in a chair behind the door with his head on his chest as it rose and fell. "He can't be comfortable," she muttered as she left the kitchen.

She quickly washed and dressed for the evening. She wanted to have dinner and still have time to talk to Blasko before she met Matthew for the séance. She wasn't sure if she would tell Blasko that Matthew was going, but she would definitely tell him about the séance. François frightened her. *There is something about him that is… off*, she thought.

Blasko came into the parlor just as the last light of day disappeared.

"You heard about the fight with the werewolf," he said after fixing a drink for Josephine.

"Bobby said you were riding him like a bull." Josephine smiled.

"I had never seen one that close. It was… impressive."

"Y'all were lucky to have survived."

"Tucker nearly didn't. I won't be going on any more werewolf forays without my sword," Blasko said in the same manner that another person would have said they wouldn't go out into the rain without an umbrella.

"That's going to be pretty conspicuous."

"I have a solution. Anton!"

Anton came into the parlor carrying a wrapped package that was four feet long and a foot wide. Obviously the sword.

"What is in the package?" Blasko asked the little man, who seemed befuddled by the question.

"Your sword, Baron."

"No, no, no. What did I tell you to say if anyone asked?"

"Ah! Rods for curtains." His gnomish face broke into a smile, revealing several missing teeth.

"Let me get this straight," Josephine said, trying to keep from laughing out loud. "Anton is going to follow you around carrying the wrapped sword?"

"Exactly. If anyone asks, he has curtain rods." Blasko took a deep breath. "I know that it is ridiculous, but it is simply the best I could come up with. If you have a better idea, I'll take it under consideration."

"No. I went to Parsons's house and saw the destruction. Having a sword handy is probably not a bad idea."

She went on to tell him about the interview with Timothy Handlin and their visit to the Taylors. "Like I said, afterward I went through Parsons's house. He and Madilyn Handlin were in love. Things might have changed recently, but…"

Blasko's eyes lit up and, with a flourish, he took a seat next to Josephine. "Maybe they were still in love. I've been doing more reading. Werewolves often seek out those they love."

"To kill them? That seems counterproductive," Josephine said.

"I'm talking about the freshly minted, undisciplined werewolves. Before they have learned to control themselves, when they change, their first urge is to seek out someone they love. Which, you can imagine, doesn't go well."

"This is all according to your French dragoon captain?"

"Duhamel. Yes."

"Parsons and Madilyn Handlin loved each other. What about the Taylor boy and the Chesters?"

"Maybe Parsons was infatuated with Molly," Blasko suggested.

"I don't see it."

"They are also known to hunt for food. Maybe he just stumbled upon Seth Taylor while he was out hunting. At five in the morning, he could be forgiven for thinking he wouldn't run into anyone else."

"Bobby and I discussed the possibility that he killed Molly and her family to eliminate Molly as a witness to Seth's murder." Josephine glanced up at the clock on the mantel and stood up. "I have to go. I'm attending another séance."

Blasko stood up next to her. "I don't think that's a good idea."

"I think it's necessary. Some of your concerns about François might be legitimate. I think he's trying to influence the selection of a replacement sheriff."

Blasko frowned. "If that's true, then his reason for being in Sumter is malevolent."

"I'm going to the séance with the express purpose of finding out." She had decided to try keeping Matthew's attendance quiet, but she realized as soon as she told Blasko about the séance that he wouldn't want her going alone.

"I will go and at least be nearby if you need me. I would go in with you, but…"

"We probably don't want François digging into your multiple generations of ghosts," Josephine said, then sighed. "Matthew will be there."

"Matthew?"

"He's agreed to go as my escort. I thought he could be some protection." The white lie would allow Matthew a little privacy. If he wanted Blasko to know that he'd sought out the séance, then he could tell him.

"A wise precaution." Blasko nodded. "How do you plan on getting more information out of François?"

"Simple, I'm going to play it by ear." She shrugged. "I need to go."

Blasko reached for her hand and brought it to his lips, kissing it gently. "Be careful. I will come by and check on you."

"Will you bring your sword?" She tilted her head toward Anton, who had sunk down on a chair near the hall with the package still in his lap.

"Of course."

"We'll be at the Robertsons'," she said and hurried out of the house.

Blasko started to tell Anton to put the sword by the door when Anna came in, wiping her hands on her apron.

"Pardon me, Baron. Where's Miss Josephine?"

"She's gone out already."

"Oh, this just came and I hoped I'd catch her before she left." Anna's usual calm demeanor was gone and she looked nervously around the room.

"What just came?"

"This note," Anna said, pulling an envelope from her pocket.

"Perhaps I could be of service." Blasko held his hand out toward the envelope, but Anna hesitated. Normally, he wouldn't use his abilities on a member of the household, but he was curious about the note. "Anna, I should probably take the envelope," he said, getting her to focus on his eyes. "It would be best. After you hand me the note, you will feel much better. Won't you?"

"Yes," Anna said.

"Excellent. You always make the right decisions. Handing me the note is certainly the right thing to do because you always do the right thing."

Staring into his eyes, she extended the note. He calmly took it from her.

"Thank you. You will feel much better now. I am sure you wish to get back to your kitchen."

"Yes, I do," Anna said, and headed to the back of the

house while Blasko turned the envelope over in his hand. It was addressed to: *Josephine Nicolson, c/o Anna.* Feeling only a slight twinge of guilt, he opened the envelope.

Inside was a brief note that read: *I have something you have been looking for. Come tonight and pick it up before I do something rash. Sissy Lylou Masson*

Blasko frowned, fully understanding Anna's odd nervousness. He and the bone doctor didn't see eye to eye. However, his curiosity was piqued.

"Anton!" he shouted.

"Yes, Baron?"

"Bring my sword. We're going for a little visit."

"You drive good," Anton said a few minutes later, as he bounced up and down in the back seat of Blasko's car.

"I do," the baron said without modesty, swerving around a fallen limb in the road and then over-correcting and almost hitting an oncoming car that blared its horn at them. Anton had only been in a car a dozen times before this and he wasn't sure if he was enjoying the experience.

Blasko was headed out of town when he changed his mind and made a rough six-point turn to head back toward Colonel Etheridge's house. He had wanted to talk with Etheridge anyway and he decided that having the colonel as backup at Masson's riverside shack might not be a bad thing. Of course, he would've had a better idea of what might be necessary if Masson hadn't been so cryptic in her note.

"We're going where?" Etheridge asked as he put on his coat.

"Down to the river. I... We received a note from Sissy Masson."

"What does that woman want?"

"She says she has something for us."

"In my humble experience, that woman is dangerous," Etheridge said, opening the passenger door of the car. He flinched when he saw movement in the back seat. "I don't believe I've had the pleasure."

"This is Anton Lacob. He is from my country," Blasko said. "I thought I might need my sword."

"Indeed," the colonel said, settling in for the ride.

"You know Masson?" Blasko asked.

"We've had dealings," was the colonel's cryptic answer.

Blasko drove out of town toward Cotton Dock and the black community beside the river. Once he reached the river, he turned and followed the road to Sissy's house, which was perched on the bank a fair distance from any other homes.

The yard was strewn with strange artifacts and held a vibrant herb garden. Even in late winter, there were a number of plants thriving outside her cottage. The cabin was made of cypress, grey and weathered. Various wind chimes were hung around the roof of the porch and they rang in a breeze from the river. Blasko and Etheridge stepped onto the porch and heard laughter from inside.

"Come in. Come in. I send for the woman and instead I get her dark side." Sissy's laugh was not infectious. Instead it sent a chill through everyone who heard it. It was the laughter of revenge.

Blasko opened the door to the odor of a hundred herbs and tonics. Sissy was perched on an old sofa with her legs crossed, wrapped up in a wool blanket. Her looks were exotic and alluring, like the edge of a cliff.

"Good evening," Blasko said, determined to remain polite so the meeting could be as productive as possible. "Josephine wasn't available. Since your note made it sound urgent, I thought I'd take the liberty of coming here myself."

"Liberty, indeed. And you brought the colonel with you." She looked Etheridge up and down. "I haven't seen you for a long time. You have no more trouble?"

"The situation worked itself out," Etheridge said, clearing his throat.

"With a little help from Miss Sissy, no?" she said teasingly.

"You were of some assistance. Not that you weren't paid

for your help."

"Pay. A good thing to bring up. As my note said, I have something that everyone has been looking for. Now, I go to some trouble to catch and keep it here and I think it only fair Sissy get some compensation," she said with a slight edge to her voice.

"We don't even know what you are talking about," Blasko reminded her.

"I want to know that Sissy is getting something before I wake it up."

"Wake what up?"

Sissy let out a huge sigh. "Okay, fine. In there." She pointed to a door that Blasko hadn't noticed before. He and Etheridge walked over to it, Blasko wondering if he should have brought his sword inside with him.

The door opened into a small bedroom. A man-size cage sat in the middle of the room. Inside, they could make out the shape of someone curled up on the floor.

"You be careful. Don't you open that cage. That's one crazy, wild woman."

"Is that Molly Chester?" Etheridge said, peering at the girl. She was wearing a strange dress and lying on a blanket.

"That my dress. You have to pay extra if you want the dress."

"What did you do to her?" Etheridge shouted back at Sissy.

"I not do anything except give her shit. I give her food. I give her a dress and a place to stay. You might want to come talk to Sissy before you do anything crazy like open that cage."

"She's breathing regularly," Blasko said, listening to Molly. He reached out and touched her arm. "She's warm and her pulse is strong." Blasko could hear her heart beating.

The two men went back into the front room.

"Where did you find her?" Etheridge asked, glaring at Sissy.

"I don't find her. A man who hunts things for Sissy

found her. That was one wild girl. I had no rest till I gave her something to calm her down."

"What did you give her?"

"You worry too much about the wrong things. She is better than when he brought her in here. You should thank Sissy."

"Why are you keeping her in a cage? You could be arrested for that alone."

"Big man who wants to be the sheriff should be very careful about who you arrest," she said, pointing a finger at him.

"We're going to take her out of here and you aren't going to stop us."

"You pay me. I'll tell you what I know. Then you take the girl."

"You are crazy if you think—" Etheridge started, but Sissy uncurled herself from the sofa and stood up.

"No!" she said to Etheridge. "I help you and you spit in my face. I should let you learn that a hot stove burns." She turned to Blasko. "You are half in the other world. You should see her for what she is. Don't you smell it?"

"She is a werewolf," Blasko stated. He had considered the possibility that Molly might be the attacker ever since he'd learned that inexperienced werewolves often kill the ones they love.

"You knew," Sissy said, clapping her hands silently. "When she was brought to me, she was changing back and forth. Unable to control her emotions. I gave her some meat laced with a potion to settle her down. When that wears off…" Sissy fluttered her hands as though raising the question up to her gods. "She might be wolf, or girl or crazy-between like when she was brought to me."

"We will need to keep her sedated until we get back to town," Blasko said, knowing that he was negotiating at this point.

"I can do that," Sissy said and held her hand out, palm up.

"Your price?"

"You aren't seriously going to pay her?" Etheridge said, astonished.

Sissy's dagger-like eyes whipped around to focus on the colonel. "Listen to me, old man. I ask for payment for the effort I expend. You wouldn't have her if it wasn't for me. I remember you coming to me, what, five years ago now? Yes. You had a problem. Not so arrogant then. You don't want Sissy as an enemy. I am no one's friend and many folks' enemy. Very unhappy folk."

Blasko saw Etheridge blanch and knew that Sissy had made her point. "So, how much?" he pressed.

"Five gold coins." She pushed her hand out toward Blasko, who stepped back.

With his eyes focused on her, he reached into his inner coat pocket and took out a small leather bag. He opened it carefully, taking five coins from it. After he put the pouch back, he stepped forward and dropped the coins into Sissy's hand, which clamped shut like a steel trap.

"I'll get the potion," she said with one last glare at Etheridge.

They heard her rattle around in her kitchen for a few minutes before coming back with a small glass vial. There was a glass dropper in the bottle.

They followed her into the room where Molly lay in the cage. Sissy opened the door and leaned in. Carefully, she opened the girl's mouth and let two drops of liquid fall onto her tongue, then she closed her mouth and held it for a second.

"You have three hours."

Blasko and Anton carried Molly out to the car. Sissy had informed them that it would be extra if she helped to carry the girl.

"What should we do with her?" Etheridge asked as Blasko turned the car around and headed back to town.

"Maybe we should have bought the cage too," Blasko said, only half joking. "The safest place would be the jail, but if she changed where someone saw her, who knows what the consequences would be."

"I find it hard to imagine that she killed Seth Taylor and both her parents."

"She'd been bitten. I think her father tried to cut the bite mark off of her. Maybe she was even willing to have it done. However, when he started to cut, the pain must have caused her to change. Once she had changed, there was nothing that could save them."

"Baron, she will not change into wolf?" Anton asked nervously.

"Not for several hours. So we'll take her to Josephine's. She can stay in my apartment. There are no windows in my bedroom and I had the door made of very stout wood."

"What can be done for her in the long run?" Etheridge asked.

"There is nothing that will undo what has been done to her," Blasko said as he drove through the dark streets.

CHAPTER TWENTY-THREE

When Josephine came out of the house, she was startled by a dark figure standing on the other side of her Chevrolet. Matthew stepped out of the shadows.

"If you don't mind, I'd appreciate a ride to the Robertsons'," he said.

"No, of course not. I should have offered in my note."

"I appreciate this," he said as Josephine drove.

"I'm sorry, but I had to tell the baron. He thinks the séance was my idea and that you are just going along as my escort." She went on to share her growing suspicions about François.

Matthew was quiet for a couple of blocks, then said, "Do you think he's a fraud?"

"He has some sort of power. What I'm worried about is that he's looking for power of a different sort."

"If he has the power to contact people who have died, why would he want to get involved in local politics?"

"Sounds crazy when you put it like that. What I fear is that he has bigger plans for Semmes County."

"There is a feeling... I can't quite put my finger on what, but I have a growing sense of... anticipation."

From Matthew's voice, it was clear that he didn't quite

know what he meant, but Josephine understood. Lately, she had also felt a combination of anxiety and expectation. Like when you hear a knock at the door and you aren't sure if it's your worst enemy or your best friend. *Dragomir is right. There is a force drawing the odd, the unique and the deadly to Semmes County. We better be ready for whatever is coming. My focus for tonight is François, who apparently doesn't want us to be prepared,* she thought.

The Robertsons' driveway was full, so Josephine parked at the curb. As she got out of the car, she saw the glow of candles lighting the front rooms of the house. Matthew walked awkwardly by her side.

"Come in! This is going to be the best séance yet," Alice said, holding the door open for them. She gave Josephine a hug and turned to Matthew. "You are looking so good, Mr. Hodge. Everyone is very proud of you."

Matthew's face flushed in embarrassment.

Alice led them into the parlor where François was holding court with the new mayor George Harrington, county commissioner Guy Copeland and their wives. Josephine couldn't remember either of their wives' names. She cursed herself for not asking ahead of time who would be attending.

"Miss Nicolson," the mayor said. "We were just talking about the unfortunate matter of Sheriff Logan."

Josephine was taken aback. Her plan had been to broach the subject when she found an opening. Now a shot had clearly been fired across her bow.

"And the murders, I'm sure," she said.

"Exactly," Copeland said. "The mayor and I have talked with many folks and I think we need to promote a young man who's been with the department to fill Logan's shoes. Of course, there will be an election in a year and a half. So whoever is appointed will just have to take control until then."

"Bobby Tucker would be an excellent choice," Josephine said, pretending she didn't know who they really meant. She noticed that François was standing back with a wicked little smile on his face. *He planned this ambush,* Josephine thought.

Mayor Harrington looked uncomfortable. "We considered Bobby, but he was too involved in that business out at Mrs. Rosehill's. Some of our most prominent citizens were killed in that fiasco, including poor Mayor Thornton."

Josephine restrained herself from pointing out that Thornton had been in cahoots with a band of whackjobs that had been using the *Necronomicon* to call up an ancient evil.

"So who did you have in mind?"

"Deputy Willard Paige. He comes from a good family, not an excitable type. I think that's what we need. Especially now with these recent murders. Everyone is getting very worked up, which is not good for business."

"Exactly my point!" said Copeland, the owner of one of the larger grocery stores in town. "We have some bear attacks and the whole town goes crazy."

Delusional was the word that came to Josephine's mind.

"I've met Deputy Paige. I'd say he has real leadership attributes," François said, and this time there was no mistaking the smile on his face for anything but a stab at Josephine's back.

"I'm not sure we're talking about the same Deputy Paige." Josephine had had enough of being demure.

"He's my nephew," said one of the wives. Josephine thought it was Mrs. Copeland and this was confirmed when Copeland reached out and put his arm around the woman.

Josephine was out-gunned and she knew it. She'd have to find another way around François and his burgeoning power structure.

"Maybe we should leave politics for the daylight hours," François said, as though he had received her surrender. The others gazed at him in a way that made it crystal clear who was in charge.

Josephine looked around for Matthew and saw him talking in a corner with Daniel Robertson. "If you will excuse me." Josephine turned and went over to them before the others could say anything.

"Daniel, are you going to sit in on the séance?" Josephine asked.

"No," he snapped, then seemed to reconsider and leaned forward close enough that he could whisper to Josephine. "Honestly, the man has started to gives me the creeps."

Josephine turned her head so that François couldn't see her answer. "Good."

Her blood froze when she saw François's reflection in the glass of the window. He'd been watching them. *Fine*, she thought, wondering what the next few hours were going to be like. *Is this more than just a political trap?* She considered grabbing Matthew and heading for the door. She wished now that Blasko had come.

"Let us take our places," Alice said as she came back and escorted them to the dining room where the large table was set up for the séance.

"That's my cue to go to my study," Daniel said, downing the whiskey left in his glass.

Alice carefully placed them around the table. François was flanked by the two wives. Next to each of them were their husbands. Josephine and Alice completed the circle, with Matthew between them.

Alice had blown out all of the candles except for a single one in the center of the table. In the glow of the light, Josephine felt François's eyes focused on her. She resisted the urge to turn away. *Damn him*, she thought, grinding her clenched teeth.

"We have a new person joining us at the table tonight," François said. "I hope that the spirits will bring him the answers he seeks."

François reached out his arms and they all joined hands. A chill filled the room. There was a different atmosphere than the last séance she'd attended. Josephine felt an oppressive presence and she glanced at François, but he had his eyes closed and head down. His body swayed slowly back and forth.

The first spirit to manifest itself through François was a sister of Blanche Copeland. They laughed and giggled about their childhood together. The spirit told Blanche how important the tie was that bound them, and how she was going to use it to pull their mother out of a miserable existence beyond the veil. Every word was used to manipulate Blanche. Josephine could tell how important this link to her dead sister had become. François had woven a web of emotion to ensnare her, like a doctor who used laudanum to keep a patient coming back to him.

Next was a spirit who came to deliver a message to Alice.

"Alice, sweet Alice. I am your friend. So many years, I suffered so. But no more. I'm free, but I worry about you."

"Who are you?" Alice asked.

"Remember the pen you gave to me? So precious to me. You were so kind."

"Judith? Oh, I miss you!" Alice's voice held a great longing.

"You are in danger," the spirit intoned.

"Danger?" Alice asked, incredulous.

"Beware of the people around you."

"Who?"

But there was nothing more. François moaned and Josephine thought it might be time for a break, but suddenly his head flew back and an unearthly scream came out of his mouth. Jolted, the women holding François's hands let go and gasped. Everyone else clutched their neighbor's hand, though they all looked up in surprise.

"The pain!" François groaned. His clasped his free hands to his chest. "I remember the pain." His body stiffened while his head rocked back and forth. "So alone. You left me all alone among the dead. The night before, we played cards and drank. The next squad down in the trenches was playing a song, *The Minstrel Boy*. We shook hands and vowed that no matter what happened, when we faced the enemy we would do it together. But here I lie in the field of the dead. Lost."

"That bullet tore through your heart. There wasn't anything I could have done for you. I stayed by your side until you breathed your last breath. I swear it," Matthew said, a deep sadness in his voice.

"It wasn't enough."

"What more could I have done? Our company was already out of sight before I left you. The living needed me more than you did at that point." Matthew sounded like a man who didn't believe his own words. "I'm here because, ever since that day, I've felt you haunting me."

"I was never found. Still lost under the mud of France," the voice chastised him.

"I had to leave," Matthew said. "Please…" It was a cry for forgiveness.

"Lost," François said and leaned forward, placing his head in his hands. After a moment, he said in his normal voice, "I must take a break."

"Please!" Matthew said, reaching his hand across the table with a desperate look in his eye.

"If the spirit didn't give you what you sought, I am sorry. They do as they want. I can't command them to answer you," François said, looking at Matthew. Then he stood up. "Now I need something to drink and a moment to recover myself before we go on."

Everyone but Matthew and Josephine stood up. She let the rest of them get out of earshot before placing a hand on his arm.

"We don't know who was speaking to you. Don't take what he said too much to heart."

"His name was Terry Yates. He was from Dothan. We helped each other get through our training. Slid through the vomit of seasick soldiers together as we crossed the Atlantic on our way to France. I know that was Terry. His body was never recovered. They classified him as deceased based on my report of seeing him shot and staying with him while he died. I should have dragged him back to our trench, or at least made sure one of the medics found him."

"I've never been to war. I don't have any idea what you all must have gone through or what it was like when he was killed. What I do know is that our duty is always to the living. We have to let the dead go sometimes before we're ready to."

"I had a duty to Terry and his family that I didn't fulfill," Matthew said. Josephine watched his hand form a half circle as if holding a bottle or a glass. He looked at her and in a low voice growled, "Damn Blasko for taking away my liquor."

"Do you want to go home?"

"No. I'll stay and see this through."

Josephine thought about asking him if he wanted a glass of water, but decided that might come across as a cruel joke, so she simply got up and went to find François.

The medium was talking and smiling with Alice at the bar. Josephine locked eyes with him and he broke off the conversation he was having to follow her out onto the front porch. She could feel him behind her.

The porch was dark except for the candlelight coming through the windows of the parlor. She stood by the railing and looked out toward the street. François let the door close quietly before coming to stand next to her.

She turned to face him. "Why did you tear him down like that?"

"I didn't do anything except open a conduit to the spirit world," he said with a faint smile.

"I don't know what your agenda is, but I'm not going to let you rip this town apart."

He laughed. "Spunky. But you don't have a choice. I will do what I want." He stepped toward her in a clear attempt to intimidate her.

She stood up straighter and looked him square in the face. "I have allies."

"So you do. And I know a lot about them. Especially the one you have living in your basement. I'd rather not destroy him until I'm ready. But if you make me…"

"How dare you?" Josephine was flustered. She had not

expected him to drop his mask like this. "Why are you here?"

"I have my reasons. Your friend is one of them."

"This is a small town in rural South Alabama. We have nothing you could possibly want." She knew that it was rash to argue with him. It was obvious that he was a menace to the community. And apparently, on top of everything else, an enemy of Blasko's.

"Is that what you think? At one time, Waterloo and Gettysburg were just quiet rural communities. Battles are fought wherever the opposing forces are drawn together."

"Are you saying that this is turning into a battleground? For who?"

"I can hear the distant war drums," he said with a faraway look in his eyes.

"Then you are not a part of these forces?"

"No more than your friend the baron. We are on the outside, not part of the forces that created us."

"What force created you?"

He laughed again. "I created myself." She thought that was all he was going to say on the subject, but then he added, "I used the power of one greater than me to become who I am."

"And who *are* you?" Part of Josephine wanted to break off the conversation, but she hoped she might learn something that could be useful. Still, talking to him was like watching the rhythmic swaying of a cobra.

"I have been many people. My parents were ignorant pigs who performed for those who were more stupid than they. I watched them do their ridiculous carnival acts. My mother told fortunes while my father did conjuring tricks. I decided to learn *real* magic. I found a group of like-minded souls and we started on a journey that led me to master some of the greatest of the dark arts."

"I've never heard of you before."

"Fame is for fools who need the adoration of their peers. All I need is the knowledge that I've reached the pinnacle of my craft."

"Than why are you trying to disrupt life in our town?"

"I have debts to be paid."

"To whom?"

"The ones that gave me my power."

"Did you commit the murders?"

"Here? No, I've killed no one since I came here. Josephine, you could join me. You have power of your own." He stepped forward until they were eye to eye. To her surprise, he flinched and stepped back.

"I see that your bond with the provincial bloodsucking buffoon in your basement is closer than I thought."

"My bond with him goes beyond anything you'd understand," she told him.

"I made a fool of him once. I'm going to do worse this time." He turned and left her staring at his retreating back as he went inside the house without another word.

Josephine again debated finding Matthew and leaving. But if there was even a small chance of learning more, then they needed to stay. François was far more dangerous than she'd thought, whether he had anything to do with the recent string of attacks or not.

Back inside, the other guests were smiling while Alice played host. From the looks she gave him, it was obvious that Alice was as enamored with François as the other guests. Josephine could visualize this scene playing out over dozens of séances. The man used his charm and his link to the spirit world to ensnare people into his net.

"We should return to the table," François said.

CHAPTER TWENTY-FOUR

Blasko pulled into the driveway, scouting the yard for any sign of their nosy neighbor, Evangeline Anderson. She would not react well to men carrying an unconscious woman into his basement. *For once she would be right to make a fuss*, Blasko thought.

Blasko, Etheridge and Anton carried the girl from the car to the steps that led down to the exterior entrance of his basement apartment.

"How should we do this?" Etheridge asked, looking at the steps. The girl wasn't heavy, but carrying her limp body was awkward and the brick steps were narrow and steep.

"Who is that?" came a voice from the hedge that separated Josephine's property from the Andersons'. Luckily the voice was male. Blasko had formed a friendly enough relationship with her son, Cyril, based on mutual secrets.

"Quit peeking at us like a child and come over here," Blasko said, knowing that it was best to deal with the situation head-on.

Cyril came timidly through the hawthorn hedge. "I didn't mean to spy on you," he said and quickly added, "really."

"This young lady has had a traumatic experience. You may know Colonel Etheridge. He's likely to be the county's new sheriff. This," Blasko pointed at Anton, "is a friend from my home country. He's going to be staying with me for a little while."

"I met Anton the other day," Cyril said, causing Blasko to glare at the old man, who just shrugged.

"We are taking the girl into my apartment where she will be safe and looked after."

"There are people who want to hurt her. We need a safe place where they can't find her," the colonel added.

"Oh, okay," Cyril said. He seemed intent on standing there while they took her into the basement.

Blasko sighed and lifted the girl easily into his arms. He'd resisted showing Etheridge his true strength, but he didn't want to be out here if Cyril's mother came around.

"Anton, get the door," he said. Then he paused after taking a couple of steps down and turned back to Cyril. "If you hear any odd noises, such as howling, or perhaps growling, she has been having some mental issues. Dr. McGuire will be attending her." He turned his back on the boy and carried Molly through the door that Anton held open. Blasko had no intention of calling Dr. McGuire. Molly Chester's affliction was incurable.

"We'll put her in my chambers for the time being."

Blasko stopped and put the girl down on a chair and turned to Colonel Etheridge. He realized that he would have to take the colonel into his confidence as far as his sleeping accommodations were concerned. He thought about shooing the colonel upstairs while he and Anton placed the girl inside the smaller room, but to do that might lead the colonel into thinking there was something unsavory about Blasko keeping the girl in his sleeping quarters.

The baron took a deep breath. "As a well-traveled man, I'm sure you've seen a few people who have some peculiar idiosyncrasies."

"Certainly. I met an officer on the Ivory Coast who only ate chicken. Odd little man."

"People can also have strange sleeping habits."

"Most assuredly. There was the mayor of a town in Texas who slept standing up."

"I must let you know that I, too, have a rather… Some might call it a morbid habit of sleeping in an unconventional bed. I don't want you to be too shocked." Blasko opened the door into his chamber, revealing his coffin on its bier.

"Well, now, that is different," the colonel said, stepping into the room. "Where did you acquire this… habit?"

"As you know, back in the day when many children could be expected to die before reaching their maturity, parents often had a child's coffin made and would store it at their home. My parents did this and one day when I discovered it as a child of eight, I decided that I would start sleeping in it." He shrugged. "All these years later and it's a habit I've never shaken off."

"Ha! Understood. Funny, that. Mum's the word."

After the awkward explanation passed inspection with the colonel, they carried Molly into the room and made her as comfortable as possible on the floor. She was still unconscious, but her breathing was becoming more rapid.

"I'd suggest we leave her alone," Blasko said, herding Anton and Etheridge out of the room. He closed the door and locked it before handing the key over to Anton.

Blasko turned to Etheridge. "We should go up and tell Josephine what has happened."

"Yes. We'll need to decide what we can do for young Molly," Etheridge said with a frown.

"*Stand by the door. Answer her questions if you can. Try to calm her. If anything goes too badly, send for Grace and have her come find me,*" Blasko told Anton in Rusyn. The man nodded and staged himself by the door to Blasko's bedchamber.

Once upstairs, Blasko was concerned to find Grace alone.

"She's still not back yet," the maid told him.

The séance got underway again with François channeling an

old friend of Commissioner Copeland, a child who had been struck down by polio.

"We were such good friends. I'm sorry that I never came to see you," Copeland said to the spirit.

"I was scared," said the high-pitched voice.

"I would have come, but Mother wouldn't let me. She told me I would catch it and be paralyzed like…"

"Like me?" the voice moaned.

"Yes, forgive me," Copeland said, his eyes cast down at the table.

"I wanted to see you before I died. I waited for you to visit for weeks."

"I know."

"We will talk again," the voice told him.

"Forgive me!" Copeland suddenly cried. His wife reached out and put her hand on his arm, but he shook it off and stood up. "I have to go," he said, wiping tears from his eyes. Blanche followed him to the door, offering apologies and picking up their hats and coats.

Everyone at the table seemed at a loss until François calmly said, "We shall continue." He put his hands out and everyone joined hands again as best they could across the gap left by the departing couple.

The next voice to come out of François's mouth sent a shiver down Josephine's spine.

"Josie, I fear for you!" the voice cried.

Josephine's emotions battled with her logic. The voice had an eerie resemblance to her father's. She ground her teeth, angry that François had ignored his promise not to use her father at a séance. But then she wasn't surprised after the conversation they'd just had on the porch.

"I'm listening," she said, trying to keep her voice as neutral as she could.

"The monster living in your basement must be destroyed," the voice intoned. There were gasps from the mayor and his wife while Alice looked up, her eyes wide.

"He's no danger to me," Josephine said.

"You have always been stubborn. I remember when you were twelve and you wanted to go riding. I told you that it was going to rain, but no amount of persuading would convince you to wait another day. By the time we got back, we were both soaked. I made you clean and dry all the tack. This time you have to listen to me. You've chosen the wrong ally."

Even knowing what she did about François, it was difficult for Josephine to deny the voice. It sounded so much like her father. The pacing, the tone. In order to combat her confusion, she gave way to her anger.

"Stop this!" she shouted, no longer caring what the others thought. She'd had enough of this emotional abuse. "You, sir, are a liar."

François looked up at her and an evil grin spread across his face. "Josie, my love, all I want is your happiness," he said in her father's voice.

"I said stop it!" she snapped.

A hand reached out and took her forearm. She whipped her head around, prepared to slap whoever had dared to restrain her. But the hand belonged to Matthew, who was shaking his head slightly back and forth. The mayor and his wife stared at Josephine in disbelief. Slowly their heads swiveled to François for guidance, but it was Alice who spoke next.

"Now we all need to take a moment to catch our breath. It's no wonder that hearing your father has upset you," she said to Josephine with a sad tilt of her head.

"This man is a dangerous charlatan." Josephine pointed at François, unable to stop her anger now.

"That is enough," François said and stood up. "I will not sit by and be insulted." His voice carried an equal mix of hurt and anger.

"I don't know what tricks you use, but you are playing a cruel hoax on these people," Josephine said, waving her hand toward the mayor, his wife and Alice.

"Now see here," the mayor said. "I'm no fool. This man

has genuine power. I'll vouch for him."

"He has power, all right." Josephine jerked her arm violently away from Matthew and walked around the table until she was face to face with François. "How is the trick done? How do you know so much about all of us?"

"Back away," he said through tight lips.

"Fake!" she said, spitting the word at him. Josephine remembered his comments about his parents and guessed that this might be a way to get under his skin. Now that it was out, she had decided that a full frontal attack was the only way to proceed. *Caution be damned*, she thought. *I'm done letting you screw with my town.*

"How dare you?" he said with such menace that everyone else in the room froze. Into the cold silence came a pounding from the front door.

"What now?" Alice squeaked and started for the hallway.

The pounding continued as she reached the door. Alice was flustered and irritated as she flung the door open, only to be knocked aside as a man pushed his way into the house.

"Where is he?" the man screamed. "I can smell him."

Alice just had time to notice that the man was wearing the oddest assortment of clothes she'd ever seen on an adult. He wore a woman's blouse, men's trousers twice as big as he needed and no shoes or hat. With the speed of a cat, he dashed into the parlor.

Everyone in the room had turned toward the hallway. As the man rushed in, each reacted in their own way. The mayor and his wife both shouted, the wife in surprise and the mayor in fear, for he recognized the man. So did François. Josephine also knew who it was and backed away from the table while Matthew stepped in front of her.

"You bastard!" Charlie Parsons said, locking eyes with François.

François stood up straight. "Parsons, what is wrong with you?"

"As if you didn't know. You told me I'd be stronger, better than before. All I had to do was control it."

François looked at the others in the room as though assessing the number of witnesses he'd have to kill. When he looked back at Parsons, there was a darkness in his eyes that transcended the world of light.

"I gave you a gift. What you did with it is no mark against me," François said in a tone so menacing that it even stopped Parsons.

The man recovered quickly. "I killed the only person I ever truly loved."

"*You* did it," François shot back.

"Because of this *gift* you bestowed upon me," Parsons said. Josephine saw his head make an odd twitching motion. François saw it too and squared up.

"A thin line often separates a gift from a curse."

"I'm going to rip your heart out…" Parsons said, and Josephine watched transfixed as he changed into a terrifying wolf form. Before the change was complete, she thought she heard him say, "…and eat it!"

What no one expected was François's reaction. He laughed maniacally and, before their eyes, changed into a creature that was even more horrifying and powerful than Parsons.

Parsons was determined and didn't let the sight of the Beast of Gévaudan stop him from leaping at the creature.

Splinters from the table flew at Josephine and the others as Parsons smashed into it on his way to grapple with the beast that was François. In a flash, François's huge claws swiped out and blood flew from Parsons's snarling face as he pushed past the reach of François's arms to come to grips with him. Furniture flew as they smashed into the wall.

Josephine felt a hand tugging her away from the flailing beasts and toward the doorway.

"We've got to go now," Matthew whispered urgently.

Just as she realized he was right, the two beasts fell apart. As François, larger and more powerful, scrambled to reengage with Parsons, whose fur was drenched in blood, they moved and blocked the way to the exit.

Matthew looked for another way out. All of the windows were locked and he looked around for something to break one of them with. But before he could find anything, a shriek of pain came from the Parsons wolf. Blood spouted from his neck and chest as the François beast stood over the prone body in triumph.

The horrible grinning snout that was François turned to each of the people in the room. He knew that they would all have to die if he was to stay in this town. He'd taken just one step toward the mayor and his wife when Josephine ran forward and shoved what was left of the table into his knees. The creature turned and looked with blazing eyes at Josephine. In that instant, she knew that her life was forfeit.

The beast started forward, saliva and blood dripping from its huge canines. Unable to look away from her imminent death, Josephine saw a flash of movement to her right.

"Not this time," she heard Matthew say as he charged past her and straight at the beast.

For just a moment, Josephine thought that Matthew might have a chance. The François beast was so surprised by the attack that Matthew managed to make it inside the reach of the monster's claws and plowed like a lineman into its gut. The impact caused the creature to stumble back for a moment.

Josephine held her breath. Matthew's luck lasted for a second before the beast recovered, then its jaws clamped down on Matthew's shoulder, shaking and tossing him across the room to smash into a bookcase.

François, the Beast of Gévaudan, again locked eyes with Josephine.

Blasko and Etheridge were standing undecidedly in the hallway after Grace told them that Josephine still wasn't home.

"I'm going over there," Blasko said. At that moment, he

felt a wave of emotion flood through him that was so powerful he felt physically ill. "Something is wrong," he gasped.

"What?" Etheridge asked, confused by the sudden change in Blasko's demeanor.

"I don't have time to explain. You'll have to trust me. Josephine is in grave danger." Blasko was already moving toward the stairs to the basement. Etheridge followed close behind him.

Blasko never stopped. He went through his apartment, startling Anton. His hand reached out and grabbed his broadsword as he headed for the outside door. The colonel had to quickstep to keep up.

"Do you know where Daniel Robertson lives?" Blasko asked without turning.

"I do."

"Drive," Blasko said, tossing his car keys to him. "We must hurry!"

The colonel had the car started and was backing up before Blasko closed his door. The colonel had lived on adrenaline in his younger days and he felt the old surge come back with a vengeance as he stomped on the gas and the large car roared down the cobblestone street.

Blasko sat in the passenger seat and unwrapped the sword, then pulled the leather sheath from the four-foot-long weapon. His hand ran over the blade, feeling the nicks and dings from hundreds of past battles. The bond that linked him and Josephine was telegraphing her fear and anger. Every fiber in his body demanded that he rush to her side.

The colonel drove with the precision of a pilot. Twice he had to weave the car around those of other startled drivers. He stepped on the brake and turned the wheel as he approached the Robertons' house, swinging the car up onto the front lawn.

"To the house," Blasko said, jumping out of the car with his sword in hand. Etheridge was slower out of the car, but was trying to keep up. He was pleased that he'd thought to put on his shoulder holster. He pulled out his old army revolver as he trotted up the stairs and followed Blasko into the house.

There were cries of fear and pain coming from inside. Blasko burst into the parlor, broadsword held out. His eyes flashed around the room and locked on Matthew, blood oozing from his shredded shoulder. The mayor was holding his wife to his chest as she cried. Alice was just standing against the wall, staring vacantly at nothing.

"Where are they?" Blasko said, pointing his sword at the mayor. With a trembling hand, he pointed toward the hallway. "Speak, damn you!" Blasko ordered.

"I think... I heard them go up the stairs," Harrington squeaked.

Etheridge was standing behind Blasko, staring in horror at the carnage in the room. The naked, battered and torn body of Charlie Parsons lay close to Matthew.

Holding his sword in one hand, Blasko grabbed Etheridge with the other. "Take care of Matthew."

The colonel nodded. "Take this," he said, holding the revolver out to Blasko.

"Keep it. You might need it," Blasko told him as he headed out of the room.

He rushed into the hall and up the stairs, listening as he went. There were faint sounds of footsteps far above him. When he came to the small third floor, he found a wrought-iron circular stairway that led to a trapdoor in the ceiling. He clattered up, his sword banging on the metal as he made his way toward the opening. Cautiously, he pushed through the small door and came out onto a twenty-by-twenty-foot widow's walk. Around it was an old, rusted railing.

"You needn't have worried. I want this to be a fair fight," said François, who stood on the north side in human form again, holding Josephine tightly in his grip. "I swear, if you bite me one more time I will simply hurl you off of the roof," he hissed at her.

Blasko could see blood running down François's arm from the various bite marks she'd inflicted on him. He was proud of her.

"Kill the son of a bitch!" Josephine screamed.

"This is between you and me," Blasko said. "Let her go."

"The hell it is," Josephine said, kicking at François.

"He's right," François said, tossing Josephine at Blasko. She tumbled across the roof, landing hard despite Blasko's attempt to break her fall.

"Stay down," Blasko told her once he was sure she wasn't badly hurt. "If you get the chance, go downstairs."

"I'll be damned if I'll leave—"

"Please do as I say," Blasko said, surprising her with a tender kiss.

François laughed heartily. "What a ridiculous pair you make!" he shouted. "This is going to be more fun than I ever imagined. I am so glad that I hunted you up, my old friend."

"You are the monster who killed the villagers in Romania," Blasko said.

"Of course. I made you look like a fool then and you haven't performed a bit better this time."

"You bit Molly and Charlie so they would turn into werewolves and wreak havoc on the community."

"They came to me with petty concerns about lost loved ones. I told them I could give them the power to speak directly with their dead relatives. All they had to do was let the beast bite them." He chuckled.

"He's using the chaos to grab power," Josephine said.

"Bravo. Exactly as I was doing in that Romanian village. And what I did so successfully in Gévaudan."

"Kill him," Josephine told Blasko.

"My pleasure." Blasko moved forward, sword at the ready.

François smiled and immediately transformed into his enormous wolf shape. Blasko was careful to stay balanced and focused as he approached him. It had been fifty years since he'd wielded a sword in combat. He let the weight of the blade swing back and forth as he judged the distance between him and François, who was snarling and shifting his weight between his powerful legs.

Six feet away, Blasko determined that he could step in and have enough reach to strike a blow. He moved and swung, only to have François swat the sword away and duck under it.

The monster counterattacked with a swing of its great claws. Blasko pulled back, but the claws snagged his clothes and ripped his vest. He stepped in with a mighty swing that managed to catch the beast in the shoulder, causing it to roar in pain and anger. It leaped at Blasko, knocking him down. He rolled away, but was now on the defensive. The beast lunged at him again and all Blasko could do was scuttle away.

Blasko kept moving until he managed to get enough distance to give him time to get in a blow. Up on his knees, he swung the sword as the beast advanced. The sword caught the creature in the thigh, just above the knee, and stuck in bone. As François fell he came down on the sword, pulling it away from Blasko, who lacked the leverage to hold onto it.

"Run!" Blasko hissed at Josephine, who could see the precarious position he was in.

She wanted to help him, but she couldn't attack the monster with her bare hands. It would just fling her off of the roof. So she turned and rushed for the trap door that led back into the house.

Blasko felt relief as Josephine escaped from the widow's walk. The monster had been distracted by Josephine's movements, which gave Blasko a chance to get back to his feet. However, he was still without his sword, which was on the ground near the wounded monster. François stood unsteadily on his damaged leg. Unfortunately, without his sword, Blasko wasn't sure how to take advantage of the monster's vulnerability. Blasko's condition gave him strength and a high tolerance for pain, but it was nothing compared to the beast's.

Blasko could hit him at the right moment and drive him off of the roof, but the fall wouldn't kill either of them. It would just take the fight to a new venue where others were likely to get involved and hurt. *It is better to let the battle play out up here*, Blasko decided.

He slowly crept around the widow's walk, trying to draw the werewolf away from his sword. François moved with Blasko, but he cut the distance between them with each step. At last, there was a moment when Blasko was closer to his sword than François was to him. He leaped and grabbed the sword. Rolling over, he pulled the sword up in time to catch the creature pouncing on him.

Blasko felt the satisfying sensation of the sword entering flesh. He raised his arms, plunging the sword more deeply into the creature's side. François howled with a terrifying sound that rattled windows in all directions. Slowly, the monster looked down at Blasko. The sword had entered at his waist, but too far to the right side. Nothing vital had been damaged. The drooling jaws of the werewolf came closer and its yellow eyes stared daggers at the baron.

Blasko tried to push the creature off of him, but François was enjoying the moment. He placed his huge clawed hands on Blasko's chest, digging into his flesh, and made a couple of coy snaps at Blasko's face. Then, just before the beast started to rip into his chest, Blasko caught a motion to his right. Something metal came forward and rested against François's head, just before a huge blast threw fire and guts in his face.

Momentarily blinded, Blasko felt the full weight of the monster settle on top of him before it suddenly became lighter and easy to roll off. Looking over François's mostly headless human torso, he saw Josephine standing above him, holding a double-barreled shotgun.

"Excellent," he said with a fierce smile.

"More than one way to remove a monster's head."

Blasko got to his feet slowly. His sword was still embedded in François's side and he pulled it free.

"Where did you get that?" he asked her, nodding at the shotgun.

"Daniel's library. He's passed out drunk and hasn't heard a thing. It's an eight gauge. The biggest gun I could find."

"Did the job."

"We better get back downstairs. There's quite a mess to clean up. Or maybe I should say, cover up."

"I don't think the people of Semmes County are ready for the truth," Blasko agreed, using his sword to finish severing what was left of François's head from his body. "We shouldn't take a chance with something this old and evil," he said, feeling great satisfaction as he administered the *coup de grâce* to his old foe.

"Do you think he was right? Is there a battle coming?"

Blasko put his arm around her. "If the last year is any indication, yes, I do."

EPILOGUE

Downstairs, they found Dr. McGuire tending to Matthew's wounded shoulder, assisted by Colonel Etheridge. "He needs a blood transfusion."

"I have some blood at the house," Josephine said and received a very odd look from Dr. McGuire.

Josephine glanced around the parlor. The mayor and his wife were gone. Alice was sitting on the sofa in what looked to be a catatonic state, her mouth half open and eyes wide.

Etheridge helped the doctor carry Matthew out to his car. Josephine agreed to ride along so they could stop at her house and retrieve the blood before taking the wounded man to the doctor's office.

When they got to the car, Bobby Tucker's car came to a squealing halt at the curb. He got out and rushed over to them, but slowed down as soon as he saw that Josephine was all right.

"I was clear on other side of the county dealing with a fatal car crash. I came as fast as I could," he said breathlessly.

"The monster is dead. Dragomir's inside and can fill you in. I need to go with the doctor," Josephine told him, climbing into the car.

A bit stunned, he watched them drive off before turning

to the house.

Blasko saw Bobby come in. "There are a few items to deal with," he said, looking down at the body of Charlie Parsons.

"What the hell happened here?"

Blasko told Bobby all that he knew. They went through the rest of the house and found Daniel Robertson still snoring on the sofa in his library. Also in the library was the open gun cabinet where Josephine had found the shotgun.

Up on the roof, Bobby looked at the body of François and turned to Blasko. "Help me get this downstairs."

After a messy trip down the circular staircase and to the first floor, they placed the body close to where Parsons lay.

"Parsons was the murderer. He shot François and then shot himself," Bobby said.

"But he doesn't have any gunshot wounds," Blasko pointed out.

"We're going to fix that now." Bobby looked over at Alice, who was still staring straight ahead. "First, take her back to her husband. And grab another shotgun shell."

Blasko eased Alice up from the sofa. She was compliant and went with him without a struggle. Blasko set her down in a chair before going over to the gun cabinet and taking a couple of shells out of a box inside.

"We'll just have to count on the neighbors not caring that there was another shot that came later than the first."

"No one's even looked out the windows," Blasko said. "I imagine that the recent murders and the howling from the rooftop earlier has everyone minding their own business."

"Good thing," Bobby said. Just as he took the shot and finished arranging the body, they heard other cars pull up outside the house.

Josephine came back inside with Deputy Paige and several part-time deputies behind her. Bobby was able to focus everyone on cleaning up the mess. They all bought the story without too much effort.

"What about Mayor Harrington and his wife?" Bobby

asked Josephine when they had a moment alone.

"I don't think it'll be that hard to convince them to keep their mouths shut," Josephine said, determined to leverage this carnage into support for Etheridge. If more trouble was headed their way, then she certainly didn't want Paige to get in the way. With François dead, she didn't imagine there would be much resistance to Etheridge's appointment to sheriff.

On a warm night in March two weeks later, Josephine, Blasko, Bobby and Colonel Etheridge were gathered in her parlor.

"I received a letter today that might be the answer we've been looking for," Blasko said.

"We can't keep Molly locked up down there much longer," Bobby said.

"We won't have to. Duhamel's book mentioned several of the werewolf clans by name and I used them to track down one in this country. I have made contact with a man who has offered to help us."

"This man is a werewolf?" Bobby asked suspiciously.

"Yes. He was born a werewolf. He had no choice about his condition and has learned to control it. He's offered to teach Molly and Matthew how to do the same."

"Matthew has managed to help Molly a bit," Josephine said.

"But he's started to have his own issues. He lost control two nights ago. I was just able to restrain him," Blasko said.

"Do you think he will go with this man?" Etheridge asked.

"I talked to him before you all got here. He will. Which will also mean that he can look after Molly."

"Has she said anything?" Josephine asked.

"Matthew is in there with her now. She mumbles, but it's unintelligible."

"Who is this man who's offered to help?" said Bobby.

"His name is Finn Malone. He said that he can be here in a day. All we need to do is send him a telegram."

"We don't have much choice," Etheridge said and there were general nods all around.

After everyone else had gone, Josephine and Blasko went outside and sat in the porch swing, enjoying the warm air as spring approached.

"How is Alice?" Blasko asked. He'd used his mesmeric powers to help her forget the ordeal of that night.

"Daniel says she gets out of bed most days. He thinks she's coming around."

"What about us?" Blasko asked, surprising her with the question. Normally he avoided any direct reference to their relationship.

"I'm sorry, but I read more of that book," Josephine said, reaching out for his hand and clasping it in hers.

"We both have things to be sorry for. I drank fresh blood a few days before our battle with François. I knew it was coming and needed to be at my strongest. I broke my oath to you."

"Whose blood?"

"Gene Hawkins," he said solemnly, prepared for her to angrily shame him.

Josephine tried to maintain her stern expression, but failed. She started to laugh and then couldn't stop.

"That bastard," she said when she finally caught her breath. "I wish I could have seen his face. That man has ruined so many good people in this town, but always just on the edge of the law. I can't tell you how many people have come into our bank begging for money to save them from his greedy clutches."

"I think his business is going to be a mite stunted since I implanted a rather nauseous aversion to taking advantage of people."

Josephine looked at him. When she realized he wasn't kidding, she burst into another fit of laughter. When she finally had control of herself again she said, "Seriously, you really can't go around drinking people's blood." She paused, took a deep breath and added, "We'll chalk this up to an emergency."

She didn't want this chance to talk about their relationship to slip away, so she wiped the last tears of laughter from her eyes and said, "The book says there are two ways in which our relationship can change."

"Stake me out and let me fry in the sun," Blasko said with a frown.

"Which would also be horribly painful for me. You know the other way."

"We've discussed this. You don't want to be like me."

"Have you ever changed anyone?"

"Once. And I won't do it again. This is a curse, Josie! To manage it the way I have… Not many people can. I know of only a few others…"

"I'm not sure it's something I want. But what I *do* want is for us to at least consider it."

"It would mean you giving up the daylight. Not to mention that you would then be just as dependent on blood as I am." He shook his head. "No, I…" Then he saw the serious expression on her face. "Perhaps."

"Am I wrong to think you care about me?"

"No."

"This imposed physical bond that ties us together doesn't allow either one of us to exercise our freewill," Josephine said in frustration. "You could remove that by making me as you are."

He took her in his arms and kissed her deeply. "*This* is what I want. But if I did anything to cause you greater pain, I could not live with myself."

"At least we could stand as equals. Then we could decide if we want a future together." She pressed her head against his chest and felt his strong heartbeat beneath his shirt.

"We'll see, my dear. We'll see."

Baron Blasko and Josephine return in:

TENTACLES
The Baron Blasko Mysteries–Book 4

Cover design by Corvid Design
Cover illustration ©2019 Duncan Eagleson

ABOUT THE AUTHOR

A. E. Howe lives and writes on a farm in the wilds of North Florida with his wife, horses and more cats than he can count. He received a degree in English Education from the University of Georgia and is a produced screenwriter and playwright. His first published book was *Broken State*. The Larry Macklin Mysteries is his first series and he released a new series, the Baron Blasko Mysteries, in summer 2018. The first book in the Macklin series, *November's Past*, was awarded two silver medals in the 2017 President's Book Awards, presented by the Florida Authors & Publishers Association; the ninth book, *July's Trials*, was awarded two silver medals in 2018. Howe is a member of the Mystery Writers of America, and was co-host of the "Guns of Hollywood" podcast for four years on the Firearms Radio Network. When not writing Howe enjoys riding, competitive shooting and working on the farm.

www.ingramcontent.com/pod-product-compliance
Lightning Source LLC
Chambersburg PA
CBHW021008120726
47905CB00009B/2914